THE EDEN TEST

||||

THE
EDEN TEST

||||

ADAM STERNBERGH

FLATIRON
BOOKS
NEW YORK

THE EDEN TEST. Copyright © 2023 by Adam Sternbergh. All rights reserved. Printed in the United States of America. For information, address Flatiron Books, 120 Broadway, New York, NY 10271.

www.flatironbooks.com

Designed by Donna Sinisgalli Noetzel

Library of Congress Cataloging-in-Publication Data

Names: Sternbergh, Adam, author.
Title: The Eden Test / Adam Sternbergh.
Description: First edition. | New York : Flatiron Books, 2023.
Identifiers: LCCN 2022031935 | ISBN 9781250855664 (hardcover) |
    ISBN 9781250855671 (ebook)
Subjects: LCGFT: Novels.
Classification: LCC PS3619.T47874 E34 2023 | DDC 813/.6—dc23/
    eng/20220707
LC record available at https://lccn.loc.gov/2022031935

Our books may be purchased in bulk for promotional, educational, or business use. Please contact your local bookseller or the Macmillan Corporate and Premium Sales Department at 1-800-221-7945, extension 5442, or by email at MacmillanSpecialMarkets@macmillan.com.

First Edition: 2023

10 9 8 7 6 5 4 3 2 1

For Julia, of course.

I think that Eve loved Adam, first of all,
Not in the garden where all things were fair,
Not in the sad time when he failed her there,
But when they were at last outside the wall
And it was night.

—BERTHA TEN EYCK JAMES, "EVE AND ADAM"

A couple is a conspiracy in search of a crime.

—ADAM PHILLIPS, *MONOGAMY*

THE EDEN TEST

IIII

PROLOGUE

The Sixth Day

The private ambulance pulls into the gravel driveway with a rattle and parks at an angle to the cabin. In the darkening evening, the throbbing light bar splashes the walls and windows of the cabin red. There are three cars already parked outside: one that belongs to the cabin's owners and one that belongs to the groundskeeper, both of whom have just arrived, and there's a third car that the EMTs don't recognize.

The two technicians disembark from the ambulance's cab, both laden with lifesaving equipment. They don't move with any urgency, though. There's no one to save tonight.

They're just here to pick up a body.

In the pulse of the swirling lights, the driver walks around to the rear of the vehicle, past the company's name, EDENIC FOUNDATION, stenciled on the ambulance's side. He tugs the back doors open and reaches in for the collapsible gurney, wrestling it free from its restraints.

It's funny, the driver thinks as he goes about his job. They've come all the way out here to the middle of the woods so they can transport a body for an hour in the back of an ambulance to the closest hospital two towns away, where it will sit in a refrigerated morgue, waiting to be examined, before being bundled up again and shipped off to a funeral home, then embalmed, then sealed up in a wooden box and buried somewhere in a hole under a granite stone.

Or they could just leave it in the woods, he thinks. Let the woods consume the body.

Dust to dust.

We can dress it up all we want with flowers and ceremony, the driver thinks, but in the end we're all just organic matter, waiting to move on to the next stage.

As for souls, who knows?

The driver struggles with the gurney, finally wresting it free from the back. He extends the wheels with a click and starts rolling the gurney over the gravel toward the cabin. His supervisor ambles around from the other side of the ambulance, in no hurry.

When she spots him, she calls out his name and holds up two gloved fingers.

"What?" the driver says, halting.

"We need both of them," she says.

"Both gurneys?"

"That's right. We're here for two bodies," she says.

The First Day

||||

DARKNESS AND LIGHT

1

It's hard to take a woman named Daisy seriously. Trust her, she knows.

She smooths out the ripples in the tablecloth by hand. Everything has to be just right. With her palm she can feel the splintery tabletop under the cool, soft cloth.

She feels anxious, nervous—she's surprised to feel nervous. After all, it's just *him*. It's just *them*, the two of them, three years together and two years married. But there's something thrilling to her in this kind of work, in the act of preparation. She knows this feeling well from all her years onstage: the moment just before the show begins, before the rush to the wings, the hush and the darkening of the lights—the moment that's ripe with anticipation and possibility, when the stage manager comes and knocks on the dressing room door, giving the five-minute call.

Five minutes, please.

Thank you, five, you answer back.

She loves that moment. The moment before the moment.

She inspects the table and gets back to the work at hand.

Maybe it's that jaunty *i*, she thinks, planted smack in the middle of her name—*Daisy*—that so successfully drains it of all seriousness. Or maybe it's the temptation to dot that *i* with a cheery, round-petaled flower—the Daisy-with-the-daisy-on-top. She did that when she signed the contract on this cabin, finalizing the agreement, a grown-ass woman of thirty-two, as a little joke to herself, she couldn't resist. After she wrote out their life stories, their problems, their issues, their histories, after she detailed their hopes and dreams as a couple, after she filled out the forms and answered the questions and signed all the waivers—so many waivers—after she paid her hefty deposit and handed it all over to the foundation's representative, who smiled and stuck her forms in a file folder and stashed it away, then shook her hand and promised her she'd just made the most important decision of her life.

Seven days. Seven questions. Forever changed.

That's the pitch.

She straightens the tablecloth.

We'll see.

None of the other floral names have this crisis of legitimacy, she thinks. *Lily* sounds stoic and elegant, *Rose* is luxurious and regal, *Iris* unflappable, *Ivy* intriguing, but *Daisy*—Daisy is a bimbo, a bumpkin, a ditz, the simplest and most common of flowers. And, sure enough, whenever she goes to an audition, hair done, makeup on, dressed in her best *please love me* outfit, her name is inevitably the first thing that anyone remarks on, that trusty icebreaker. She enters, smiling, eager, *Hello, hello*, they peer at her headshot, they glance up at her, and all too often someone says it: *Daisy—like* The Great Gatsby? Or, even worse: *Daisy—like Daisy Duke? From that old TV show?* Every once in a while, she'll get a real old-timer, someone who sings tunelessly, *Daisy, Daisy, give me your answer, do—I'm half crazy, all for the love of you!*

She usually just laughs, nods, gives them the same practiced smile, she's skilled at that—she's an actor, after all. Sure, I'll be your Daisy, any Daisy you want, she thinks, and then she gets down to the serious business of selling herself, of saying someone else's words like they're her own, of losing herself, of being who they want her to be, of dazzling them.

She's skilled at that, too.

She picks up the two ornate silver candleholders she found packed away in a cupboard in the cabin's kitchen, hidden among cobwebs and mismatched coffee mugs. The candleholders feel substantial in her hands, like trophies. She catches her reflection in the rippled glass of the cabin's window and she imagines her award-show speech, the one she's practiced in every bathroom mirror since she was a little girl. *I just want to thank everyone who believed in me—who believed in a girl with a dream from Wisconsin.* She clutches the candleholders, regards them with convincing surprise. *What, two? For me? Please. I'm just happy to be nominated.*

Then she sets them down in the center of the table, their intricate silver sides inlaid with the ancient wax of a hundred previous evenings. She wonders how many of the cabin's prior occupants did exactly what she's doing now: setting the table, lighting the candles, hoping against hope for a miraculous change in their lives. She wonders how many other troubled couples have stayed in this cabin before, have booked this retreat before, have escaped to this lake in these woods before, to look for some kind of rejuvenating spark that will salvage their relationship.

She's not sure how old this cabin is, but it must have been on the edge of this lake forever, she thinks. It seems less like it was built here than that it grew up out of the forest floor. It's old enough to have warped wooden floorboards and a kitchen full of drawers that don't quite close and leaded glass windowpanes that distort the view of the lake beyond. Outside she sees the sky is entering that moment of darkness that blurs the horizon line; black pines in silhouette ring the far edge of the lake. As she watches, she realizes that it's quiet, so quiet that she strains to listen to the silence—a silence beyond anything she's ever experienced back in Brooklyn. If there's another soul on the lake at this hour, she thinks, they're keeping themselves well hidden.

She imagines herself as a different woman, long ago, someone wearing an apron and bonnet, living in this cottage by her wits and rustic skills, lit only by candles and kerosene lamps. Instead, she's got her dirty-blond hair pinned up messily and she's dressed in denim overalls, an actor's trusty rehearsal uniform, baggy and comfortable. She calls these overalls her *fuck it* outfit—fuck it, she thinks every time she puts them on. There's literally nothing you can't get done in overalls—that's her motto.

In the beginning, he liked the overalls. He *loved* them. Still thought they were somehow sexy. He loved how they fell away easily, just two unfastened snaps away from pooling around her ankles on the floor. In their first year together, that whirlwind year, she wore them with him to lounge around in with nothing on underneath. They spent their weekends together, in exile, huddled and hidden from the world, holed up in one or the other of their tiny Brooklyn apartments, clothing very much optional. He'd only venture out for croissants and coffee from the corner bakery. Otherwise, they'd cuddle together and read the fat weekend paper, the actual newspaper, its sections unfurled all around them like blueprints for some brazen upcoming heist, their bodies curled into each other on her thrift-shop sofa, their fingers dirty with pastry butter and printer's ink. That was in the beginning, the first year, the good year. Then they moved in together. Then they got married. Now here they are, three years later, two years as husband and wife, on the edge of a week in which they'll decide together if it's even worth sticking it out. They never get the weekend paper anymore, he got an iPad, he's cut out carbs, and they long ago left her thrift-store sofa at the curb.

She arranges the tarnished silver cutlery at the table settings. She pauses. Should she and he sit side by side or facing each other across the round table? The purpose of round tables, she read once, is that there's no head, no hierarchy. On their first date, they sat at a tiny round table in a sushi restaurant below street level, the walls of the subterranean bar scribbled with Japanese graffiti. She sat in the booth and he sat in the chair facing and it was so dark in the bar that his face kept fluttering in and out of the light from the single sputtering candle. Am I going to marry you? she thought absurdly, watching him in the guttering flame. That night, after several orders of sake, he came around and slid into the booth beside her. They sat and ate like that, crammed together, shoulders touching. They shared one dessert. On a whim and long past drunk, she licked a curl of crème brûlée from his chin. His chin was stubbly. He blushed. She was brazen. She laughed. She knew right then he was the one. Better yet, she knew he knew she was the one.

They got married a year later, in the Hudson Valley, under an apple tree.

Actually not too far from here, she thinks.

As for tonight: facing each other, like diplomats at a negotiation.

She can smell the chicken roasting in the kitchen, almost finished.

Look at her. Being domestic.

She'd stuck the trussed bird in the ancient oven an hour ago, then unpacked her bag in the bedroom upstairs, along with the clothes she'd packed hastily for him. The note she'd left him on their kitchen table said eight p.m., but she knows that traffic from the city will be a nightmare. It's creeping toward nine and getting dark, and he hasn't called yet, hasn't even acknowledged the invitation, not that her phone service is reliable way out here.

The whole thing being a surprise, of course. Her anniversary gift to him.

She's not sure what she'll do if he doesn't show up. But then she's not entirely sure what she'll do if he does.

It's getting dark enough that if he's not at least off the thruway by now, he'll have a hell of a time finding her. She herself had headed up during the day while he was at work, hopping a bus upstate, then getting picked up by that same smiling representative of the Edenic Foundation, the organization that's hosting them this week, the organization to which she handed over a shockingly sizable portion of her TV acting check. She'd seen their ads in New York for years, in the subway, on billboards—*Seven Days, Seven Questions, Forever Changed,* the constant promise, the faithful motto—and on each ad there they were, the smiling faces of the beatific therapists, Drs. Kit and Bridget Arden, promising to save you, themselves a fiercely married couple, that's how they described it on the TV morning shows and on podcasts, "not happily married, *fiercely* married," they always said, clutching each other's hands— and each ad tempted you with a getaway, a fresh start, a refuge for troubled couples just like you.

After a long and winding drive deep into the featureless woods, the representative pulled into the cabin's gravel driveway, passed over the keys to Daisy, along with a map to the nearest grocery store an hour away and two special sacks with instructions to stash their phones for the week, no outside contact, no distractions. The representative walked Daisy to the door, and as a final flourish in the doorway she handed Daisy a long white envelope.

Written on the front of the envelope in florid gold script: *Q1.*

The first question. Of seven questions.

Daisy glances over at the envelope that she left sitting on the coffee table, now waiting for her husband to arrive.

She twists the corkscrew and uncorks the wine and sets the bottle in the middle of the table. She'd contemplated whether to serve wine at all, since she knows they have a lot to talk about and she knows she won't be drinking. But she also knows he'll want a glass as soon as he arrives, after such a long drive, it's the first thing he'll ask her about.

She lights both candles in the heavy silver candleholders with a long wooden match. She shakes the match dead and watches as a trail of smoke twists toward the shadowed ceiling.

Then she steps back and inspects her handiwork.

Perfect.

Showtime.

Seven days. Seven questions.

Forever changed.

That's the pitch.

One week to save a marriage.

A radical step, she knows, but sometimes radical steps are what's required.

She thinks of open-heart surgery, the kind her grandfather once had. They knock you out, crack your rib cage, pull your heart free from your chest and stop it, all to fix it.

Then they put you back together, carefully.

Okay, she thinks, wiping her hands on the front of her overalls.

Let's crack this patient open and stop its heart.

2

He's lost and he's late—of course he is. The GPS failed him miles ago and his high beams are only showing him trees. Trees, trees, and more trees: Who knew there were so many trees? It rained all week, a late-summer rain, so the dirt road is good and muddy, the car slipping and lurching in the muck. He creeps along at fifteen miles an hour. He thinks this is the right road, but who knows? How anyone got anywhere before satellite technology remains a vague puzzle to him, a time that seems as long ago and as full of mysteries as when people guided sailing ships by the stars.

Her note sits unfolded on the dashboard, its whiteness reflected in the windshield against the darkening sky. The note reads *Dear Craig* with a brief explanation, along with a time, an address, and a little hand-drawn heart, and her name below that—*Daisy*—with a cutesy little flower dotting the *i*.

He hates when she does that.

Happy anniversary.

Surprise!

She's going to be pissed, he knows that, but it's not his fault she changed the whole plan. He'd done exactly what they'd agreed on: He left work early, ducking out of the office at four, dodging the watchful eye of his manager, then headed home to meet her at the apartment so they could dress up and grab dinner at their favorite local restaurant at five. Not the best restaurant in their Brooklyn neighborhood, not even the second-best one, but the one where you can reliably get a table if you're willing to eat before six p.m. After that: an early movie—at the local theater or, if they weren't up to that, at home. Then: a nightcap, probably, maybe two. That was the plan. And Daisy loves nothing more than making, and sticking to, a plan.

But when he walked into their apartment—boom. No Daisy.

Apartment's empty.

For a second—for one dizzying, sickening second—he thought that maybe she'd left him. On this, their anniversary night. How ironic would that be? Then he spotted it: the note. Laid out on the kitchen table, as banal as a reminder to get milk.

Is she gone? he thought, his chest still constricted, as he approached the table and eyed the note warily.

He opened the note.

Dear Craig.

An invitation. An address.

An anniversary surprise.

As soon as he read it, he called her. No pickup. Then he punched the address she'd left him in the note into his phone. When he saw the route, he groaned. Are you fucking serious? Estimated travel time: three hours, twenty-two minutes, with nothing but red-line traffic along the way. The arteries out of the city all clogged, angry, throbbing red like some dire diagnosis your doctor shows you.

He called her six more times while standing fuming in their empty apartment but still no answer. This was not how he'd expected the night to unfold. But he grudgingly got in the car and hit the road. Of all the days. What choice did he have? He spent the next hour and a half in excruciating gridlock, wriggling free of the straitjacket of New York.

On the dark country road he checks his phone again—still no signal; fucking boondocks, he thinks—then tosses it on the passenger seat. He struggles to open the glove compartment while keeping one eye on the winding road ahead. He's pretty sure there's a map in there, an old-fashioned paper map. He shuffles through the glove compartment contents—a tiny flashlight with dead batteries, some expired insurance cards—and finds nothing. He glances back up at the road just in time to jerk the wheel wildly and avoid trundling off into a ditch. Goddammit. The headlights swing across a crowd of spindly trees.

These trees, he thinks, look like witches. Hunched over with their crooked fingers, waiting to snatch up the wayward and the lost.

An anniversary surprise. Why is she making such a big deal of it? It's only their second wedding anniversary. For your first? Sure, pop the champagne. Your fifth? Go on—ring the bells. But your second? What even is the traditional gift for a second anniversary, anyway? Paper? Cardboard? Tinfoil?

Not that he'd managed to bring a gift.

She's going to be pissed about that, too.

And to think he'd had to maneuver so hard to slip away from the office early, something his shrew of a manager, who's already on his case, definitely frowns upon. *Adios,* he thought to himself as he ducked away and slid out the door. Craig doesn't speak Spanish but *adios,* he recalls from a college comp-lit course, is a contraction of "*A Dios vais,*" or "You're going to God," a phrase that appears in *Don Quixote,* a novel Craig carried around campus for weeks and tried to read but never finished.

Well, if his manager fires him, he thinks, she can virally market their viral marketing without him, find someone else to comb social media accounts and reach out to potential influencers. He was a writer—right? Once? When he first moved to New York from Michigan after college? Mid-twenties? Moleskine notebook in his pocket? Dreams of tweed jackets and drunken debates with the ghosts of Henry Miller and Hemingway in his head?

But Henry Miller and Hemingway were long dead, tweed was long out of style, and even though he'd dreamt of writing novels in New York, he got a job in magazines for the steady paycheck. Then a job in advertising for the bigger paycheck. Then a job in—well, whatever it is he does now. Persuasion? His business card reads *Brand Advocate.* The only writing he does on a regular basis are the texts he sends to social media influencers trying to recruit them to get paid to show up at events and pretend to like some new vodka. *Hey, just circling back on my last text. Did you get it. Hey, what's up. Just a simple yes or no.*

As for the Moleskine notebook, he still carried one but only for collecting women's names and numbers. Ladies are drawn to the antiquarian charm of a Little Black Book, he's found, in this cold world of apps and swipes. They love the flourish of a pen, the scribble on a page, the theater of it—and he enjoys flipping back through the notebook at all the names and numbers he's collected over the course of thirteen years in New York. He's never had trouble attracting women's attention—that's something he learned early on. Some boys have talent. Some boys have smarts. And some boys have looks that act like a hall pass. It's nothing he can take credit for, but he doesn't see why he should ignore it. He also realizes, as he edges toward forty, that the hall pass is getting a little frayed around the edges.

Still, sometimes he pulls out the notebook—even though he's married now, *out of the game*—just to riffle nostalgically through a decade's worth of conquests. Half the names in his notebook are married now, half have left New York, and a handful are fake—fake names, fake numbers; no one in New York is who they pretend to be, he learned that pretty fast.

Then he met Daisy.

Their romance was similarly swipe- and app-free; they were set up, old-school-style, by a friend of a friend. Dinner and a movie and a drink. How courtly is that? And she was mysterious, too, at first, like everyone, mercurial, unreadable. He'd learned that in New York the trick for most people is to be as elusive as possible so that no one figures out how boring you are. But she was never boring; she was—what's that word? *Inscrutable.* She refused to be scruted, while he, of course, was an open book, an honest man, highly scrutable, or so he said to her. *I'm the most scrutable person you'll ever meet*—he made that joke to her early on, and she laughed, a real laugh, he remembers. He also remembers how she licked crème brûlée off his chin on their very first date, how surprising that felt, how brazen—he actually shivered. He remembers how she used to lounge around his apartment in the early months on weekends in overalls with nothing on underneath, and how those overalls were more often off than on.

And he remembers how, little by little, stubbornly, persistently, improbably, he, Craig, won her over, all while falling deliriously for her.

It's true. He fell. Here it is, he thought then: the Big Romance, the Whirlwind Affair, the Falling in Love That's Like Sailing off a Cliff. The kind of romance you read about in novels, see on the big screen, and dream you might encounter when you move to a place like New York. And he was nothing if not a romantic, right? Didn't he have a notebook full of names to prove it? But none of those women was Daisy, not one, not then. Daisy was beautiful. Daisy was funny. Daisy was outgoing and clever, and she charmed all his friends. And Daisy was talented—holy shit, she was a dynamo. An amazing actor with only success ahead. Even he could see that. Their first year was magical. Epic. Wild enough that they decided to get married.

Now here they are.

Year three.

She's still beautiful, of course, still funny, still charming, occasionally, when she wants to be, when she's not anxious, sullen, or withdrawn. And he's still waiting for her to take that next step in her career, to grab that brass ring, so that both of them can ascend to whatever destination her talent had promised at the start—even as she refuses to do anything but shitty downtown black-box theater for little money, in front of half-empty audiences comprised of pretentious assholes. Even as she declines to audition for any TV or movie roles, not her, she's too *pure* for that. So that's a thing they fight about.

And he, of course, is still stuck in the same deadening day job, the same compromise to a compromise to a compromise, because New York is expensive and she makes no money—so that's a thing they fight about, too.

And it's funny, he thinks, how quickly three years together and two years of marriage can feel like a lifetime, a sentence, especially to him, a guy who, now at the advanced age of thirty-eight, had never before been in a relationship that lasted longer than eighteen months.

Maybe the whirlwind isn't meant to spin forever, he thinks, his hands gripping the steering wheel. Maybe when you fall in love and it feels like sailing off a cliff, eventually you fall through the air far enough that you hit bottom with a thud.

He shifts in the driver's seat, eyes on the road and hands at ten and two. Thinking about the night ahead. A night that's already been full of surprises. With one more surprise to come.

The bright rectangle of his upturned phone on the passenger seat jumps to life with a shudder.

The lit screen illuminates the car's interior.

A text.

Where R U?

Another text.

Is it done?

Not from his wife.

He clicks the phone back to sleep, turns it facedown, and starts once again to mentally rehearse the speech.

He knew this would be a hard night, he knew that, and he'd prepared for it. He'd planned the night out to the last detail. Leave work early. Dinner. A movie. A nightcap.

Then: *We have to talk.*

The speech, he knew, was crucial. He'd been practicing the speech for weeks. At work he'd sneak off to the bathroom between meetings, check under the stalls for shoes, then deliver the speech to the mirror, muttering the polished lines over and over. Consistently struck by how sincere he seemed. She's not the only actor in this relationship, he thought.

And why not—he *was* sincere. He was sincerely sorry that things had come to this. But life is a journey, after all. A winding road, and we don't always know where it will take us. Sometimes we travel together. Sometimes we have to part ways. *But we'll always live on in our hearts*—no, that sounds like somebody died. *We'll always be together*—except, well, they wouldn't be, that's the whole point of the speech. But she's young, just thirty-two, and he's still young, just thirty-eight—youngish, anyway, young enough to still get out there, but not so young to be willing to be stuck in something that's not working for the rest of his life.

They'd had three great years together, but now maybe it was time, he'd tell her, for both of them to go and have great years with someone else. Or great months, at least. Great nights.

He'd kind of jumped the gun on the *great nights with someone else* part.

He wasn't planning on mentioning that.

Thirty-eight is not too late, he thinks now in the car, his motto, his mantra, as he scans the deepening darkness for some sign of his destination. He'd considered not coming at all, just not showing up, but that seemed wrong. You can't do that on your anniversary. It's going to be shitty either way, he thinks, but he has to do this face-to-face. He owes her that much. And everyone has their own sense of right and wrong: *I'll do this, but I won't do that.*

Isn't that the definition of morality? Your personal list of will- and won't-dos?

At least they don't have kids, he thinks. My God, kids would complicate things. Thank God that particular entanglement was never on the table for them.

The phone buzzes again, facedown on the seat.

Should he text her back?

No. Deal with this first.

Then it hits him—wait. If he's getting texts—

He flips the phone over and opens the map app.

Hallefuckinglujah.

Connected to civilization again, if only for a moment, a sweet pocket of electronic intervention from above, like an answered prayer, like God finally turning his face toward you and saying, *Yes? How can I help?*

Except the voice he hears is not God's; it's a woman's voice, and she says:

In 250 feet, turn left.

His headlights jerk hard across another coven of trees, and he finally hears the words he thought he'd never hear.

In point-three miles you will reach your destination.

Point-three miles later, driving at a crawl, he misses the driveway once, twice, it's nothing but darkness now, but on his third pass, in reverse, the car whining over the mud ruts, he spots it and turns in slowly, then follows the winding drive and sees a cabin. Lights blazing in the living room. Framed in the window, Daisy stands over a table. Set for dinner. With candlesticks.

Wearing those fucking overalls she always wears.

The gravel crackles as he brakes. Gets out, road-sore, and stretches.

Rehearses the speech under his breath.

He pockets his phone but not before reading one more time that plaintive text he never answered—*Where R U?*—and wondering how long the writer of said text will wait for a reply. He's got bars, temporarily, so he texts back *talk soon* with a heart, hits send, then stashes the phone. He should be back in hailing range of civilization in a couple of hours. Then they can get this plan underway. He figures Daisy booked this place for, what? The night? The weekend? A surprise anniversary getaway?

It's a sweet gesture, he has to admit.

Just shitty timing.

He swings open the trunk and considers the two fully packed suitcases inside.

A week with Lilith, just the two of them, in Cabo San Lucas, let everyone cool off, then move his things out of his place with Daisy and into Lilith's place for good. Not her actual place, she has a husband and a kid, but into the Airbnb love nest they'd rented for a month while they get everything sorted out. He'd packed just enough clothes in the two suitcases to be gone for two weeks, plus everything in the apartment he cared about and thought Daisy might be inclined to break or destroy after he'd gone.

Plus his copy of *Don Quixote*. He'd finish it this time, on the beach.

Thirty-eight is not too late.

He slams the trunk and heads into the house to face his soon-to-be ex-wife, hoping she at least thought to open a bottle of wine.

3

"You made it."

"Barely."

"I'm happy to see you."

"I nearly got lost. It's been pitch-black for an hour."

"Traffic must have been terrible."

"The city was a nightmare. And my phone—" He holds up the dark rectangle helplessly.

"I know. Mine, too." She smiles sympathetically and offers him a glass of wine. She's poured two glasses, at the ready. One for him, one for her, though she won't sip hers.

She raises her glass. "To surprises."

"To surprises."

They toast and the glasses ring.

He takes a big sip, looks around the cabin.

"You like it?" she says.

"The wine?"

"The cabin."

"Sure. It's cozy. It's great." He tosses back another long gulp, and soon, she notices, he's done that trick of his where he makes his entire glass disappear.

"We have it for the whole week," she says, watching for his reaction.

He looks at her, shocked. A week? he thinks. "But what about work?"

"It's a vacation. We need it. Don't worry, I already cleared it with your boss. Come on. Sit down. Let's relax."

Now he's done that other trick he does, she thinks, where he makes a new glass of wine appear. You don't ever quite remember him pouring it. His glass is just a magic glass, draining and refilling itself.

"How's the wifi up here?" he asks, taking another sip. "I need to stay in touch."

"There's no wifi. No phones. Just us." She holds up the pouches she got from the foundation's representative. "We're supposed to put our phones in these. And then we're not supposed to check them for the week."

"But what if there's an emergency?" He thinks of the texts on his phone right now. Of Lilith—*Is it done?*—and how she's packed and waiting to go.

"The foundation can reach us," she says. "Otherwise, it'll wait. It's a week. People used to do this all the time—take off and disappear."

"But what if we need help?"

"There's a landline." She points to the ancient red rotary phone on a side table, displayed like a relic in a museum. "It's a direct line. The foundation will send someone."

"What's 'the foundation'? Have you kidnapped me into a cult?" He attempts to say this last part as a joke, but the reality of the situation is just starting to dawn on him—the extent of this "surprise" she's planned for them. When he saw the note, he assumed he was headed for dinner in some rustic town upstate, maybe an overnight stay at some charming B&B. But she's rented this cabin for a week and is expecting them to stay here, together, alone? Meanwhile, he's booked on a flight to Cabo that leaves from JFK tomorrow night at 8:40 p.m.

"Trust me. It's going to be good for us," she says, smiling, trying carefully to dole out just enough information that he doesn't completely melt down. "Let's have some dinner and I'll explain everything."

"But I have clients. Accounts." He's sputtering now, trotting out business jargon as a kind of get-out-of-jail-free card.

"Come on, you hate that job." She pulls out a chair at the table. "You must be famished. And guess what?"

"What?"

"I cooked."

He eyes her over his glass, disbelieving. "You cooked?"

She laughs. "I know, right? Me—Our Lady of Perpetual Takeout." She hopes a joke will relax him. This is not how she wanted the evening to go. Yet it's how she knew it would unfold. How could it not? A surprise note? A long drive? She knows Craig well enough to know a curveball of this magnitude will only leave him antsy, agitated, hostile, on his heels. He hates surprises. More accurately, more than anything, he hates feeling like you know something he doesn't.

Still, she thinks—he's here. That's the first step.

"You can't see it, but there's a lake out there," she says, gesturing to the darkened windows. "It's beautiful. And private. We have this whole place to ourselves. We can hike. There's a canoe."

"How did we afford this?" he says.

"Don't worry. I covered it with my money from the TV show. It's my anniversary gift to us."

He looks at her, puzzled. "How did you even get up here?"

"Someone from the foundation dropped me off."

"What is this *foundation?*" he says, but she's already set down her still-full wineglass and disappeared into the kitchen.

He sits alone at the table in a hard-back wooden chair. The table setting does look nice, he thinks. She really did go all out. She spent her TV money—after years of him nagging her, she finally booked a TV gig—on this weeklong vacation, just the two of them. She's really making an effort, he thinks. Then he thinks about Cabo, and Lilith, and the impending flight, and the texts that are no doubt arriving right now and jangling around inside his sleeping phone. So what's his plan here, exactly? He downs his second glass of wine.

It all seemed so clear to him when he left New York, but that was four hours and an excruciating drive ago. Now he's here, and it's late, and he's going to—what? Deliver the speech, break her heart, then get back in the car and drive all the way back to the city? In the dark? Half drunk?

If he's going to do that, he needs to stop drinking, and the one thing he knows for sure right now is that he does not want to stop drinking.

Calm down, he thinks. You have a day. The flight doesn't leave until tomorrow night. Lilith is waiting, yes, but she'll understand. You can't trash three years of your life on a whim—you have to be deliberate. We'll have our dinner, no need to ruin it, then we can talk all this through in the morning.

Okay. New plan.

Satisfied, he pours himself another glass of wine.

She reenters wearing oven mitts and an apron and carrying a whole chicken in a deep roasting pan. Her hair, which in winter retreats to a reliably indistinct brown, is at the peak of its late-summer blond radiance, and she's piled it on her head, pinned up, in the exact style he likes best. Her green eyes seem lit by the glow of the candles, and her cheeks are flushed red from the heat of the stove. She looks happy to be here, truly, happy to see him, he thinks. Excited for the week.

And, he has to admit, the dinner looks good. He's not sure how she did it, but the roast chicken is golden brown and perfect, skin crisped and garlanded with thin lemon slices, like it could be on a magazine cover, which is the highest compliment he can pay to anything.

"Impressive," he says.

"We needed something like this, don't you think?" She takes off the mitts and sets them aside, drapes her apron over a chair, and tops up his glass.

He flaps the heavy cloth napkin over his lap. "We needed chicken?"

She sits. Holds up her glass again. "No. This. A chance to get away. To leave everything behind. To be together. Just the two of us. Like there's no one else in the whole world. Happy anniversary."

He toasts, takes a long swig, then grabs a carving knife. "Shall I?"

"Please."

He holds the knife, poised.

Pauses.

"So what is this foundation?" he says.

"Have you ever heard of the Eden Test?"

"No," he says. "Should I have?"

She smiles. "Just carve," she says.

IIII

He's on his third glass of wine and in a better mood now, she thinks, as he relaxes into the faded sofa with floral cushions, the dinner done and the dishes cleared away. She knew he'd need a glass or two—or three—when he got here, just to let the shock of the surprise dissipate. He hates surprises, but this is important, she thinks, this week, this retreat. This will be good for us. It's what we need.

This, and the test.

She stands in the door of an open closet on her tiptoes, running her finger over a tall stack of weathered board games. She wriggles free an ancient faded Scrabble box from the pile, lifts the lid off, and sets it on the coffee table before him.

"I hate Scrabble," he says. "You know that. All those stupid nonexistent two-letter words like *x-g.*"

"You mean *x-i,*" she says. "*X-g* is not a word." She leaves the Scrabble box open and heads back to the closet. "How about Ouija? Maybe it will tell us our future."

"No way," he says. "We're in the middle of nowhere. I don't want to be summoning ghosts." He glances into the Scrabble box and spots a folded piece of paper. "What's this?"

"I don't know. You tell me."

He unfolds it. "It's just a typed list of words."

"Like what?"

"*Cleave. Left. Weather. Bound. Temper. Refrain.*" He looks up at her. "Maybe they're secret Scrabble clues."

"Let me see," she says. He passes her the paper. She glances over the list, the typed letters slightly askew.

"These are Janus words," she says finally, proudly.

"What are Janice words?" he says. The only famous Janice he knows is that obnoxious girlfriend from *Friends.*

"They're also called antagonyms—words that have two different meanings that are the opposite of each other. Like this first one: *cleave.* It

can mean to cut or sever, like a cleaver, or to cleave something in half. But it can also mean to stick to closely, to adhere or hold on to, like in *The Tempest* when Ariel says, *Thy thoughts I cleave to. What's thy pleasure?*"

"God, you're such a show-off," he says.

"Hey, graduate theater school was very expensive. I have to use that knowledge somehow." She hands the paper back to him. He's annoyed, she can see, that this is yet another thing she knows about and he doesn't.

"What about *left?*" He glances at the list, a bit petulant. "*Left* doesn't have two opposite meanings."

"Sure it does," she says, taking a teacher's tone—she can't help it. "*Left* can refer to leaving, as in 'He left.' But it can also refer to remaining, like 'She got left behind.'"

"So what do these words have to do with Scrabble?"

"I don't know. Maybe someone *left* that list here when they *left* the cabin."

He mock-claps for her. "Okay, Little Miss Genius—so who's Janice?"

"Janus—he's the Roman god with two faces. He looks to the past and the future. He's the god of beginnings and endings."

"Oh, yeah," Craig says with some satisfaction. "Like comedy and tragedy. The theater masks."

"No, that's something different."

Craig regards her, his smile frozen, frustrated, as if she's tricked him into a conversation the only purpose of which is to make him feel stupid. "See, I knew I made a mistake by marrying someone smarter than me," he says finally. He replaces the note, puts the lid back on the Scrabble box, and holds it out for her.

"I don't think you had a choice," she says—leaving him to wonder whether she means he had no choice but to marry someone smarter than him or no choice but to marry her.

On tiptoes, she stashes the Scrabble box back in the closet and returns to him with another box—the old plastic fighting game Rock 'Em Sock 'Em Robots. She unboxes the game and places it on the coffee table.

It's a yellow boxing ring with two plastic robots, fists raised, one robot red, one blue, facing off. With little controllers, so you can make them punch each other until one of their heads pops off.

"Put up your dukes," she says.

"I'm sorry. I think I'm too tired for a game. Or too drunk." He holds up his empty wineglass like, *Guilty.*

"No problem," she says. She picks up an envelope that's been sitting on the coffee table the whole time. On the front of the envelope in gold script it says: *Q1.*

"What's that?" he says.

"This," she says, "is the Eden Test."

"Okay, spill it. What's the Eden Test?" The wine's whispering to him, *You've been tricked. This is a trap. You're in trouble. Run.*

"It's a system to help couples, couples like us. It was invented by these therapists, Kit and Bridget Arden. They're doctors, they're married, and they started this foundation called Edenic years ago. The Eden Test is seven days and seven questions, one per day. This is number one."

"Wait—we're going to have to see therapists while we're here?" he says. "I thought this was a vacation."

"It is," she says calmly. "A retreat. We just have to do the questions and then the rest of the time is for us."

"What kind of questions?"

"Think of them as—conversation starters. I don't know what the questions are, specifically. The questions themselves are a big proprietary secret. You have to do the program, that's the point."

He looks at her, agitated. *Seriously?* "We've been together three years, Daisy. Don't you think we know each other pretty well?"

She holds up the first envelope. "Let's find out."

She rips open the envelope and pulls out a folded sheet of paper, printed on heavy stock, like an invitation to some grand event.

She unfolds it. "*Question One.*" She turns to him. "Are you ready?"

"Is that the question?"

"No," she says. "This is the question: *Would you change for me?*"

And then she reads the rest.

Question One.

Would you change for me?

We fear change. Especially when it comes to relationships. When we fall in love, we want that magical moment of transformation to be preserved forever. We like to say, "Love changed me!" or "I met him and everything changed"—but then we want the change to stop. Later on, when dark clouds gather and we sense love careening off course, what do we blame? Change.

"You've changed!" we cry. Or "Don't try to change me!"

But change is life. So is growth.

So is love.

So start your journey today by turning to your partner and asking the first simple question.

Would you change for me?

Only by acknowledging the necessity of change can we start to understand what change requires.

And it will require a lot. From both of you.

Welcome to the Eden Test.

This is the first of seven questions that will start you and your partner on your journey to a better life.

A better love.

Together.

Would you change for me?

Just by asking it, just by being here, you've already changed a little bit.

You've taken the very first step.

And we've only just begun.

She finishes reading, folds the paper, and turns to him, expectant.

He looks at her, slightly agitated, slightly drunk, and says, "So what am I supposed to say now?"

The Second Day

||||

HEAVENS

4

The sun wakes her. She's alone in the bed. The sheets are crisp and white and smell clean, and the room is cool and bright. In the open window, a white curtain swirls in the late-summer breeze like the skirt of a flamenco dancer.

She thinks of the long conversation they had last night, a conversation about change. All of which went surprisingly well, she thinks. Eventually, Craig opened up a little bit—about his fear of change, about the need for it—overcoming his initial hesitation, his well-established aversion to "working on the relationship." He comes from a school of thought, she knows, that believes that good relationships don't need work; that's what makes them good.

But they got past that. And once they did, they connected. Or started to.

Sure, he seemed a bit distracted, a bit antsy, but who can blame him? After a surprise note, a long drive, a bottle of wine.

Look at us, she thinks. Making progress. And we're only on day one.

Seven days. Seven questions.

Six to go.

Promising.

She lies back with her hands folded behind her head on the white pillow. Revels for a moment in the bright birdsong trilling just outside the window.

So far, so good.

As for him, he's nowhere to be seen.

But she smells coffee.

||||

In the kitchen, he stands by the burbling coffee maker, head throbbing, rummaging through the drawers for his phone. How much wine did he drink? Too much—always an accurate answer.

And where did she put the phones?

The flight to Cabo doesn't leave until tonight just after eight p.m., so he's still got time—a little time, he thinks. They chose a night flight on purpose to give them a whole day to square everything away. That was always the plan—tell Daisy on Friday night, spend Saturday packing up and moving out, then head for Mexico that evening. The anniversary surprise threw a wrench into everything, obviously, but there's no reason he can't get back on the plan. His Friday night drive up here had been long and hellish, but on a Saturday afternoon he figures he can circumvent the city traffic and make it to JFK in two hours, maybe three, tops. So long as he leaves by early afternoon, he can still make it to the airport to meet Lilith. He just has to text her now to tell her what's up.

Which means he needs to find his phone.

He tries to recall where she put them. He remembers driving, entering, drinking, the board games, the question, the long discussion afterward.

He remembers something about—pouches. For the phones.

He ducks out of the kitchen, listens for a moment to hear if Daisy's awake, then glances at the small side table on which sits a red landline phone.

He yanks a drawer open and rummages around through the usual detritus: twine, rusty scissors, a few strips of old stamps, a bunch of weathered brochures for local attractions, and then, *boom*, there they are, the smartphones.

He grabs his phone and slaps at the dark glass with his thumbs. It wakes up.

No bars.

Shit.

He knows from the drive up here that cell service is spotty, but if he finds the right place, he should be okay. Still listening for signs of Daisy stirring upstairs, he walks toward the windows, holding the phone up, no luck, then heads toward the door of the cabin, then out to the porch, his phone held in front of him like a divining rod, like he's following its insistent tugs toward buried water.

Once outside, he glances over his shoulder to make sure Daisy's still upstairs, then heads down the steps to the gravel driveway in his flip-flops.

Slap slap slap.

Still no service.

Fuuuuuuuuuuuuck.

He'll have to concoct an excuse to head to town, then smuggle the phone out to text Lilith.

At least it will give him time to think of what to say.

Plus, the speech. There's still that.

He still has to tell Daisy.

He thought of doing it last night but abandoned that notion pretty quickly once they got into their long conversation about change. It seemed a bit abrupt—if not downright cruel—to pop that in: *Change, it's so important, it's what keeps a relationship strong, and, oh, by the way, speaking of change—*

Besides, he has to admit, it was kind of nice, just the two of them. It's been so long since they've been able to get away. Between her with her shows and him with his work, not to mention his various extracurriculars, they almost never take the time anymore to just focus on each other, the way they used to in that dizzying first year. It's actually kind of a shame that it's happening now, he thinks. Oh, well. Too little, too late.

He heads back inside the cabin and hears the coffee maker chiming. He spots his jacket from last night slung over a rocking chair. He slips his phone into a jacket pocket and holds the jacket up to see if the phone bulge is too obvious.

Should be fine.

Okay.

That's done.

Now he just has to figure out how to get a bit closer to civilization. Maybe he can invent some errand. Some work emergency he just remembered. An excuse to head into town. He assumes they're close to a town.

He hears feet, padding softly.

He looks up. She's on the stairs, smiling.

"You made coffee!" she says brightly. She's paused, mid-stair, in her flannel nightgown, like a vision. Well rested. Hair sleep-tossed.

Goddammit, he thinks. She looks adorable.

"I was just going to start breakfast," he says.

"No, no," she says. "Get your clothes on. I'm taking you out for the best pancakes in the world."

5

They get dressed together in the bedroom in silence. He watches her bend over topless in her underwear as she rummages through the bureau drawers for clothes. One thing about marriage he never expected was spending a lot of time with someone you find exceptionally attractive in various stages of undress and not acting on it. It seems unnatural to him. Which bolsters his argument that marriage itself is unnatural, which is what he's come to believe, which has led him to his current situation. In the beginning, he recalls, they couldn't keep their hands off each other. She didn't so much undress him as *unwrap* him, voracious, and he felt that way, too—like every moment they spent together that they *weren't* naked, they were just biding their time. From those early dates, they were compatible—they just *fit*. And over time, they learned each other. What they liked, what they didn't. And what they liked was each other.

Now they get dressed together in silence with their backs turned.

He checks the clock. It's still early. Not even ten a.m. They'll have brunch together, be back by one, maybe two, he'll give the speech and hit the road.

Still plenty of time, he thinks.

As they head out the door downstairs, he grabs his jacket, which is rolled up in a bundle. He carries it in one arm awkwardly, cradled like a football.

"I don't think you'll need it," she says. "It's supposed to be nice out today."

"Just in case."

"Okay, Mr. Practical."

On the porch, he pulls the door closed. "You have keys?"

"Just leave it," she says. "It's the country. No one locks their doors around here."

In the car as he drives they debate the etymology of pancakes versus flapjacks. Like whether these are two distinct foodstuffs or simply two terms—maybe regional in origin—for the exact same thing. Neither of them has any knowledge about the subject or any investment in the answer, but it's the kind of fun, mock-serious argument they used to have all the time when they first started dating. Amusing banter with a sitcom cadence. It feels nice, to both of them.

"I'm just saying, *is* there a difference?" he says. "Like, a pancake I can understand. It's a cake in a pan. But what the hell is a flapjack?"

"Clearly, someone named Jack was involved," she says, looking out her open window at the passing woods. "And then there was some sort of flap."

The woods in daylight look so different to Craig—he can hardly believe this is the same road he drove last night. The trees now tower bright and inviting, a canopy of late-summer green, and the occasional glimpse of late-morning sunlight dazzles through the branches. The air outside is cool and pleasant, the new day full of promise. Last night, his drive felt like a long descent into darkness, like he was entering a cave or a trap. This morning, these woods truly do feel like a place to escape to, a chance to get away from it all.

"If anything," he says resolutely, "you'd call it a flipjack. Like, maybe some guy named Jack flipped the cake and then everyone started calling it that."

"I can picture him," Daisy says. "Burly dude, like a lumberjack. Leather apron. Paul Bunyan–esque. They call him Flip Jack. And he carries a huge, handcrafted spatula, carved from the trunk of a single tree."

"He's got a handlebar mustache, for sure."

"Oh, of course, my love." She turns to him, smitten, her eyes earnest, full of passion. It's a playful performance, he knows, this look of unabashed adoration, but he still enjoys it.

"From now on," she says, "we'll forever call them flipjacks, just you and me. It will be our little secret."

"All hail the mighty Flip Jack," he shouts out his open window, and laughs, the car speeding into another twist in the country road.

They pull into town forty minutes later, having followed a map they'd found in the cabin. The village itself is darling, like the Platonic ideal of a Cute Small Town: basically, a main street with some alluring vintage shops on one side and an enticing bookstore located in an old firehouse on the other. That bookstore looks cool—I'll have to stop in later, Craig thinks, before remembering that he's supposed to be dumping his wife later and heading off to Mexico. For the first time, the prospect of that sequence of grim confrontations—and even the sunny getaway to follow—drops a heavy lump of dread in his gut.

"The name is Plain," she says. "This town. Plain, New York. Humble, right?"

"And not inaccurate." Craig pulls up and parks the car, no problem, right in front of the town's apparently famous pancake restaurant. This is one reliably good thing about small towns, he thinks. Abundant parking.

As they exit the car, he grabs his jacket from the backseat.

"You won't need your jacket," she says.

"You never know," he says, which makes little sense to either of them, but she leaves it at that, for which he's thankful.

Inside, the restaurant is charming in an upstate kind of way: cozy booths and local art and a laid-back vibe. Everyone here is laughing, relaxed, and looks like they might linger for hours. Brunch in Brooklyn, Craig thinks, is an Olympic event, stressful, competitive, and highly choreographed, requiring advance planning and strategy: the right hour to arrive so you're not stranded in line; the right table to grab so you're not shoehorned in by the kitchen; the best techniques for navigating the crush of people who, just like you, are there to aggressively chill on the weekend after aggressively working all week. But apparently life in the country is different.

There's a short line at the front of the diner, so Craig asks the hostess about the wait. She gives an apologetic shrug. "Sorry, it may be a while."

"How long?" he asks in a city-weary voice.

"Ten, maybe fifteen minutes?" she says tentatively, like she's delivering terrible news.

Craig almost laughs. In Brooklyn, *it may be a while* reliably means an hour and a half or more, and if the announced wait for brunch isn't at least forty-five minutes, he'll usually turn on his heel and leave because clearly this spot isn't popular or good.

He turns to Daisy. "What do you think?"

She steps past him and says to the hostess, "We're Daisy and Craig. I called ahead."

"Oh, of course!" the hostess says, her eyes lighting up. "Right this way. Follow me."

As she leads them to a booth, Craig can swear the other waitstaff are watching them, like they're honored guests, celebrities. He even thinks he spots a cook peek out from the kitchen. The hostess hands them two menus.

"This good?" Daisy says once they're seated.

"Seems great," he says.

She's so glad he likes it.

Craig, Daisy knows, as she watches him carve into his towering stack of pancakes, can be needlessly finicky about restaurants—it's one of his least endearing traits. She remembers their early days of dating, when they'd walk arm in arm in Manhattan and pass some inviting dive bar and she'd try to nudge him toward the promise of perfect cheeseburgers and he'd make a big show of resisting—*No, no, I know exactly the place*—and then he'd drag her to some cramped and insufferable bistro down the block with the hot new chef and a ninety-minute wait.

The real irony is that he thought he was impressing her. Well, it certainly left an impression, she thinks. She's since learned that Craig grew up in strip-mall suburban Michigan, eating at Chili's and Olive Garden and calling it a fancy night out. Maybe that legacy is what he is trying to escape, but something about living in New York curdled him into a wannabe amateur gourmand, the kind who uses *plate* as a verb. The kind who feels moved to constantly comment on the décor, the wine pairings, the head chef's employment history, the appearance (or lack) of amuse-bouche before dinner, as though he'd studied in the finest culinary schools of Europe rather than being just another dude in Brooklyn with a credit card and a subscription to *Bon Appétit*.

Of course, the game in New York is to never be satisfied—she understands that—not just with restaurants, not just with meals, but with apartments, neighborhoods, jobs, offices, friends, and romantic partners—partners most of all. New York: the city that offers everything but promises nothing, except a continual itchy sense of dissatisfaction and the suspicion that someone, somewhere, is having a better time, in a better restaurant, with a better meal, in a better outfit, with a better companion than you are.

That's why they had to get out of the city, to someplace like this, someplace quiet, a getaway.

And Craig, she knows, has always benefited from being nudged out of his comfort zone.

If nothing else, she's introduced him to some knockout cheeseburgers.

He looks up at her, his mouth stuffed, lips glazed with gooey syrup.

"Oh my God," he groans. "These are fantastic."

"I know, right?" She smiles. "Would I ever lead you astray?"

Craig's general attitude about restaurants is this: He lives in New York City, one of the most celebrated food destinations in the world, so the notion that some far-flung backwater outpost in the middle of the woods has an out-of-this-world offering seems improbable to him, even laughable, and yet goddamn, if these pancakes aren't delicious. He chews ecstatically and carves another bite from the fluffy, inches-thick stack of buckwheat goodness, nutty, flavorful, soaked in syrup—and not the fake kind of syrup but real maple syrup that tastes like trees. The kind of syrup that's harvested by men with beards in plaid shirts whose breath forms clouds on frosty winter mornings. He searches for the right word for that distinct syrup flavor.

Maple-y, he thinks.

When the waitress checks in to fill up their coffee mugs, he asks her, "Can you tell me what the difference is between flapjacks and pancakes?"

"Sorry?" the waitress says. She's young, maybe mid-twenties, and she's got jet-black hair piled up in a Medusa's crown of curls with sharp bangs cut across her forehead. Tattoos ribbon up and down her pale white arms, classic rockabilly tattoos, pinup girls and sideshow devils and Day of the Dead flowered skulls, the kind of tattoos Craig has always found particularly alluring. She wears an old-fashioned waitress outfit with lace trim at the low-cut collar; it looks like a costume, like she's playing the role of a waitress, like she's Flo on the old TV show *Alice.* Her name tag reads LORELEI.

"Flapjacks," Craig says again. "See, we have this theory about a burly man named Flip Jack. Leather apron, spatula, enormous griddle." Craig glances mischievously at Daisy and sees instantly she's not on board with this playful chitchat—which, he realizes now, might seem to her more like brazen flirting. He suddenly feels kind of stupid, exposed, and he's hoping Daisy will jump in to save him. She doesn't. "I mean, how are flapjacks different from pancakes?" he repeats.

"Can't help you, friend. I'm gluten-free," the waitress says, then gives him a cold smile, her black lipstick jackknifing into a sharp V, before turning and sauntering away.

He can't help but notice as she exits that her slightly too-short skirt bounces up in the back to reveal she's wearing thigh-high stockings, along with a pair of high Doc Marten lace-ups. Good Lord. Tattoos, Docs, attitude—it's like she was designed to tick Craig's boxes.

"Old friend?" says Daisy acidly. It's a long-standing joke between them, whenever one of them catches the other's gaze lingering too long on someone else. To be honest, she was the one who introduced this joke to their relationship, and she has occasion to say it a lot more often than he does.

"Thanks for leaving me hanging," he says, a little surly.

"Hanging how?"

"Flip Jack. You made me look like an idiot."

"You were doing a pretty good job of that yourself."

"You could have chimed in," he snaps.

"That was supposed to be our joke, remember? Just you and me? Not flirtation fodder."

Craig sneaks one more glance at the retreating waitress. Sometimes he forgets that there are cool people living upstate, too. Authentic people, salt of the earth, not posers like in the city. He imagines himself moving upstate one day, leaving the superficial city behind, writing his novel, bearded, in a log cabin by lamplight.

Which is when he notices a guy in a nearby booth, eyeing him. Young guy, well-built, wearing one of those bright orange fluorescent baseball caps you wear when you go hunting. The guy's seated with a wiry friend whose back is to Craig, hunched over his menu. The young guy stares daggers at Craig—Craig wonders for a moment if they somehow know each other—and then the guy looks away. Then back up at Craig again, pointedly.

Craig breaks eye contact and looks down at his plate. Okay, that isn't a friendly look, he thinks. Maybe the waitress is this dude's girlfriend? Craig's neck is hot now, his ears itchy. See, this is why he can't live upstate. For every cool person, like that tattooed waitress, every hipster refugee from the urban rat race who escapes up here to start a puppet theater or craft artisanal candles in an abandoned barn, you've got some hair-trigger yokel, some bored racist hayseed, looking to start some shit.

Daisy, seemingly oblivious, has spread a few brochures she found at the cabin out on the tabletop. She studies them earnestly like tarot cards. "Okay—we've got a week. What should we do first?" She pushes a few pamphlets forward. "They've got inner tube rafting not too far from here. There's great antiquing, too. And there's tons of hiking trails."

"You decide," he says, forcing a smile. He glances at a wall clock—it's inching up on noon—then slides one hand into the balled-up jacket on the booth beside him and slips his phone free and into the front pocket of his jeans. "I've got to hit the men's."

Daisy nods, distracted, and turns her eyes back to the brochures.

The bathroom, as expected, is tucked away in the back of the restaurant, beyond the kitchen, right next to a screen door that leads outside. Craig looks back into the restaurant to make sure he's not in Daisy's sight line, then slips through the screen door, down a set of back steps, and into a large gravel parking lot.

More parking, he thinks.

He pulls out the phone.

It sparks to life immediately.

Three bars. Thank God.

Civilization. Sort of.

He watches as the phone downloads. An unfurling history of angry texts. And twelve missed calls.

He swipes through the texts but doesn't bother to read them all.

He gets the gist.

He opens the text box to reply, then wonders what he should say.

I'll see you—I couldn't—I'm sorry. He shuffles through excuses. Thumbs poised. For a moment—just a moment—he thinks, What if I just ignore them? He's here, he's having a surprisingly nice time, Daisy has no clue about any of this yet. He could just stay upstate with his wife—

"Urgent business?" someone says, and he looks up, spooked, and sees the same waitress watching him from the steps outside the screen door, pulling a cigarette from a pack.

"I just—yeah. Work." He flashes a guilty grin and slips the phone into his pocket.

Her cigarette lit, she walks down and stands next to him. "We have a local term for people who are visiting from the city. You want to hear it?"

"What makes you think I'm from the city?"

She laughs, as if this is the stupidest possible question. Her black lips part to reveal pearly teeth. She's so pretty, Craig thinks. "We call them citiots," she says. "Short for—"

"City idiots. I get it. Nice. Very hospitable."

"And usually pretty accurate." She taps ash from her cigarette. "My name's Lorelei."

"So I see." He points to her name tag. "I'm Craig."

"Hello, Craig. You like music?" She reaches her hand into the neckline of her dress and pulls out a folded piece of paper. Craig's gaze lingers on the spot from which she retrieved the note: On her breastbone she's got a tattoo of a rose-red apple, encircled by a flaming serpent.

"I always thought that was cool," he says. "That kind of tattoo."

"What kind?"

"Right over where your heart is."

"How do you know where my heart is?" She holds out the piece of paper. It's a flyer for a band called Blaise Orange. "We have a show tonight," she says. "At the roadhouse. You should come. Sample the local color."

"Are you always so shameless about recruiting an audience?"

"Look around." She gestures with her cigarette at the empty parking lot, the diner, the town. "I live in the middle of nowhere. Believe it or not, there's not an abundance of art lovers up here. So we have to beat the bushes." She catches his gaze and holds it. "You ever beat a bush before?"

He's caught off guard by the brazen question; his mouth goes dry; he glances at the flyer. "Blaise Orange—what's that? I thought your name is Lorelei."

"It's my band. It's a pun on blaze orange, that color of hunting gear you see a lot up here," she says. "It's that high-visibility orange color people wear in the woods to make sure you don't shoot them by mistake."

"Like the guy inside with the baseball hat?" says Craig.

"What guy?"

"There was a guy with an orange hat like that. Seemed surly. I thought maybe he was your boyfriend."

She laughs. "No, I'm devoutly single. Plus, I don't really vibe with the local youth." She looks at Craig. "And I don't like hunting. I just like the idea of being highly visible." She tosses the cigarette to the ground and grinds it out with her boot. "So are you coming to my show or what?"

"I'd love to. Maybe my wife—"

"Or alone." She puts a flat hand on his chest to balance herself. "You look like you need to take a night off from whatever you're out here doing. You know, to unwind."

Okay, this is weird, he thinks. He's not unaccustomed to female attention, but this waitress who just blew him off coldly inside the restaurant is now coming on to him in the parking lot. Maybe he's wrong. He's been wrong before. Then again, he's also been right.

His phone buzzes in his pocket.

That would be Lilith.

He holds up the flyer. "I'll try to make it."

Another buzz.

"Either way, I'm sure I'll see you again." Lorelei nods toward the restaurant. "Back to the grind. I'll leave you to your business. Though I'm guessing your wife is starting to wonder why you're taking so long in the bathroom."

He's flustered, Daisy sees that, as Craig returns from the back of the restaurant, fumbling with something in his pocket. She's not unaware of how he likes to sneak off, step away at inopportune moments, conduct his furtive business—it's just that he's so bad at hiding it. She actually wishes he were smoother, more competent—it would make it easier for her to pretend not to notice it. As it is, she has to work very hard at seeming oblivious.

Summon all her considerable acting skills.

Thankfully, she's a very good actor.

And that's okay, she thinks. That's why we're here.

Seven days. Seven questions.

She has faith in the process.

Starting with: *Would you change for me?*

Change is what this week is going to be all about.

"All good?" she asks sweetly as he slides back into the booth.

"All good." Glancing around, Craig notes with some relief that the guy in the blaze orange cap and his friend have left. He gestures at the brochures she has fanned out on the table. "So—what do you have planned for us?"

She purrs at him in a sultry voice, "You want to hear a pornographic idea?"

Craig, his thigh still tingling from the vibrations of the incoming text and his mind still befuddled by the waitress's unabashed parking lot flirtation, says, "Yeah. Always."

She looks him straight in the eyes, loosing a seductive grin. "We could take a nap. When's the last time we took a nap?"

Back at the cabin, in the bedroom, she turns down the cool white sheets.

He checks the clock. It's just past one. He's got to leave soon if he's going to make it.

She giggles and unsnaps her overalls and lets them drop to the floor and stands before him in her T-shirt and underwear.

"Nap time!" she exclaims and jumps onto the bed.

And he decides that this probably isn't the right moment for the speech.

He pulls off his jeans and T-shirt and joins her. She pulls the white sheet over their heads to make a cocoon.

"Naps are like sex for New Yorkers," she whispers. "Naps are our secret fetish."

"You know in Spain they take naps in the middle of the day," he says.

"We should go to Europe. We should do so many things." She smiles at him, their faces now inches apart. Her breath smells like maple, earthy and sweet, he thinks.

"The best thing about this place is we have it for a whole week," she says. "So plenty of time to nap."

"We can become napoholics."

"Napomaniacs," she says. "Napophiles."

"We'll move to the Napa Valley."

"You're terrible," she says, giggling. "You're the absolute worst."

She slides closer to him, right up against him, under the tented sheet. Her hand finds its way into his boxers.

"We could even nap later," she whispers. "Tire ourselves out first."

He thinks of the folded flyer in his jeans pocket, the one for the concert at the roadhouse by Blaise Orange, and the black lipstick on the cigarette filter before it hit the ground, and the tattoo on the waitress's forearm of the smiling devil with a pencil mustache.

And as Daisy acts surprised to feel how aroused he is already, he thinks this probably isn't the right moment for the speech, either.

6

They take an afternoon walk in the woods, arm in arm. As they stroll, he names everything.

He used to hike in the woods with his mom as a kid in Michigan. His mother knew the names of all the trees. Chestnut, birch, maple, oak. She was a natural naturalist, he always says. He couldn't help but pick up some of it, and if he doesn't know the name of a tree, he just makes it up, and Daisy laughs.

"That's definitely not a palm tree," she says.

"Trust me," he says.

After a while on the path, they enter a clearing. An orchard. Row upon row of gnarled trees. At the edge of the clearing a rusted tangle of barbed wire, strung between ancient wooden posts, snakes around the perimeter. An old crooked sign says in no uncertain terms: KEEP OUT.

Maybe this is the place to do it, he thinks. He knows he's running out of time—if he's going to make it to the airport for his flight, he has to tell Daisy now. He imagines turning to her, taking her hands in his, intoning: *Daisy—we need to talk.* Her fallen face. The tears. He dreads all of it—

"Okay, what kind of trees are those, genius?" she says playfully, clutching his arm.

"Let's take a look."

They hop over the low fence and walk hand in hand among the rows.

Apple trees, it turns out. Small, sour fruits dangle from the branches. The runty apples are mushy, the leaves spotted brown.

"Upon closer inspection, I don't think these are edible," he says.

"God, disgusting," she says.

He picks a mottled apple, pretends to bite it, clownishly chewing. She laughs. Then he hurls the puckered fruit into the distance like a baseball and decides that this also isn't the right time for the speech.

They hike back. A whisper of wildlife trails them as they make their way through the woods. The day is ideal, he has to admit.

But he's got to do it. He's *going* to do it. He's just waiting for the right moment, the right spot. Some wooded glade. A shaded grotto. Then we'll sit down and do this like adults, he thinks.

"Take *weather*," she says.

"What?"

"*Weather*—it was one of the words from the Scrabble box, the words with double meanings," she says. "The antagonyms."

"Oh, yeah." He suddenly feels itchy, annoyed, like this is a pop quiz. "Sun. Rain. Snow. Wind. How does *weather* have two opposite meanings?"

"To weather something means to survive it, right?" she says. "Like weathering the storm. But it can also mean to be worn down over time—like a weathered jacket, weathered by the elements."

"I see." He tries gamely to engage.

"Or *bound*," she says, enthused. "*Bound* can mean tied up or constrained, like 'You're bound by the rules' or 'Don't go out of bounds.' But it can also mean to depart on a journey—like 'We're bound for the promised land.'"

"That's true," he says. Maybe over there, by that stump, he thinks. Maybe that's the place—

"The thing that's cool about antagonyms," she continues, sounding like a tour guide now, "is how they suggest two different perspectives, two different ways of seeing the world—like, no matter what, there are always two paths, two possibilities. You can *cleave* something apart or you can *cleave* to it. You can run *fast* or you can hold *fast*. You can be the one who *left* or you can be the one who's *left* behind."

"I never thought of it that way," he says, as he thinks of the idling airplane, the furious texts, the ticking clock. He scans the forest around them. They're much closer to the cabin now—if it happens here, it's just a short walk back, he can grab his things, start the car, hit the road—

He regards her. Poor Daisy. She looks so pretty in this light. He hates the idea of causing her pain. It's just—it is what it is, he thinks. Sometimes we travel together. Sometimes we have to part ways. What did she just say about those double words? Antago-somethings? Two points of view, two paths...

She stoops and picks up a rock, just big enough to hold in her palm. Sizing it up, she runs a thumb over its surface to test its smoothness.

"What's that for?" he says.

"To put our names on." She turns to him. "It would be romantic, right? You know, *Craig plus Daisy.* As a keepsake."

"Why not just carve our initials in a tree?"

"Trees burn. Stumps rot. But rocks—" She presents it for him to consider. "Rocks are forever." She hefts it lightly, considers the weight of it, then tosses it into the underbrush where it lands with a wet thump.

"What's wrong with that one?" he asks.

"I need to find one that's big enough that I can paint on it but small enough that I can carry it home. We'll put it on our mantel in Brooklyn, next to our wedding photos. A souvenir of our anniversary surprise."

"How cute. Our little pet rock," he says. "Our kid. Li'l Rocky."

"It has to be perfect," she says, then adds melodramatically, laughing, clutching his arm, batting her eyes at him. "Perfect, just like our love."

They emerge from the tree line together and walk toward the cabin. This is it, he thinks, his gut twisting. Now or never. Lilith is waiting— she's no doubt apoplectic. He's only known Lilith for four months, and now he's going to have to spend half the week in Mexico whispering apologies to her, begging forgiveness for messing with the plan. But what could he do? He steels himself, hands clammy, gathers the speech in his head—and that's when an errant thought appears unbidden in his mind, like a late arrival to a show slipping in through a closing door.

One simple word.

Or.

Or—he could stay.

He tries to shoo it away, this undermining word, to shake it—this pesky *or,* this doubt—and picture instead the ocean and the calming sands of Cabo. To imagine Lilith stretched lean and oily in the sun on a beach chair in her bikini, her face shaded by the brim of a floppy hat. But instead all he can imagine is the looming airport, the cavernous terminal, the echoing announcements, the twitchy, impatient passengers milling at the gate. He sees Lilith fuming, hunched over her expensive hard-shelled carry-on, expecting his pathetic supplications for having ghosted her all day. He envisions the hours-long flight to Cabo, the cool darkness of the airplane, the hushed excuses he'll have to make to her intermittently for the entire flight, all the conciliatory explanations. He considers the hot ribbon of asphalt highway he'll need to drive just to get from here to the airport, crowded with honking traffic as he reenters the squalid city, sitting cramped and guilty in the car for hours, all while burdened with the knowledge that he's just broken his wife's heart, shattered her and left her alone in the woods, on the very week of her big anniversary surprise.

Or.

Not to mention, he thinks—he's here. He's already here in the woods. This is one of the rare instances in life where to do the right thing, all he has to do is … nothing. Say nothing. Do nothing. Just don't leave. Just stay here, in the woods, with her.

Daisy never needs to know about any of it; it can all just dissipate like a dream. He can turn off his phone, deal with Lilith later—what's four months, really, in the grand scheme of life; it's not like they're, you know, *married*—and relax and enjoy this week. Enjoy his *wife.*

It does seem so peaceful here, so tranquil, just the two of them. Like there's no one else in the entire world. Maybe there is something to this whole idea? Maybe a week away, together, just the two of them, is all they really needed?

Doesn't he owe Daisy that much? Shouldn't he at least give it a chance?

As he considers this, he slides his hands idly into the pockets of his jeans and with his fingertips he feels the folded flyer the waitress gave him in the parking lot.

He fondles the flyer. Recalls her invitation.

After all—the week is just beginning, he thinks. Why run away right now?

And that's when he decides: He's staying.

Fuck Cabo.

He's going to do the right thing for once.

He's going to stay. With his *wife*.

And just like that, it all vanishes: the halting drive, the awkward flight, and, of course, the prospect of tears, of betrayal, of a terrible confrontation.

He glances toward Daisy—he almost wants to shout the good news to her, *I'm staying!*, though of course he can't; he can't say anything, ever—and he sees that she's detoured off happily toward the lake, lost in a world of her own.

He finds her standing in the small sandy inlet where the lake water pools, staring out at the view, a wooden dock stretching out before her, the pilings mossy where they meet the water.

He puts his arm around her shoulder—feeling no small amount of relief and self-satisfaction at his surprising and enlivening turn toward virtue—and he peers with her across the calm water at the opposite shore.

Sure enough, there's not another cabin in sight. It's just the two of them here. Alone.

He clutches her. "We really have this all to ourselves?"

She slides her arm around his waist. "That's what they promised."

"How in the world can we afford this?"

"I told you, I'm paying," she says. "And now—I want to go swimming."

"But we don't have suits."

She turns to him, her eyes dancing, a rascal's invitation. "Who said anything about suits?"

She sticks out her tongue—she's so happy right now, he can tell, almost as though she senses somehow that their marriage just barely avoided total ruin—and she strips off her clothes like a boisterous kid and dashes, laughing, naked into the water.

He watches her splash, loose-limbed, as she ventures out fearlessly. She dives headfirst and disappears. He marvels at her. At the idea of her. At the idea that she's in his life. For the first time in a very long time, he feels lucky. Lucky to be with her.

See? You made the right decision, he thinks. You did the right thing for once.

Then he yanks off his shirt and kicks off his pants and, naked, unburdened, he happily follows her.

They swim like that for hours. The lake is cool and murky. He writhes through the water like it's his natural habitat, and when he emerges near her and grabs her from behind, she laughs in shock and splashes him. He tightens his slippery arms around her and holds her like a drowning man gripping a buoy. With his eyes closed in the quiet of the lake and the sound of his own splashing in his ears, at first he doesn't hear the voice calling out.

Then he hears it.

"Hulloooo!"

Craig looks up and blinks the water from his eyes, and there at the edge of the shore, standing in the little inlet where the lake meets the woods, is an elderly man with shaggy white hair and a generous beard, wearing a tweed blazer and a cream-colored turtleneck, waving at them with big, broad swipes in the air. A few feet behind him, farther up the shore, stands a woman, tall and regal, in a brightly patterned caftan that skirts the ground, a cascade of tight gray curls falling down to her shoulders.

They look like moneyed hippies.

The man cups his hands to his mouth.

"Hullooooo!" he calls again.

Craig is suddenly and bracingly aware of the fact that both he and Daisy are naked. He dangles uncovered in the water, churning his legs rhythmically. He looks around for Daisy and finds her, treading water, too, a few feet away, her arms clutched awkwardly around her breasts in an attempt at modesty.

"Hey! What's up?" Craig calls out to the man.

"Sorry to interrupt!" says the man. "I'm Kit." He nods toward the woman. "This is Bridget. We thought we'd pop in to say hello."

Daisy laughs. The tableau strikes her as absurd. This man in his blazer, his wife in her gaily patterned gown, both looking like they're dressed for a garden party, while Craig and Daisy bob naked like horny teenagers, walked in on, interrupted.

"You'll have to excuse us," Daisy answers. "We weren't expecting visitors."

"Hello," says Craig. Then he laughs, too.

"We can come up," Daisy calls out. "We just have to—"

"We'll need to get dressed," says Craig.

"No trouble," says Kit, now laughing himself. "We didn't anticipate a midday dip. But it's a beautiful day for it. Maybe we'll join you ourselves." He makes a show of doffing his blazer.

"Kit, stop it," says his wife, then calls out to them, "We can come back later. You kids enjoy yourselves."

"No, no," says Daisy. "Just give us a moment."

Craig shoots her a look. She shrugs, smiling. *Why not?*

"If you're sure," says Bridget.

"Of course," Daisy calls out.

"All right then," says Kit. "We'll wait for you up on the porch."

After the couple retreats back into the woods, out of sight, Craig and Daisy emerge, naked and glistening. They giggle, standing together at the edge of the lake, giving each other silent looks, like *We're not in*

Brooklyn anymore. They towel themselves off as best they can with their discarded clothes and then pull the damp clothes back on.

"I thought you said we had this place to ourselves," says Craig.

"We do," says Daisy. "But we should at least say hello."

"Why? I was having fun. That was nice, just the two of us. Now we have to entertain some random neighbors?"

"They're not random neighbors," says Daisy, tugging her shirt back on over her head. "They're Kit and Bridget."

"Okay," says Craig. "Who's that?"

"They're the doctors, the Ardens—the therapists who invented the Eden Test," says Daisy. "They started the Edenic Foundation. They run this place. We're their guests for the week."

7

Daisy brings fresh coffee and a pitcher of lemonade out to the porch on a silver tray. Kit sits slung in a wicker chair, relaxed, jovial, his long legs crossed at the knee, wearing khakis and moccasins with no socks. Bridget sits perched nearby on a chaise in her long patterned caftan, her legs bent together and folded to the side, demure. A chunky necklace hangs around her neck like a celebratory garland. Craig sprawls on the rickety wicker sofa in jeans and a rugby shirt, nursing an afternoon glass of wine. Daisy pads toward them in a slip dress, barefoot, hair still damp, sun on her bare shoulders, and sets the tray between the four of them, a proper hostess.

She likes this.

Country life.

She slides in next to Craig, curling her legs up beneath her as he wraps his arm possessively over her shoulder.

"So how long have you two been living up here?" Craig asks Kit.

Kit glances at his wife. "Seems like forever—like we've been here since the dawn of time." He leans in toward Craig, conspiratorial. "We did the New York City thing." He shimmies his hands as though to indicate a wild, bohemian bacchanal. He's got a large, generous, uninhibited smile, like someone who's always in the middle of recounting a raucous anecdote. "But the country life was calling us."

"It seems perfect up here," says Daisy.

"It's Paradise," says Bridget. "There's a spirituality here in the woods. A peacefulness. Do you feel it? I guarantee you that you can discover everything you're looking for up here, as long as you're open to finding it." She reaches over and pats Kit's knee. She wears large costume jewels on her fingers, a remnant of a different time, thinks Daisy, a time when even an afternoon walk was an occasion for finery. Daisy envies that.

Bridget pulls a pack of cigarettes from the folds of her caftan like a stage prop and holds it up for their inspection. "Do you mind?"

"Not at all," says Daisy. "There's an ashtray out here somewhere." She rises, searching, then spies it, a ceramic ashtray in the shape of a fig leaf, with a plastic Bic lighter in it, left behind by some previous resident. She sets it close to Bridget, who smiles politely and lights her slender cigarette.

"What about you two?" Kit says, taking a coffee cup from the silver tray. "Whereabouts do you hail from?"

"Brooklyn," says Craig proudly, matter-of-factly, like a boast. He gestures to Bridget's pack of cigarettes. "You mind?"

"Be my guest," says Bridget.

Craig taps a cigarette from the pack. He doesn't recognize the label. Maybe they're European, he thinks as he puts one to his lips and lights it. He takes a deep drag, exhales, then coughs. "Smooth," he jokes. No one laughs.

Kit leans in. "And what is it you do to occupy yourself in the great heathen city, Craig?"

"I'm in marketing."

"He's a writer," says Daisy, correcting him.

Kit smiles. "We're so conditioned to associate ourselves with our jobs, aren't we? We don't say *How do you do?* anymore, we say *What do you do?*" He chuckles and sets his coffee down. "But we have our careers and then we have our *callings*, am I right? They're not always one in the same." He gestures toward Bridget. "We got lucky. As you may have guessed, we're therapists. I'm sure the turtleneck and beard gave me away." He delivers this line like a borscht belt joke.

Craig looks them over. Now that he thinks of it, they do look somewhat familiar. Like maybe he's seen them smiling on a talk show once or on a subway ad. He tries to picture it: *The Eden Test: Seven Days. Seven Questions. Forever Changed.*

"And you?" says Kit to Daisy. "What's your calling?"

"I'm an actor," says Daisy.

Bridget squeals. "Oh, how delightful! Might I have seen you in something?"

"Daisy refuses to do TV or movies," says Craig. "She only does *thee-atah*"—drawing the word out in mock pomposity.

"Do I sense some tension around this subject?" says Kit warmly.

"I just prefer theater to film work," says Daisy. "The live interaction, the electricity of an audience. It's just more—intimate."

"What about Broadway?" Bridget asks, shifting, Daisy notes, into the effortlessly inquisitive mode of the therapist. Prodding without prying.

"She's had plenty of Broadway offers," says Craig. "Turns them all down."

"Broadway's not really my taste, to be honest," says Daisy tactfully. "I've always found it kind of—corny."

"You see what I'm dealing with?" says Craig. "She went to one of the fanciest theater schools in the country, but she refuses to let her light shine." He leans in toward Kit and Bridget, his legs spread wide and his elbows on his knees. "As far as I'm concerned, she deserves to be seen by *everyone*. She deserves to be *famous*. I want to see my wife's face on billboards."

"My biggest cheerleader," says Daisy with a tight smile.

"She just did a guest spot on *Legal Remedies*," says Craig, reaching to tap his cigarette in the ashtray. "Do you know that show? With the cops and the lawyers?"

"Sounds like every television show, honestly," says Bridget, smiling beatifically. "We don't have a TV. I know, I know—we're *those* people."

"Well, it paid her more for six lines than she makes in theater in a year," says Craig. "It paid for this week."

"Not an inexpensive proposition!" jokes Kit boisterously.

"And she was good," says Craig. "*Really* good. And I only had to bug her for three years to convince her to do it."

Daisy turns to Bridget, hoping to redirect the conversation. "Did you ever act?"

"Trust me—being a therapist requires plenty of acting," she says.

"Mostly to look interested. But we don't see private patients anymore. Not since we moved up here. This program keeps us very busy." She taps her cigarette and glances at Kit. "It's our life's work."

"A calling *and* a career," says Kit.

"So I guess we're going to be seeing a lot of you?" says Craig. "I guess we have to report in every day?"

"No, that's not how this works," says Kit. "We designed the Eden Test to be very hands-off. You have your questions. You have your cabin. You have each other. And, hopefully, you have the space and time to dedicate to really connecting. We'll check in again at the end of the week, but beyond that, you don't need a lot of intervention from us."

"We want to give you the space to find the answers you came looking for," says Bridget.

"Answers? I don't even know what the questions are," says Craig.

Kit chuckles. "You leave that part to us."

"Do you miss it?" says Daisy to Bridget. "Seeing patients?"

"Honestly, it got rather hard," says Bridget. "When you're a couples counselor, you often hear the same stories again and again. Variations on a theme. Some of the themes can be quite ugly. Sometimes you just want to look at someone and yell *Run!* You want to intervene. To save them. But you can't." She laughs a hollow laugh.

"We weren't so different from you once," says Kit. "Working away in the city, dealing with all of the craziness and chaos. Bridget had her patients, I had mine, billable hours in a tiny office, houseplants, mood lighting, plenty of nodding, no real progress."

"One week, we rented a cabin up here, near Plain, just to get away," says Bridget. "And being up here, it just—clicked."

"That's why we started this foundation," says Kit. "To give other couples a place, and a process, where they can truly find themselves."

"Why call it the Eden Test?" asks Daisy.

"Upstate was a very different place back then," says Kit. "No city money, just exiled hippies like us, searching for Paradise."

"Seven days, seven questions. That was our blueprint," says Bridget.

"Our only promise to each other was to ask a new question every day—and be totally, nakedly honest with our answers."

Craig shifts uneasily, like they're trying to sell him a time-share. He wonders when they'll actually explain what this test is all about. He's not even sure what the test *is* other than some questions in an envelope. "What did you learn?" he asks.

"We learned that we loved each other, but we didn't really *know* each other. We didn't know what we were willing to do for the relationship."

"So it's successful? This program?" says Craig.

"Successful enough that we own everything you see in all directions," says Kit with a satisfied smile.

"No, I mean—does it work? This test? Do couples always patch things up?"

"The point isn't to patch up anything," says Kit. "The point is to truly understand what kind of relationship you're after. And how committed you are to creating it."

Craig scoffs. "So that's it? That's the whole experience? Just a bunch of questions to answer every day?"

"It's much more than that," says Kit, somewhat mystically. "It's the whole experience—it's holistic. It's everything you see around you, everyone you meet. It's the sound of the woods in the morning and the sight of the stars at night."

"You'll have to excuse my husband—he likes to wax poetic." Bridget rolls her eyes conspicuously, their repartee like a well-rehearsed comedy act.

Kit guffaws, then says, "All we ask is—keep your eyes and ears open. Be prepared for any possibility. Let yourself be surprised. The Eden Test isn't just questions—it's a series of steps. And the good news is, you've already taken the most important one."

"Yeah? What's that?" says Craig.

"You're here!" Kit slaps his knee and cackles. "Felicitations! Welcome!" He jumps to his feet. "It's been so good to meet you both. We should really let you get back to—whatever it is you were up to when we arrived."

"Don't worry, we've walked in on worse," says Bridget.

"People get up to all kinds of shenanigans when they think no one is watching. But that's all part of the appeal, isn't it?" Kit sweeps his hand toward the lake and the woods. "By all means, enjoy the property—all of this is ours, which means all of this is yours, for one week at least." He leans in, as though making a confession. "I only ask one thing—stay out of the orchard."

"That little boondoggle has been Kit's personal project for years, trying to get that orchard to flourish," says Bridget. "As a therapist, he's a genius. *But as a gardener…*" She gives her voice a comic Yiddish lilt.

"You might see my arborist, Mr. Alwyn, nosing around this week, but pay him no mind."

"Stay away from the apple trees," says Daisy. "Got it. Just like Eden. I assume we should avoid snakes, too."

"The Garden of Eden was the very first love story," says Bridget. "Adam and Eve invented the idea of love. What must that have felt like for them? To experience those feelings for the very first time and not even have a word for it?"

"But didn't they fail their Eden test?" says Daisy. "After all, they got kicked out."

Bridget smiles. "That's right. But they ended up together. Had children together. Built a life together. That certainly sounds like a happy ending to me."

"Secrets! Revelations! Breakthroughs!" Kit declares, like the game is afoot.

Bridget stubs out her cigarette. A last twist of smoke ascends. Not looking up, she says, "Don't worry. By the time you get to Question Seven, you'll know."

"Know what?" says Craig, finally rising to stand.

She looks at him. "Who you are. Why you're here. What you want. And what you're willing to do to achieve it."

At the edge of the gravel driveway, Kit and Bridget banter with them warmly, saying goodbyes, granting well-wishes, Kit grasping Craig's shoulders, a manly squeeze, like they're all old family friends. Bridget kisses Daisy on both cheeks. Then the older couple give a last wave, turn right at the head of the driveway, and walk off down the road at an unhurried pace, hand in hand.

Once they're gone, Craig says, "Well, that was weird."

"They were sweet," says Daisy.

"They saw us naked."

"They sort of saw us naked." She nestles up against Craig, clutching his arm. "Just think—that could be us one day."

"What? Weirdo hippies living in the woods?"

"No," says Daisy. "Happy."

Daisy heads inside to start dinner. Craig gathers the dishes from the porch. The lake is at a perfect hour and he pauses for a moment, watching. The late-afternoon sun hangs heavy, twinned in the water. Animals chatter in the trees. He thinks of Kit and Bridget and stands and wonders what the hell he's gotten himself into. What Daisy's gotten them both into.

Well, he's here, he thinks. That decision's been made.

He bends to collect the tray and that's when he hears it.

A shot.

From the woods.

He looks up.

The echo ricochets past the porch.

He straightens. Waits a moment, still listening.

Daisy sticks her head out the French doors. "What was that?"

"I don't know."

"It sounded like a gunshot," she says.

"Yes, it did."

"Do you think it's hunters?"

"Maybe. I'm not sure."

"Come inside."

"I'll be right there," he says.

She ducks inside and closes the door, and he stays outside, alert, a moment longer.

Finally, he turns with the tray in his hands toward the door. As his gaze sweeps the woods, he spots it.

Blaze orange.

Can't miss it.

A blaze orange baseball cap. Deep back in the trees. A smear of bright fluorescence against the underbrush.

Highly visible.

He puts the tray down and walks to the edge of the porch.

Whoever it is, they're awfully close to the cabin.

He calls to Daisy. "I'll be right back."

8

The woods have an obvious border—Craig sees it as he walks slowly down the steps from the porch. There's a small clearing that surrounds the cabin, a carpet of yellowing pine needles and tamped-down dirt, and then the woods begin in a tangle of roots.

He looks ahead and spots the orange cap again, far off among the shadowed trees.

"Hello," he calls out.

No answer.

He heads forward but pauses at the tree line. He's lost sight of the cap now, and it's hard to tell if what he sees are figures moving in the distance or simply changes in the broken light.

He steps forward, into the woods, following what passes for a path. The difference in darkness once you're under the canopy of trees is palpable. He glances back at the cabin, which now feels like it's fifty yards behind him.

He turns back to the woods. "Hello!" he calls again.

He pauses to listen. Nothing. This is silly, he thinks. If there's someone out there, they're out there. No reason to think there are no human beings for a hundred miles. People hunt in the woods, right? It's not illegal. No doubt it's just someone who strayed a little too close momentarily and now is on their way. Big deal, he thinks. In the city, you're surrounded by strangers all the time. He routinely stands jammed up against people on the subway, or walks within a few feet of ranting men screaming at the top of their lungs on the sidewalk, without even flinching.

Besides, what's he going to do, exactly, now that he's in the woods?

He's suddenly aware of his own empty hands. Why did he walk out here without grabbing a stick or something heavy, or at least his phone? But then—what exactly would he do with it? Craig doesn't even live here. In a sense, he's the trespasser. He should get back to the cabin. Back to Daisy.

He turns to head home.

As he turns, a man appears, a few feet away.

The man's arms and shirt are smeared with slick and shiny blood.

Craig startles.

It's the guy from the diner, wearing that blaze orange baseball cap, his flannel shirt rolled up to the elbows as he holds his arms loose at his sides. His forearms and hands are glistening with dark red gore, like he's been elbow-deep in something.

"Hey, buddy," he says calmly. "My friend and I just bagged a twelve-point, back a ways. One shot. Do you know the way to the nearest road?"

Craig stares at him, speechless. Heart rabbiting. He says finally, "Yeah, that way," and nods toward the cabin, then regrets it. Why is he pointing this guy closer to his house?

Blaze Orange smiles. Maybe a leer. Hard to tell in the wooded darkness. He lifts a slick and shiny arm and points a finger toward the cabin. "Nice setup," he says. "View must be spectacular. Lake all to yourself. You live here?"

"For the week, yes."

"So you're just passing through. From the city."

"You were at the diner this morning, weren't you?"

"Got to start the day off right," the man says. The way he holds his hands is menacing, awkward, arms bent slightly at the elbows, blood-coated, like a surgeon interrupted. He notices Craig noticing the gore. "You ever field dress a buck before?"

"Me? No," says Craig.

"Gets messy." The man pulls a knife from a leather scabbard at his belt. The knife is long with a serrated edge. The blade is smeared with blood. He holds it out for Craig to consider. "This does the trick, though." He turns the knife in the vanishing light. "Blade for the flesh, teeth for the bone." He wipes the blade on his pants. "Well, back to it, I guess." The man turns away.

"You're too close," Craig says.

The man turns back. "What'd you say?"

"To our house. I heard the shot from the porch."

"Well, shots are loud. Didn't mean to scare you."

"Look, we came up here to be alone. We don't want to be disturbed. And I don't think you're supposed to be on this property."

"Says the tourist."

Craig hears a third voice now, disembodied, calling from deep in the woods: "*Let's go.*" The call is angry, insistent, stretching out that last word, *goooooo*, like a plaintive howl. So there are others around, Craig thinks. A group party. Craig wonders if the voice is the other guy he saw that morning in the diner, the wiry one. It's hard to tell from the echoing exhortation if he means *Let's go* like *Let's depart,* or *Let's go* like *Let's get things started.*

Blaze Orange looks up at Craig and brings his blood-slicked hand to the brim of the orange hat and, absurdly, tips his cap to Craig. Like a gentleman. "Got to run. Until next time," he says.

"Just—stay away from this cabin." Craig's not sure why he's pushing it, not sure why he doesn't just let the man leave; he feels like he's mimicking a forcefulness, a bravery, he's seen elsewhere. But as long as it's effective, who cares if it's sincere. "Are we clear?"

The man stands perfectly still. "Crystal," he says.

Craig senses the man backing down. He feels exultant, triumphant. The man starts to walk away, then looks back. "Oh, and I hope you and your pretty wife get your issues sorted out." He lobs this last part with an easy malice, then tromps off, undeterred, back into the tangle of the trees.

Craig walks back to the porch, his heart slowing to a thud. What were you *doing,* he thinks. In the city, there's a reflexive pushback, a necessary armor when confronted, but then, in the city, there are other people everywhere. That's the great safety net of the city. You're *surrounded*. Sure, all kinds of crazy shit can happen, but you're nearly never alone.

Once Craig stepped into those woods, he'd never felt more alone in his life.

But he did it, he thinks. He made his point. The guy backed down. Right?

As he mounts the steps to the porch, he feels better, relieved. Fortified. He handled it.

He's about to head inside when he stops. Looks down.

"Honey?" he calls out.

Daisy opens the French doors for him from the inside, regarding him quizzically. She follows his eyes downward.

"Was that there before?" he says.

She bends down and plucks the white envelope from the welcome mat.

On the front of the envelope written in gold: *Q2*.

"Let's do the question now," she says inside the cabin. She's changed into a cable-knit sweater and sweatpants, girding against the dusk's encroaching chill.

He's hunched by the hearth, goading the fire. He feels better now, calmed by a glass of wine. He pokes the logs. Here's another little-used skill he half remembers from his Michigan Boy Scout youth. Newspaper, tent of twigs, then logs placed just so. Strike a match, get it started, feed it fuel, watch it roar.

The fire's going pretty good when she appears over his shoulder, holding the envelope.

"Come on," she says. "Question Two."

This feels to him a bit like finding out he can't watch TV until he finishes his homework, but he rises and follows her to the couch.

"All right," he says. "Let's see what those nutty hippies have in store for us tonight."

They sit and nestle into each other. She rips open the envelope, pulls out the sheet of paper, and reads aloud.

Question Two.

Would you sacrifice for me?

Love *is an action verb, but what exactly is the action? Love is a gesture that costs nothing. We say it all the time: "I love you." But how do you demonstrate love? In ancient cultures, to* love *your God was not enough.*

You had to offer up a sacrifice.

These days, we think of sacrifice as something small, something petty, an act of self-denial. You sacrifice *the last piece of cake or your Saturday evening plans.*

Once, sacrifice was the ultimate tribute: the giving of a life to prove loyalty. And not your life. That would be too easy. You had to give up something precious, something pure. You had to lay it on the altar. You had to say goodbye.

Sacrifice is an offering. One that comes with a cost.

Love is the emotion, but sacrifice is the action. Sacrifice *is both the verb and the noun: It is both the act of offering a sacrifice and the offering itself, the thing you are willing to surrender, to destroy, as evidence of your love.*

The proof. The sacrifice.

Think of it both as an offering and *an act.*

Now turn to your partner and tell each other what exactly you're willing to offer up.

9

In the clawfoot tub in the dark of the bathroom, lit only by a scattering of candles, he sits back, lets his eyes close, and thinks, I was never really going to go to Cabo. Let that be my sacrifice.

Reclining with his arms propped up on the sides of the tub and his head resting on the hard iron rim, he feels like a righteous Old West gunslinger after a long, dusty day. The kind of man who *fights for justice*, who *steps up*, who *does the right thing*.

Hadn't he done the right thing today? Can't he take a moment to feel good about that? And it was, all in all, a good day—the swim felt good and Daisy felt good and she was fun and funny and the lake water was perfect and skinny-dipping was, he admits, a blast. The weird old hippie therapists were weird but fine, with their corny jokes and promises of Paradise. He even feels okay about the man with the blaze orange baseball cap lurking in the woods. Didn't Craig *step up*, after all? Didn't he chase that guy away?

After which he built a fire in the hearth and he and Daisy read the second question. They had a good dinner and opened a bottle of wine— which, weirdly, she barely touched—and they had a long talk about what it really means to *sacrifice* for someone. And suddenly a different future started to unfold for him: not him on the beach in Mexico but them, him and Daisy, together, *working things out*.

Craig had never really *worked things out* with anyone, not really, not before meeting Daisy, because no one ever seemed worth the trouble, honestly. Or, more specifically, no one ever seemed worth forgoing all the alluring illicit possibilities that inevitably pop up and that commitment would only curtail.

But *she* is, he thinks—Daisy is worth it. He'd always believed that; he'd just forgotten. Just been momentarily beguiled by Lilith, with her brazen advances—but now he's back, he's here, he's ready to *do the work*.

Because he loves Daisy. He does.

Maybe this week is all we needed, he thinks, satisfied. How lucky that this week happened when it did!

The best part is, he never mentioned his plan to leave Daisy, not once, never gave the speech (as good as it is, and it's really good, really heartfelt, he thinks)—so Daisy never needs to know how close he came to leaving, to trashing everything, to throwing it all away.

And they've got five more days and five more of these questions to answer.

Would he change for Daisy?

Sure. Of course. People change. Right?

Would he sacrifice for Daisy?

Well, he has already, hasn't he? He gave up a trip to Cabo, after all.

Now he's left to wonder: What else would he do for Daisy?

He dips farther into the tub, his stubbled jaw dropping just below the warmth of the waterline, and his eyes flutter open and he sees candle flames dancing in the darkened bathroom and the steam on the surface of the water . . . dancing . . . idly across the surface of the water as the candlelight dapples the—water's . . . surface. As the candlelight dapples the water's—as the candles dapple the—damn it, he thinks. What's another word for surface? *Top?* The top of the water?

Daisy lit these candles and then disappeared upstairs, and he assumes she's going to join him any minute. But he's happy for this moment of calm, of stillness, of *reflection,* given all he has to think about.

His new life. *Their* new life. Starting now. Just the two of them. A reset.

No more surprises. No more evasions. No more lies.

And at the end of this week they'll go back to the city and he can see how it goes from there, he thinks. See if they can somehow recapture that elusive excitement from those first few months when he was dizzy with longing for Daisy. When she appeared in his life like a lottery windfall, when he couldn't stop thinking about her—how wonderful she was, how talented, how funny, his good fortune, the luck of it all, this incredible woman, not like anyone else—before, you know, things got *hard*. Before life tapped them on the shoulder and cut into their romantic waltz. Before her tendencies toward secrecy hardened into sullen withdrawal. Before most of their nights were occupied with arguments. Before, you know, the relationship became *work* and that ever-present voice started whispering that pesky word to him:

Or.

Or you could be with that woman over there.

Or works both ways. He knows that.

For example: He can stay right here with Daisy tonight—*or* there's that concert in town with that band with the girl from the diner, that very hot waitress with the tattoos. But that's not really a thing he's going to do, obviously. He's not actually going to get out of this tub, towel off, get dressed, concoct some lame excuse for Daisy, maybe something to do with work, maybe something about needing to get on a wifi connection right away, then drive forty minutes in the dark to some cinder block roadhouse in the middle of nowhere to sit through a concert by some half-assed backwater goth band on the off chance he can hook up with the lead singer in the greenroom afterward.

Old Craig would definitely have maybe thought about doing that, but no, he will not do that. Of course not. He's changing. He's sacrificing. He's becoming a new man.

New Craig.

Starting now.

After all, she invited him up here for a reason, right?

A fresh start.

He settles back into the water and closes his eyes again, content.

Forget the city, forget the past, forget it all, he thinks, and focus on you and Daisy.

Changing for her.

Sacrificing for her.

And whatever is coming next.

IIII

Daisy sits on the edge of the bed upstairs.

Gathering herself.

She clutches a small item in her fist.

The room is lit only by a table lamp that spills an insufficient light. The corners of the room are dark, obscured. She considers this moment—the moment before the moment. She knows this feeling intimately. It's not nervousness or dread, exactly; nothing as simple as that. It feels more like anticipation, a tingling sense that something momentous is about to happen—it's a feeling she often has onstage, right before the show begins. Like she is poised to open a door that she can't close again.

She shuts her eyes. Enacts her usual preshow ritual. *Calm yourself. Take a breath. Find your mark.* She thinks of how this unfolds in the theater: A hush falls. The lights come up. Upturned eyes shine in the darkness to greet you. You feel that sudden exhilarating surge as you step from one world into another.

She opens her eyes.

Squeezes the item in her closed fist tightly.

Craig's waiting for her in the bath downstairs.

As she rises to stand, she thinks: Poor Craig.

He has no idea the turn that this evening—and their lives—is about to take.

When he hears the old wooden bathroom door creak, he pries his eyes open and there she is, in the doorway, naked and ready for the bath, her body shadowed by flickering candles.

"Room for two?" she says.

"Of course." He shifts himself up to make space.

She steps into the bath carefully and sits against him, her back against his chest, cradled, secure.

Only now does he notice she's holding something small hidden in her hand.

"What about three?" she says. "Is there room for three?"

"Three what?" he says.

She opens her hand and reveals the pregnancy test, and he knows even before looking at it what its twinned blue lines are going to tell him.

10

Does she want to have a child with Craig?

It's a reasonable question to ask. Given the circumstances.

But it's a question she's never had to consider before, not once, not seriously.

Not because she wasn't interested in having a child. She's never had to ask it because she believed she couldn't get pregnant. That's what the doctors had told her. So that's what she told him. They had the conversation, not long into their relationship, settled the issue, and moved on.

I can't get pregnant.

She told him that because she thought it was true.

But it's not.

And she is.

Now what?

Daisy lies awake in the bedroom in the late-night hours, long past midnight, her head resting lightly on Craig's chest. She gazes out the window at the gnarled branches of the tangled trees that stir in silhouette against the darkened sky. She likes to do this—to lie awake at night, silent, thinking, long after he's fallen asleep. These moments seem like stolen moments, her thoughts belonging only to her.

Tonight she fixates on one thought in particular. The same thought she's been fixating on for, oh, the last ten weeks or so.

She wonders if Craig can change.

In the three years that they've been together, she's never wanted Craig to change before. She's always known exactly what kind of man he is—it was clear to her from the moment she met him that night in the sushi bar.

Craig: handsome, charming, inattentive, self-absorbed, one eye always searching for the next conquest and one foot forever pointed toward the door.

In other words, her perfect match.

Until ten weeks ago.

Ten weeks, by the way, is how long she's known that she's pregnant—just enough time to take the pregnancy test, confirm it, confirm it again, reconsider her entire future, then hastily arrange for this retreat: fill out the forms, answer their questions, sign their waivers, put down the hefty deposit, then lure Craig out here to the middle of nowhere for a week to try to salvage their relationship.

She was sure she couldn't get pregnant. That's what the doctors told her. The legacy of old scars.

And yet.

Twinned blue lines.

An impossible baby.

A pregnancy she'd kept secret from him, until now.

Thankfully, it's never been too hard to keep her secrets from Craig. He's not exactly the inquisitive type. He's usually too busy clumsily scrambling to hide his own hapless indiscretions.

Like at the diner, she thinks. Excusing himself to the little boys' room, fumbling to hide his phone as he exits the booth, texting like a teenager from the parking lot, of all places, thinking he's out of sight, unseen. It would be comical if it weren't so sad.

Yes, she knows about the affairs. Of course she knows.

She's not stupid.

And she's always accepted his indiscretions and infidelities as part of their deal. Unlike most people, she doesn't need her partner to be faithful. She just needs him to be predictable. And incurious.

Craig, reliably, is both.

For Daisy, emotional security doesn't come from doe-eyed devotion or unwavering adherence to old-fashioned notions about fidelity. For her, emotional security comes from the rock-solid assurance that you understand your partner so well—that you know him and his decisions, his motivations, his predilections, and his behaviors so completely—that he can never, ever surprise you.

And Craig—handsome Craig, happy Craig, flirtatious Craig, faithless Craig—has never, ever surprised her. Not once. Not in three years together.

Does she love Craig?

Good question. Also a reasonable one to ask. Given the circumstances.

She does. She has. She won't deny it: He ticks boxes. Funny? Frequently. Good-looking? Undeniably. Charming? Intermittently, when he wants to be, though he definitely doesn't restrict his famously alluring charm only to her.

Warm, caring, helpful? He can be all three some—even most—of the time.

Supportive? He unfailingly comes to every one of her shows, no matter how small the theater, how obscure the play, how far-flung the venue. He's always there, alone, smiling, clapping, cheering her on. In fact, he never seems happier, never more infatuated, than when she's onstage, being someone else.

Devoted? Now that's a tricky one.

Faithful? Absolutely not.

But she was very clear-eyed about Craig from the beginning. Honestly, she could read him on that first date in the dim light of that subterranean sushi bar: his insatiable need for affirmation, which he tried hard to disguise with a bluff and practiced charm. She's smart enough to understand that she or anyone can only placate that level of need for so long before his eye starts to wander—before he yearns again to feel validated by the cheap satisfactions of new flirtations, new entanglements, new intrigues. He's sadly predictable in this way. And she mostly just feels sorry for the new women he ensnares, tossed like virgin sacrifices into the raging volcano of his insecurity. She just hopes they know what they're in for.

She certainly did.

She and Craig were set up by a mutual friend. Someone from a play she'd starred in whose partner had met Craig once through work and thought he was cute. She said, *Why not?* On their first date, Craig told her he'd been meeting people online, how fruitless it all was, how empty. She never dated online. She stayed off social media entirely. He jokingly called her a Luddite, a Puritan. She laughed. He didn't pursue it.

She thinks of how she must have seemed to him that night, sitting across that table: Daisy, cute actress, funny, pretty, the ideal date. Yet another role, another character study. How he got up and squeezed himself in next to her in the booth, and she leaned over and playfully licked the curl of crème brûlée from his chin, to his delight. That was the moment he fell for her, she knew it, she could see it happening. Craig longed for someone impetuous, someone surprising, someone *fearless*. Someone who made him feel like she could help him become the better version of himself that he had long since lost faith in but that he still yearned to be.

With that one brash act, she became that person to him.

And he fell. Hard.

He was so happy to take her at face value, she thinks. Daisy: the cute girl who's the friend of a friend of a friend. Daisy: smart, talented, funny—she'd moved to the city from theater school just a few years earlier, still looking to meet new people, still seeking her New York tribe. Daisy: shameless, fearless, frightfully talented, not many college friends to speak of or, for that matter, long-term friends at all; Daisy, who came to New York to reinvent herself just like a million people before her, Midwest childhood, normal background, at least the parts that she'd told him about, which weren't many.

As for the rest of it, the details, she never elaborated. He never pressed.

Each of them exactly what the other person needed.

For her, that's ideal.

That's love.

Of course, most women—smart women—would have fled from Craig that first night, given his obvious deficiencies. But most women think romance means attention, devotion, being *fully seen* and *deeply understood.*

She doesn't want attention. She doesn't require devotion. And she doesn't crave to be *seen* or *understood.* In fact, all of her past romantic relationships in New York had reliably derailed at the moment when her suitors, thoroughly smitten, tried valiantly to push past her vaunted defenses, to encourage her to *open up,* to unearth her secrets, to truly *get to know* her.

She didn't want that and she never invited it.

With Craig, she doesn't have to worry about that at all.

She recognized it on that very first date. How easy it would be to keep secrets from him. She knew that he would take her at face value and never look at her too closely or scrutinize her too deeply or long to know her too completely.

Like she said.

A perfect match.

But now everything's different.

The impossible has happened.

This impossible baby.

Surprise!

It's a very strange feeling, she thinks as she lies in the stillness of their room, his breath rasping in his rib cage beneath her ear, to believe that something is impossible and then to have it actually happen. It bowls you over and knocks the wind out of you, yes—but once you've picked yourself up and gathered yourself, it also opens your eyes to the world and reacquaints you with the notion of *possibility.* It makes you wonder what other things in your life that you thought—or were told—were impossible might actually be possible.

For example, saying yes to a TV role.

Breaking her one hard-and-fast acting rule: *No movies, no TV.*

Craig knows about this rule. Craig hates this rule. He just doesn't know why she has this rule. Or why she decided to break it.

To be fair, she didn't chase the TV role she landed. It fell unexpectedly in her lap. And when it did—with her newfound belief in the possibilities of the impossible—she found herself saying the one word she never allows herself to say. That pesky word.

She said *yes.*

She'd met the casting agent at an opening-night party for a friend's play. The agent mentioned she was looking to fill a last-minute part on *Legal Remedies*—an actor had dropped out that day, the agent said, flown off to LA at a moment's notice for a big film with a huge director.

The joke among theater people, of course, is that *Legal Remedies,* with its decade-long run and endless demand for guest stars, is the reason most New York stage actors manage to stay alive. This role was a one-off, a guest spot—an honest cop who gets gunned down for *saying too much,* killed just to *shut her up.* "But don't worry, you don't just die," said the casting agent, sizing up Daisy on the spot. "You get six lines. You'd be perfect."

Six lines.

Perfect.

And Daisy would make more money for one day of shooting than she'd make for a six-month run in a hit downtown theater show.

She knew exactly what she'd spend that money on, too.

So she said the word she never says. Never allows herself to say.

That forbidden word.

Yes.

Craig was ecstatic, of course. His wife had finally heeded his nagging, embraced his advice, and broken her stupid rule. She'll be famous. *They'll* be famous. Or at least he'll be unshackled from his terrible career.

My wife, the TV star.

She shot the episode. Stood in the chill of the early-morning fog in Brooklyn, in Red Hook by the bay, on the day of her big scene.

Said her six lines.

Nailed it.

Later, she died.

Cut down in a hail of bullets, sitting behind the wheel of a car, the bad cop killing her to keep her quiet, blood squibs exploding, her body jerking, the windshield of the car seeming to splinter and crack as the special effects coordinator, Mike was his name, standing just off-screen, fired glass hits at the car from a paintball gun. Tiny plastic capsules filled with Vaseline and glitter that make a shatter effect when they impact on glass and look just like bullet holes. Utterly convincing.

Bang, bang, bang, bang, bang.

Her body spasming rhythmically. Fake blood everywhere.

Vaseline and glitter.

The director yelled, "Cut."

Everyone praised her for how committed she was. Cheers all around. Mike the effects guy was ecstatic about how the whole thing had gone off. Daisy thanked them all, then wiped the blood off her face with a cotton ball in the makeup trailer. She changed her clothes and went home in a cab, a little bit of prop blood still spattered in her hair.

A few weeks later, she cashed the check.

She sent off the hefty deposit to the Edenic Foundation for a hastily arranged weeklong retreat in the woods.

Seven days. Seven questions.

Forever changed.

She glances up at the face of her blissfully sleeping husband.

She thinks of all the things that Craig—for all his little secrets, his clandestine sneaking around—still doesn't know about her.

For example: He doesn't know that she had a different name before she moved to New York and started calling herself Daisy. Or that she had a different name before that.

He doesn't know why he's never met her family. Or why she dropped out of college so abruptly in Wisconsin and moved overnight to Boston, then moved again overnight from Boston to theater school in Connecticut.

If *moved* is really the right word.

When you take a single bag and disappear and don't even tell your friends or family where you've gone, then show up in a new place with a new name where you don't know anyone, is that called moving?

Or something else?

Running.

Intermission

The man steps inside an apartment and locks the door behind him and hangs the keys on a hook on the wall. He stows his black coat on a wire hanger in the closet but leaves on his fingerless black gloves, the ones he calls his "driving gloves" as a little joke with himself. He unlaces his black combat boots and places them neatly inside the closet, next to the tower of unopened packages that arrive periodically in the mail. He's in no rush to open these boxes. He knows what's in each one and he doesn't need any of it yet.

In the dimly lit kitchen he opens the fridge, the icy blue light of the interior bulb bathing over him. He grabs an energy drink, twists it open, and downs half. Half now, half in an hour, that's the regimen. The clock in the stovetop glows red—just past 11:30. It's late, later than he'd like, the show ran late tonight, through no fault of his own. He did what he always does, alone in the booth: run the board, raise the lights, bring up mikes, cue blackout. Hanging lights, haunting the catwalk. Dressed all in black so as not to be seen.

No, tonight it was the actors who blew it, he thinks; they were sloppy, baggy, thirsty for applause, steeping in every extended laugh break like greedy little children. The audience, of course, ate it up, they always do—so happy to get served some warmed-over Broadway retread that's limped its way across the country to a regional theater in the middle of nowhere, cast with local has-beens and never-weres.

When he's up in the booth at the back of the theater watching it all unfold, he amuses himself with the notion that, at any time, he could plunge the whole production into darkness. He likes to imagine it. The stage going suddenly black. The sound system squealing to inaudibility, the audience murmuring, looking around, and the actors—the sad actors—scrambling, panicking on the newly darkened stage, starved of the only thing they crave.

Maybe one day, he thinks. Until then, it pays the bills. And offers plenty of downtime to pursue other passions.

He replaces the half-consumed energy drink in the fridge and sets the timer on the stove for sixty minutes. He crosses the room to his desk and settles into the ergonomically sculpted gaming chair that cost him a full two weeks' pay but was absolutely worth every penny.

He toggles the mouse to shake the flat-screen monitor awake.

First up: the email newsletters, dispatches from the Hollywood trades. Variety *breakdowns and* Deadline *announcements. He opens each email, scrolling, searching for casting news, production updates, job openings, positions filled. Finding nothing in the newsletters, he checks* Playbill *for Broadway bulletins. Casting announcements. Shows opening. "Spotlight On." "Faces to Watch."*

Then he heads to Facebook, which is pretty unpromising these days, a blizzard of pop-ups and kooks, but he's had success there before, and old hunting grounds are hard to quit. He searches his reliable keywords: classmates, known friends, stage names, theatrical establishments.

No luck.

So he does a good old-fashioned Google reverse image search just for fun, another old standby trick, even though the few photos he has are now nearly a decade out of date. Sure enough, everything that comes up he's already seen before.

Next up: the message boards. 4Chan and 8Chan and beyond. He thinks of how, years ago, he used to waste hours on these boards, talking military gear and girl trouble and insurrection. Now he's only interested in the endless ribbons of expert commentary on rising young actresses, emerging starlets, hacked photos. He scrolls.

The timer on the stovetop goes off.

Has it been an hour already?

He rises from the chair, twists at the waist, bends his wrists back, first one hand, then the other, then walks back to the fridge. The red stovetop clock now blinking long past midnight, coming up on one a.m.

He drinks the second half of his energy drink and rinses out the bottle. He glances at the unchanging night beyond the bedsheet curtains. He thinks of the vastness of the country, stretching out in both directions over prairies and plains and highways toward the overcrowded chaos of the coasts. He thinks about the search, the discipline of it. It's a matter of patience, he thinks. He imagines a man standing knee-deep in hip-waders in a long, curving river, his long line cast, fly-fishing, the hours passing, the patience required. He imagines a man stationed deep in a nuclear silo, at a console setup not unlike his own, with little contact with the outside world, awaiting that message, that code, that sign from the surface that war has begun.

This feels no different to him.

Endless patient hours in the service of a purpose.

He does not yet know that this night, so similar in all its particulars to the many nights that have preceded it—that this night is the night he will circle in red on the calendar, the night that will change the direction of his life.

The tug on the line.

The signal to launch.

He settles back into his chair.

He toggles the mouse and heads to his next destination. Fan sites, he's learned, are invaluable repositories of knowledge, the true keepers of wisdom. This is where you find not just plot discussions and character breakdowns but rumored future guest stars and cameos and one-offs—complete with each actor's bio, height, weight, hobbies, hairstyle, hometown, relationship status, gossip, hookups and breakups, appearance schedule, autograph availability, memorabilia marketplace, and more.

He starts with a stalwart network drama. Not the best show, but a show that's been on forever, that reliably cranks out weekly episodes, and that absolutely churns through guest stars, many of whom are longtime New York theater actors. This legal melodrama, he's learned, has particularly obsessive fans who gather after each episode to post notes to one another online like Remember how in season eleven, episode eighteen— or Oh, if you like this actor she also appeared in a five-episode arc on— or I saw this actress live onstage in New York, here's a selfie from the autograph line—

These people need to get a fucking life, he thinks.

He clicks through to the show's official site, where he knows that even now online fans of the fourth-highest-rated network TV drama are assembling to scrutinize the details of that particular evening's episode—and that's when he finds it, that signal, that sign, the one that he's spent the last eight years searching for.

The Third Day

||||

SEEDS

11

She can't get pregnant. That's what she'd told him, he's sure of it.

Craig swipes wet leaves from the hull of the canoe that leans up against a tree near the lake. Daisy's inside changing into her bathing suit. She's eager to get started on the day's activities. That's how she's always been: a planner, a scheduler, the drill sergeant of the vacation. If the point is to take a week away, rest up, relax, do nothing, Daisy will reliably have an itinerary for every minute of every day, drawn up for the whole week with tasks duly assigned.

But how, he thinks, is he supposed to pop out of bed and just jump right back into this vacation, knowing that—well, knowing what she told him last night? He can hardly bring himself to think the words, let alone contemplate what they mean. *We're having a baby.* Their whole lives have been upended. As far as he knew, as recently as twenty-four hours ago, having a baby together was not even a possibility. Now they've apparently skipped right over the *Guess what, maybe we* can *have a kid* conversation and gone straight to the *Guess what, we are actually having an actual kid* conversation.

She can't get pregnant. He thinks back to the night when they had the conversation. They were on date number five, maybe six, about two months in and everything was going great. He liked Daisy a lot, he knew that already, he thought he might even be falling for her. Like, actually falling in love with her—a strange and unusual, if not unwelcome, feeling for him.

She'd sat him down in a noisy bar in the West Village and told him she wanted to have a talk.

He remembers that he actually got scared for a moment, his heart clenching, because he thought that she was going to break things off with him.

She can't get pregnant. That's what she'd told him, some genetic condition she had, she just wanted to let him know now in case the relationship continued to progress. She seemed nervous when she said it, but the only feeling he felt was relief. Not about the news—as for kids, he was agnostic. Kids seemed . . . fine? No, he felt relief that night because this news meant he'd never have to face the one big test he knew he'd fail. He'd never have to endure that future moment where she decides he's not the kind of man she'd *want* to have kids with—that he's not good enough, not worthy, to take that step with her.

And that was a huge relief.

Because the one worry he had—that he wasn't interesting enough, wasn't smart enough, wasn't good enough, wasn't *worthy*—was one he felt often, especially since moving to New York. And not just with her. Whenever he found himself in a roomful of strangers, or meeting someone new, he could be clever and entertaining, sure, even charming, but he always felt—always *feared*—that he was just a few moments away from being exposed as a ludicrous fraud. He couldn't shake the suspicion that these people were simply humoring him, indulging his presence, and, when he wasn't looking, secretly or not-so-secretly mocking him. And, really, who could blame them?

So he always kept it light with people—especially with women. Kept the banter flowing, kept the conversation clever, kept everyone safely at arm's length. Which had been fine for friendships, he'd found, and work life, and casual dating. But it made real relationships tricky since it meant that you'd eventually hit that moment when you've mutually decided to take things more seriously and try to, you know, *really get to know each other*—and he dreaded that moment. For him, it was the signal to bail. To sabotage everything, find someone new, someone whose only requirements of him were a handsome face, a clever joke, a charming smile.

Miraculously, Daisy seemed to see him differently. She laughed at his dumb stories, and told him dumb stories of her own, and he laughed, and they got along great. And she was gorgeous and smart and talented in all the ways you'd hope someone might be, and she seemed to value him and she didn't mind at all that he found it so hard to open up. And she was *fearless*—fearless in a way that astonished and inspired him. Like that moment on their first date—he can remember it so clearly—when she leaned over and licked custard off his stubbled chin. This woman is *undaunted*, he thought, in a way that he'd never been. But maybe he could learn to be. Maybe she could teach him.

He also knew that, if you asked her, she'd say that was the moment he'd fallen for her. But it wasn't.

The moment he fell came a few weeks later, when he was alone in the dark, watching her.

She was starring in a downtown show in a tiny theater in some far-flung precinct of Brooklyn, the kind of show that comes and goes with little notice. She'd invited him to see her, and he'd settled in alone in the third row of the nearly empty audience. The few other attendees hushed and the lights came up and there she was.

And she was flawless.

He sat rapt and watched her and felt breathless. At how good she was. The whole room could feel it.

And she was, improbably, his.

The thought baffled him. She was too good for him, that was obvious. He'd never deserve her. That was obvious, too.

Yet she liked him. Apparently, she loved him. Eventually, she *married* him. And each passing month in this improbable circumstance only made him more certain—more fearful—that one day the bubble would pop, that she'd wake up as though from a dream, that she'd *figure it out*, see him for who he really is, which is not much at all, and then she'd leave him—which only spurred him to preemptively disappear.

If it hadn't been Lilith, it would have been someone else.

And all that was before this news.

Surprise!

He'd said all the right things to Daisy in the bathtub, of course. He's very good at saying all the right things. He'd said "Great" and "Oh my

God!" and "This is unbelievable" and "I'm just so excited to have this adventure with you," and he held Daisy tight against his chest in the bath and tilted his face into her hair and kissed her softly on her skull and tried to forget that just moments earlier he'd been fantasizing about escaping to a roadhouse greenroom with a goth-band waitress he'd met in a parking lot.

All the right things. He knows exactly how to say them.

He just isn't sure he knows how to do them.

He stands and considers the curved hull of the canoe, leaning up against the tree, and he thinks of the bags in the trunk of the car.

Still packed.

Not that he could run back to Lilith.

Lilith's furious.

But somewhere. With someone.

There's always *someone*. Right?

But he won't do that. Not now. Especially not now. After this news?

Run?

Right?

Is he the kind of person who'd do that?

Or he could, he thinks, try to do the other thing.

The right thing.

Be worthy.

He hasn't fully chased the tempting thought of flight from his mind when he steps forward and finally flips the canoe with an effortful tug, attempting to angle it toward the sandy inlet and the lake, and that's when he sees it—the snake, black and coiled and glistening, lurking in the shadows of the canoe's interior.

He jumps back.

A voice comes from behind him and startles him: "Careful now."

Craig spins and sees a man who looks as though he's been lingering there silently for hours. The man wears khaki trousers and a red windbreaker with EDENIC FOUNDATION stenciled on the front. He's young—

early thirties, younger than Craig—and handsome (more handsome than Craig? Hard to say), his sandy, shaggy hair hanging to his jawline. He's smiling broadly, friendly. Craig's first thought is that this guy looks like a missionary come to share the Good News.

The man steps forward and holds out a hand by way of introduction. Craig shakes it.

The man points at the snake, still coiled inside the canoe. "You never know what can happen when you least expect it."

Daisy appears at the railing of the porch in her bathing suit. "Hey," she says to both of them, waiting for someone to explain. When no one answers, she looks to Craig. "Who's this?"

The man gives her a cheery wave. "Pardon me—good morning—I'm Shep. I'm in charge of security for the Edenic Foundation. You two mind if I have a word?"

"Sure," says Daisy. "Just let me get a robe."

As Daisy heads back inside, Craig looks toward the canoe and sees the snake uncoil with an unsettling shudder, then disappear with a rustle into the underbrush.

The three of them convene on the porch, standing in an awkward huddle. Craig and Daisy cling closely to each other, watching this strange guest like he's a doctor who's about to deliver life-altering news.

"I want to assure you, everything's perfect, everything's fine," says Shep, which, Craig notes, has the opposite effect of reassurance. "I just like to stop by periodically and see if there's anything you might need. And to ask if maybe you've seen or heard anything—unusual."

Daisy glances at Craig, then at Shep. "Unusual like—how?"

Shep considers this, glances toward the tree line, then says, "Look. I'm going to be straight with you. Dr. Arden would never tell you this because he's a little too"—he waves a hand—"head-in-the-clouds. Don't get me wrong. The Ardens are brilliant. But very optimistic about human nature. That's why they keep me around. I'm more of a realist."

"Are we in some sort of danger?" says Daisy.

"No. Absolutely not," says Shep. "I mean—we have had a few in-cidents." Craig notes that Shep is clearly choosing his words carefully. "When the Ardens moved here, it was all hippies chasing Woodstock. The biggest danger you faced was an incense overdose." Shep waits for a reaction to his joke, doesn't get one, proceeds. "These days—some of the locals can be a little inhospitable to visitors. Especially visitors from the city."

"The ones who call us 'citiots,'" says Craig.

"Some of our guests have had hostile run-ins," says Shep.

"What exactly do you mean by 'hostile'?" says Daisy.

"Vandalism. Broken windows. Slashed tires. The occasional confron-tation. Sadly, it's the nature of the country we live in. So divisive. So polarized. We used to all get along. Now it's red state, blue state, even within the same state. Anyone different is an enemy."

Daisy's face clouds with concern. "They didn't say anything about this when we signed up."

"The foundation's been very careful to keep word of these incidents quiet. You know—compensation, NDAs, et cetera. You signed one your-selves before you arrived."

Craig shoots Daisy a look. "We signed an NDA?"

She shrugs. "There was a lot of paperwork."

"Look, I'm not trying to spook you," says Shep. "For the most part, folks up here are very friendly. There's just a few bad apples. So we've stepped up security. That's why I came by—to let you know you might be seeing me around."

"We're just here to spend the week alone," says Daisy. "We're per-fectly happy to keep to ourselves. That's kind of the whole point of this."

"I appreciate that," says Shep. "Just don't hesitate to get in touch if you encounter any—unpleasantries." He gives them both a conciliatory smile. "Oh, and one more thing. You didn't bring any sort of protection, did you?"

At first, oddly, Craig thinks he means birth control. Which makes

Craig think of the baby, and of the news of his newly pregnant—impossibly pregnant—wife. But how could Shep—then it clicks for him. "You mean, like a *weapon?*"

Shep acknowledges the seeming absurdity of it. "It's not at all uncommon for people up here to keep something on hand for self-defense. Sometimes city people get ideas in their heads, too."

"No, we don't have anything like that," says Daisy sharply.

"Do we need it?" says Craig. Daisy glares at him. But he had to ask.

"Of course not," says Shep. "Protection—that's my job. And in my experience, having that sort of thing—a firearm—on hand will only just complicate the situation."

"Wait," says Daisy. She looks to Craig, her face now shadowed with worry. Craig feels like she's waiting for him to say something, but he's not sure what. Finally, she says, "What about yesterday in the woods?"

Craig turns to Shep. "We heard a gunshot. But that was just hunters." Craig expects Shep to shrug this off as a perfectly rational explanation, but instead Shep also looks troubled.

"This property extends for miles in all directions," Shep says. "So there definitely should not be anyone hunting back in these woods." He peers back at the tree line, then turns to Craig. "What did this hunter look like?"

"He was young. Maybe twenty. He had a bright orange baseball hat," says Craig. "Does that sound like one of your bad apples?"

The three of them stand for a moment in silence while Shep seems to process this new information. Then he says, "Did this guy seem confrontational to you?"

Did he? thinks Craig. "He certainly wasn't friendly." He glances at Daisy, then back to Shep, suddenly feeling like he's the one being grilled. "I also saw him at the diner yesterday. Same guy. Eating with a friend."

Now Daisy's alarmed. "*What?*"

"Did he happen to say anything to you at the diner?" asks Shep.

"No, but he was definitely—inhospitable, like you said. Just a vibe."

"I'm glad you told me," says Shep. "If he or anyone else comes around, you let me know right away, okay? You definitely should not have unexpected visitors."

"Except for you, of course," says Craig.

"Exactly. Except for me." Shep laughs, a tension breaker. He pulls a business card from his pocket and holds it out to Craig. The card says simply EDENIC FOUNDATION with a phone number. "Anything else comes up, anything at all, just call my cell. I'll answer, twenty-four seven."

Craig takes the card. "What about that landline in the cabin? That red emergency phone?"

"Better to just call me directly. Don't worry, I'll come running." Shep claps Craig on the shoulder. "Just one more thing. Please stay away from the orchard. I expect that Dr. Arden already explained it to you. Apparently, it's a very delicate ecosystem." He leans in confidentially. "I know you two paid a visit already, but we'll keep that between us."

"We didn't realize—" says Craig.

Shep stops him. "No worries. My lips are sealed. Nice to meet you both." He gives them each a curt wave, then heads off down the steps toward the woods.

Craig watches him leave, in his bright red windbreaker with SECURITY written on the back. When he turns to Daisy, he's surprised to see unmistakable anger in her eyes.

"What?" says Craig.

"Why didn't you tell me?"

Craig's confused. "About what?"

"That you saw that guy *twice* yesterday?"

"The hunter? I didn't think it was a big deal."

"You didn't think it was a big deal that you saw a hostile stranger at the diner and then he turned up here in the woods?"

Yes, and with blood all over his arms, thinks Craig. And a knife. A very long knife.

He doesn't mention that to her.

"I'm sure it's fine," he says, holding up the business card. "It's like Shep said: He'll protect us."

She says nothing further, simply fumes.

Craig watches her, waiting for the moment to pass. Then he says finally, "You okay? Look—I'm sorry."

"No, it's not that," she says darkly, distracted.

"What is it?"

She looks up at him. "How did Shep know that we were in the orchard yesterday?"

12

They shelve their day's plans, the hiking and rafting, and decide to hunker down at the cabin. They don't discuss the decision directly, they just agree, unspoken, to stay secluded in the woods. Make lunch. Read. Take out the canoe.

Once they're out on the lake, the day feels more peaceful. He sits in the stern of the canoe and strokes evenly like he remembers learning to do as a boy. She sits in the stem, watching the water ripple as the keel cuts swiftly through the lake.

Finally, in the quiet, he says something that's been on his mind all day. "Should we leave?"

She looks back at him. "You mean go home? Why?"

He pulls the oar from the water and rests it across his knees. The canoe drifts. "Because it's not safe here? It *is* creepy about that hunter. And also—" He pauses.

"Also what?"

"There's just something off about this place," he says. "Don't you think?"

"Off how?" she asks patiently.

"Like you said at the cabin, about the orchard—how did Shep know? Do you think they're watching us?"

She turns her whole body toward him now. "Craig, when you say 'they're watching us'—who do you mean by 'they'?"

"Those hippie doctors," he says. "And, you know, Shep. And that waitress from the diner."

Daisy laughs. She looks genuinely confused. "The waitress from the diner? With the tattoos? What does she have to do with it?"

"Just this whole experience," he says, sullen now at her dismissive tone. "This supposed 'test.' I mean, how are they testing us, exactly?"

"They're just questions."

"But what did Kit say about it being a 'holistic experience'? What does that mean?"

"That's just hippie talk," she says, looking to comfort him. "He just meant"—Daisy turns again to the glassy lake, the distant tree line, the rolling hills—"*this*. He just meant all of this. It's all part of the experience. That's why they leave us alone for the week. That's why they don't just send you the seven questions in the mail to answer at home."

Craig stews in the stern. *Would you change? Would you sacrifice?* This fucking test, he thinks. *Would you leave? Would you shit your pants and run back to the city?* Maybe those are the next questions. "Okay. But still," he says.

He's getting stubborn, petulant—she can hear it. "Craig, we're doing great."

"I just mean—it's an option to leave. It's not like we're prisoners."

"I know. But we chose to do this."

"No—*you* chose," he snaps.

And now she hears it—that unmistakable edge, that bitter bite, that signals an impending fight. She watches him. He sits huddled and glowering, gripping the oar. The oar's blade trails a steady drip, disturbing the placid surface of the lake.

"I just mean we're here," she says calmly. "We did this for a reason. And we're making progress. Right?"

"I guess."

"So let's stay." She smiles warmly. She rests a hand on her belly. "This is important for us. Especially now."

"Of course," he says. He's softening now. She sees it. The conflict averted, for now.

"Let's just make sure we watch out for each other, okay?" she says. "We're all we have up here."

"Okay. You're right," he says.

She can't quite tell from his voice if she's convinced him or merely defeated him.

He lifts the oar again and dips it deep in the water, turning the canoe now to point them back home. With each stroke, as he steers them toward shore, he looks like a man with a shovel, digging a deepening hole.

That afternoon, she gets started on her painting project.

She changes into her overalls and carries her supplies to the porch. She lays down newspaper, then methodically sets out the bottles of paint before her. She lays out her brushes and sits, splay-legged, among a semicircle of her carefully curated rocks. Each rock is about the size of a softball. She hefts them in turn and inspects them, then begins to paint. Bright colors, garish letters, childish patterns: arcing rainbows, fluffy clouds. A letter *D* on one rock, followed by a plus sign. Then a letter *C*.

D + C.

Daisy plus Craig.

She regards it, then puts that rock aside to dry and reaches for another. On this one, she paints *D + C* in bright colors, then adds *Forever* underneath in florid script.

Behind her, Craig leans in the doorway of the open French doors, half in, half out, watching her. "*D + C. Forever.* That's encouraging. Are those your souvenirs of our week?"

She keeps her eyes trained on the rock in her hand, her paintbrush poised. "Let's see how the week goes first."

He looks out at the lake. "If we're going to stay, do you think we need to get something?"

She glances up. "Like what?"

"Protection. Like what Shep said."

She puts the brush down. "Absolutely not."

"But if there's a chance of trouble—"

Her expression goes suddenly flat. "Craig, have you ever even fired a gun?" Her tone is derisive, mocking.

"Yes," he says, defensive. "When I was a kid, in Michigan. My uncles took me hunting." A slight lie. His uncles would sometimes take him along to their cabin, where they'd drunkenly shoot at beer cans in the woods. But they never let him touch the guns, let alone fire one. "I mean, we're obviously not going to use it."

"If we're not going to use it, then why have it?" She turns back to her rocks, then adds firmly, the matter settled, "I don't want to hear about it again."

By evening, they're restless. She's tired and doesn't feel like cooking. She suggests that they make dinner plans. Something special. The fancy anniversary dinner date they never got to have in the city.

She rummages in a drawer under the red phone and unearths a brochure for a rustic farm-to-table restaurant on the town's main street, and they agree to get dressed up and take the drive into town.

The restaurant is dimly lit and empty, tea lights flickering on the wooden tables. Craig glances at the hay strewn artfully by the handful on the rough plank floor, the rusty decorative scythes hung on the walls. Well, at least they got the farm part right, he thinks.

Daisy's in better spirits now, he sees that. As for him, he's trying. This day feels tainted, ruined by Shep's warnings. But they can still manage to salvage the rest of the week.

After they've finished their dinner, the plates cleared away, she pulls out a small gift bag. "I got you something. Happy anniversary."

He looks at the bag. Shit—they're doing gifts? He has nothing for her. "Before you say anything—I have a present for you, too." This is a lie. "But when I got your note back home, I left in such a rush, I forgot it." Also a lie.

"It's okay. It's just something small."

He takes the gift bag and reaches inside, pulling out a wooden cigar box. "Ah, I get it. For the—" He gestures toward her belly. "For our news. Congratulations! I love it." He's never smoked a cigar before in his life.

"It's not cigars. Open it."

He glances at her, intrigued. He opens the hinged top of the wooden box.

Inside, there's a small pocketknife with a worn bone handle, nestled in tissue paper. He holds the knife up.

"Wow," he says. "Thank you."

"It was my grandfather's pocketknife. He passed it down to me. Now I'm giving it to you. Given our anniversary, and our good news this week, this seemed like the perfect occasion."

Craig inspects the knife in the candlelight. He feels awkward. What will he do with an heirloom pocketknife? "Why don't you keep it?" he says finally, and offers it back. "You should. It's yours."

"It's *ours*," she says.

He nods, then opens the blade—it's a substantial knife, he sees, the blade about five inches long. Though he can't help but recall the hunting knife that man showed him in the woods, the one he turned in the light, the blood-smeared one with the blade and the teeth. The one that man carried in a scabbard on his belt. Compared to that knife, this pocket-knife looks puny.

"Let me show you a trick," she says and holds out her hand.

He passes the knife to her, and she folds the blade closed, then holds the folded knife lightly in one palm. "Watch this," she says.

Wedging her thumbnail into the notch on the blade, she flips the blade open effortlessly with one hand. "The things you pick up when you hang out with the stage crew in high school," she says. "Totally useless, but it impresses all the girls."

She hands the knife back to him. "You try."

He takes it and closes the blade, then tries to open it one-handed, but it's surprisingly hard, the blade stubborn, and his fingers fumble, and he fails.

"Don't worry," she says. "You'll learn." She points to the gift bag. "There's one more thing in there for you. For us."

He pulls out an envelope with *Q3* embossed in gold on the front.

"I found it on our doorstep," she says. She takes the envelope and opens it, unfolds the paper, and starts to read.

"No fair," he says. "You said it's for both of us."

She doesn't answer. She keeps reading.

He can't quite tell in the guttering candlelight, but her eyes seem to be newly moist.

"What does it say?" he says finally, impatient.

She hands him the paper and he reads it aloud.

Question Three.

Would you fight for me?

What does it mean to fight? In relationships, we fight all the time. We fight with each other. We fight back tears. We fight our worst instincts. We fight to keep love alive, or so we say.

But how often is our strength truly tested? We have romantic ideas about gallantry and chivalry, scores settled and slights avenged. But if a person insulted the honor of your partner, what would you do? If someone approached your spouse looking to lead them astray, how would you react?

Would you fight?

"Fight or flight" is the most basic human instinct, but modern life has taught us to quell these impulses. Instead we negotiate, compromise, equivocate—anything but stand up for ourselves and for each other. It's permissible to feel passionate about love, we're taught, but not to apply that passion to the struggle to keep that love strong. Fighting with each other is a failure of communication, a sign of love gone sour. But fighting for each other is essential for love to thrive.

So what will you do when the moment comes, whatever that moment might be?

Will you cower and cave? Will you flee?

Or will you fight?

Go ahead. Ask your partner the same question a general would ask any foot soldier. And expect the same answer, without hesitation.

Would you fight for me?

He hands the paper back to her.

"Good thing we have this knife," he says, a feeble joke. When she says nothing, her wet eyes still fixed on the question, he waves to the waitress and signals for the check.

13

"Let's grab a nightcap."

Her mood is seemingly buoyed a bit by their retreat to the cool night air. They walk arm in arm up the sidewalk of the main street. She nuzzles against him, the happy couple.

"You sure?" he says. "You're not even drinking. And I've already had a few."

"Come on." She tugs his arm. "We're celebrating."

The hour is late and the street is quiet, shuttered, save for one storefront, a bar that's lit up and jubilant. The tavern windows are frosted, fogged. Warmth and noise beckon.

Daisy nudges the door open and leads him inside.

The place is crowded but not packed, local regulars from the looks of it. Craig's not certain, but he feels like their entrance occasions a few unfriendly glances.

"I'm going to hit the bathroom," he says. "Order me a whiskey neat?" He rests his gift bag on the bar, then edges his way toward the back of the room, navigating the huddles of people who seem unhappy to let him pass.

He makes his way slowly, and that's when he sees it, in the far corner, unmistakable: the bright orange baseball cap.

Shit. Oh, fuck, he thinks. Of all places. The hunter's back is turned to him, the man huddling with a small knot of friends. Craig glances away and hustles toward the rear of the bar. As he moves, he thinks he spots the hat tilting and turning his way.

He scuttles with his head down and bumps accidentally into an old man wearing a heavy flannel shirt.

"Watch yourself," the old man says.

"I'm sorry," says Craig.

"No, I mean—be careful in here," says the old man, then steps aside to let Craig pass.

Daisy slides between two people huddled on barstools and waves the bartender over.

The bartender approaches and leans with two ropy arms on the bar, a wet rag in one hand. "What can I get for you?"

She's a pretty woman, thinks Daisy—a little frayed at the edges but with a pleasant patina of rough experience. The actor in Daisy notes the bartender's no-bullshit stance, her seen-it-all readiness, her bluff confidence—all character traits she can mimic one day. "One whiskey neat and a seltzer, please."

The bartender nods. "You here with a date?"

"My husband. It's our anniversary."

"Good—because I would not recommend hanging out here alone."

Daisy smiles, wary. "Not a friendly crowd?"

"A little too friendly, if you get my meaning." The bartender gives her a look and moves away to fetch the drinks.

Daisy leans on the bar and surveys the patrons. An upstate mix of elderly regulars, hunched over and drinking alone, and younger folk in rural wear, trucker caps and Carhartt jackets, the kind of outfits you might see worn ironically in Brooklyn but which up here just mean that people didn't bother to change after work. Some of them could be refugees from the city, she thinks, idealistic hipsters starting organic farms, but they mostly just look like kids who grew up here and never found the energy or inspiration to leave. Either way, there's a hard edge to everyone.

Daisy's eyes settle on a particular woman, sitting alone at the bar. She's young, maybe eighteen, blond with pale skin, a neglected drink sitting in front of her, something colorful with a little umbrella. Her hair's done up tight in a ponytail, the edges of her scalp pulled pink. She wears tight jeans and a loose white blouse, and her gaze is fixed intently on her lap. She looks scared, on edge.

The bartender sets the drinks down. "You must be up here for the Eden Test."

Her mention of it surprises Daisy. "How'd you guess?"

"It's our number one draw for outsiders. Not much else to do in Plain except fuck and fight. How are you two liking it?"

"So far, so good, I guess."

"What question are you on?"

"Question Three."

"So it's just getting interesting," the bartender says. "I did it once myself, you know. Changed my life."

"It saved your relationship?"

"Nope—ended it. We only made it to Question Five. Then I dumped his ass and bought this bar. A fair exchange, I'd say."

"Mostly regulars here?"

"Sure, save for the few stray citiots. No offense."

"None taken." Daisy nods toward the young woman at the end of the bar. "You think she's doing okay?"

"Her? Why?"

"She looks—spooked," says Daisy, glancing at the girl. "I know that look. Sitting in public, hoping not to be seen."

"Can't say I recognize her, to be honest," says the bartender. "But don't worry—I keep an eye on everyone, friend or foe."

Sure enough, as if on cue, a man from the back of the bar, the man in the blaze orange baseball cap, peels off from his circle of friends and approaches the girl. She stares down into her drink. He says a few jocular words to her, looming, and she tries to politely dismiss him.

Daisy watches. He persists. The girl shrinks as he towers over her. He leans an elbow on the bar, grinning, his mouth now hovering close to her ear, whispering something, likely lewd. The girl cringes and folds even further into herself.

The bartender shrugs, weathered. "Like I said: a little too friendly."

Craig reappears at Daisy's elbow. "What I miss?"

Daisy hands him his whiskey. "The bartender was just telling me that she did the Eden Test."

"Really? You did?" says Craig, sounding more surprised than he should.

"Indeed," says the bartender. She looks at Daisy. "Hey—I know you, don't I? From that TV show. The one with the cops and lawyers."

"*Legal Remedies,*" says Craig proudly. "That's right."

"You were good," says the bartender. "Though you sure came to a bad end."

Daisy thinks of the blood squibs, the bullet holes, the Vaseline and glitter. "Thank you, that's kind," she says.

The bartender leans in and points her rag toward Daisy's belly. "By the way—congratulations."

Daisy laughs. "How'd you—"

"Two drinkers, one drink. Bartender's intuition." The bartender straightens up. "You two have yourselves a fruitful week," she says, then steps away toward a waiting customer.

Craig glances back toward Blaze Orange, who's still hovering over the cowering girl. "You know what?" he says. "Let's just finish up and head home. I'm a little more tired than I thought."

Daisy grips his arm, her eyes back on the girl. "No—look at that guy's hat. Is that the guy you saw from before? In the woods?"

"Him? I don't know. Maybe. I barely got a good look at him," Craig lies.

"Look what he's doing to her."

"Seems like a clumsy pickup attempt. I'm not sure he needs an audience."

"No, it's not that," says Daisy. "Watch."

Blaze Orange is crowding the girl now, using his full height to fence her in. The mood between the guy and the girl has palpably soured, and the people around them start to murmur and step away.

"Someone needs to help her," says Daisy. "Someone needs to step in."

"She's a grown-up. She's fine," says Craig. "Who knows about these townies and their mating rituals?"

But Daisy's already let go of his arm and stepped toward the couple. Oh, boy, thinks Craig. Here we go.

"I think she wants to be left alone," Daisy says to the man in a firm, unwavering voice. Her forceful declaration silences the murmuring crowd.

The man in the blaze orange ballcap straightens up. He's got a good six inches on Daisy. He sneers, amused at this feisty intervention. Even from a few feet away, in the darkness of the bar, Craig can see that the man's cheeks are flushing red, either drunk or angry or both.

"No one wants to be alone," the man says to Daisy.

"You want to come with us?" Daisy says gently to the girl, placing a hand on her shoulder. "My husband's here with me."

The man in the blaze orange cap looks up at the mention of a husband—and now, finally, spots Craig. He laughs. "Who—this little bitch?" His eyes now lock on Craig. "Hello again."

The blond girl keeps her eyes fixed on her lap and doesn't move.

Daisy turns to Craig. "So this is the guy?"

"I guess so," says Craig.

"You don't remember me?" says the man. "Out in the woods watching you and your little wife in your cozy little rental cabin. Why don't you weekenders just fuck off back to the city?"

The man in the ballcap is beaming now, Craig can see it, the man looks so happy now. He seemed clumsy around the girl, but when another man steps up to challenge him, in front of everyone—it's like his favorite song just came on the jukebox. He knows this tune. He loves this dance. He knows all the steps.

"We're just trying to enjoy a drink—" says Craig, stepping up to stand with his wife, but the man's already mocking him, repeating his words back into his face—*jutht trying to enjoy a drink*—with a lisping, simpering voice. From the crowd, Craig hears a few chortles. People have noticed the show. A chilling silence pervades the bar, the sound of a curtain rising, an audience settling into their seats.

Why doesn't the bartender step in here? thinks Craig. But no one's saying anything.

The man stares him down. "What, you're not happy in your fancy cabin? You decided to come slumming in town?" He takes a half step toward Craig. "Get the fuck out of here, you little pussy."

Craig knows well what he's supposed to do here. He knows he's supposed to toss a drink in this dude's face, then drop him with one punch. He's supposed to fight his way out of this bar like Bruce Lee, tossing bodies through the plate-glass window.

But it won't end that way, will it? he thinks. Bar fights aren't like in the movies. They're violent, ugly, and brief. He's seen this whole scenario go down before, late nights at bad bars, dark streets in the early mornings in the collegiate neighborhoods of New York, where posturing frat boys run afoul of actual hardened thugs, some of whom don't like the way you looked at them, some of whom have simply been spoiling for a fight all night. He knew a guy back in college, a promising trumpet player, who got jumped in a parking lot behind a bar after some assholes mistook him for someone else. They stomped his skull and broke his jaw, sent him to the hospital, and he never played the trumpet again.

"Come on," Craig says to Daisy, quietly but firmly. He grips her shoulder to guide her away, while doing his best to hold eye contact with the man. The man's jean jacket barely fits him, stretched over a methodically developed physique. On one shoulder of the jacket, Craig notices, is a Confederate flag patch. Oh, great, Craig thinks. Racists, on top of everything else.

The bar is watching, hushed.

"That's right, little bitch. Walk away," says the man.

"Look," says Craig. "Have your drink. Enjoy your night. Leave this woman alone. No one needs to get hassled. She's obviously not interested."

"Or what?" says the man.

And now another guy steps up, a sidekick of sorts, a wiry, wild-eyed man, shorter than the first man but older, meaner-looking, junkie-taut, lean, and crazy, too, that's obvious. The kind of guy who's always lurking at the edge of a brawl and can't wait to jump in. Craig's seen this guy before, too—it's the other guy from the booth at the diner. Craig's eyes pass from Blaze Orange to the wiry man, the one who seems so anxious to unload, and on the smaller man's neck, where his corded veins are pulsing, Craig sees it, unmistakable—motherfuck, he thinks, is that a swastika tattoo? Is that half a swastika, just visible, rising up from under his collar?

Blaze Orange reaches out and prods Craig hard with a finger. "I said, or *what*, motherfucker?"

Daisy, meanwhile, has her eyes and both hands on the folded girl. "It's okay," she whispers softly. "It's okay."

The girl twists her head toward Daisy and hisses, "Fuck off and leave me alone."

Daisy pulls back, stung.

"Come on," says Craig. "Let's just go."

"No." Daisy turns back to the girl. "We can help you."

"I said, fuck off, weekenders," says the girl. "Or my boyfriend here is going to stomp your skinny city ass."

And now the whole bar has turned against them, Craig can feel it, they have no allies here. It's a townie bar, and they've wandered in where they're not wanted, and the whole crowd seems poised to pounce and pummel them both.

He puts his arm around his wife—his newly pregnant, fragile wife— and realizes that all that matters is getting her out of here, getting them both back out safely to the street.

The man, without taking his eyes off Craig—he's all about Craig now, the crowd's murmured encouragements coming to a crescendo— smiles and says, "What's good, little bitch?"

"All right, that's it, you two," shouts the bartender finally, pounding on the bar and then pointing toward the door. "Take that macho posturing outside."

"We're good," says Craig, not taking his eyes from the man. "We're leaving."

"I guess we'll settle this later then," says the man.

"I don't think so." Then Craig says to Daisy, "Let's go."

"I'll see you again. Count on it," says the man, his voice rising, shouting after them as they retreat to the door. "Count on it, motherfucker—"

Daisy's muscles are coiled beneath his hands, tense, Craig can feel it, as he leads her away. She's full of latent energy, she's ready to pounce, wild, he's never seen her like this, but he's got a hold of her now. Craig wonders as he gathers her into his arms if this is what Shep the security guard was warning them about that morning—if this is what he meant when he talked about *inhospitable incidents.*

They retreat out the door and with relief Craig feels the cool air of the outside enfold them. The figures in the bar recede, the man in the ballcap still shouting, arrogant, jabbing a finger in the air toward Craig, the seated girl's face twisted toward them in a hateful grimace.

As Craig pulls his wife through the doorway to safety, Daisy stops and stands still, holding the door open. Gazing back into the bar, she says softly, "Look."

And Craig looks.

They both stand there and watch it all unfold.

In the bar, a tall figure steps out from the edge of the crowd, a lanky man with shaggy hair.

Holy shit, Craig thinks. He recognizes this figure even without his red windbreaker—it's Shep, the security guard.

Shep moves swiftly from the periphery of the crowd toward the man and strikes him swiftly with a rabbit punch to the throat. The man's blaze orange cap jerks backward, teetering, then falls off his head as he staggers. In a blur, Shep strikes him again, then again, and Blaze Orange slumps to his knees, coughing blood. The bar erupts. Craig tugs Daisy back toward him, and as the door closes softly on its hydraulic hinge, they both watch as the chaos unfolds, until the door shuts and the steam-fogged glass obscures the mayhem inside.

"That was Shep," says Daisy quietly, in wonder.

Craig hustles her across the empty street toward their waiting car.

"Fucking townies," mutters Craig, furious, humiliated, spitting the words like a curse. "I told you we should have gone straight home."

He opens the passenger-side door for her, a gentlemanly gesture, but she just stands there, holding out her hand.

"I'm driving," she says. "You've been drinking."

He hands over the keys without complaint.

14

The silent drive through the woods soothes his jitters a bit and now he wants to explain himself. But what is there to say? he thinks. He saved her. He got her out of there, right? He did what he had to do. He kept them safe. That's what he wants to say. But he doesn't. He says nothing.

She says nothing, too. Just keeps her eyes trained on the road ahead, dirt clouds swirling before them in the funnel of the headlights as they drive.

He sits and looks out the window at the passing woods in the dark. He figures that maybe one day together they'll remember this night, years from now, as a funny story and a near-miss misadventure. Maybe they'll even tell this tale to incredulous friends back in Brooklyn, maybe heighten the danger a bit, add the flash of a knife—*did someone have a gun?* Maybe laugh about the time they almost got into it with a gang of riled-up, tattooed, white-power townies in a faraway rural bar.

He's almost assuaged himself when he remembers Shep, appearing from the crowd to fell the man.

And Daisy's face as she watched him from the street.

She seemed—what?

She seemed *intrigued.*

Craig can't help but feel the hot fingers of jealousy constrict around his throat.

Well, he's got his waitress, she's got her security guard, he thinks, spiteful. Maybe that's how this week ends, he thinks, with them split up and paired off with their rural lovers. The tattooed waitress and the shaggy-haired security guard—it's almost as though they were figures conjured from Craig's and Daisy's respective fantasies. Maybe that's all part of the test, he thinks, this so-called Eden Test: a week's worth of temptations thrown at them to see if they will crack.

He looks over at her, hoping to catch her eye, maybe start a conversation, but she just drives, her face lit from below by the glow of the dashboard, reflected and twinned in the windshield, as though she's staring back at herself, both of her faces frozen, unreadable.

They pull into the cabin's driveway and she kills the engine but keeps the headlights on.

The car's bright beams lance the night, spilling in two brilliant pools against the cabin's walls. A sudden frenzy of moths and night flies form and flutter in the twin spotlights, their enormous shadows projected against the cabin.

She sits staring forward. "Thank you for stepping in back there."

"Yeah, of course," he says. "How are you? Are you okay?"

"Yes. It's just—there's something I should tell you." She's still looking straight out the windshield. "That guy in the bar—he brought something back for me." She pulls the keys from the ignition and clutches them in her lap, worrying them in her fingers like she's holding a rosary. "There's something I never told you before. Something that happened to me. Before we met."

He leans in. "What is it?"

"There was a guy. Back in grad school." Her eyes are now trained on her lap. The night stills around them. Moths flutter in the bright beams. "It's the reason I had to leave school early."

Craig shifts toward her, straining against his shoulder belt. "What guy? What happened?"

She looks up at him. "He was a high school boyfriend from back home. When we broke up and I moved away to college, he didn't take it well. I didn't have any contact with him, but he tracked me down at school and he made my life—untenable."

Untenable—she says the word like it's one she's considered for years, one she's chosen after rejecting many alternatives, a word whose nuances and implications she's studied like a scholar. "That's why I had to leave school so suddenly," she says. "That's why I moved to New York when I did."

"My God. Did he—did he hurt you?"

She stares into her lap. "It was just important that I get away."

"I'm so sorry," he says. "Why didn't you tell me about this before?" He doesn't mean for his tone to sound accusatory, he's just trying to unravel what she's telling him, but it comes out sounding slightly like a recrimination, and he wishes he could take it back.

"It all happened long before we met," she says. "That was the whole point of moving to New York—to start fresh. But tonight—that guy in the bar. The way he was bullying that woman."

"Do you ever hear from this guy anymore? Is he still out there?"

He's trying to be supportive, she thinks. She's known him long enough to give him that benefit. But she also wonders, as he prods her now, whether he's asking these questions solely out of concern for her or as some sort of risk assessment for himself.

"No. It's been years. He doesn't know where I am, I made sure of that. But seeing that guy, how he acted, it just—it shook me." She braves a smile. "I just wanted to try to explain."

He unbuckles his seat belt and tries awkwardly to hug her. "Daisy, I'm so sorry," he says as he pulls her closer.

She exhales, a steadying breath. "I'll tell you the whole story sometime, I promise." He sees her eyes are wet again. "That was another thing I wanted to bring up this week, actually," she says. "To just lay it all out, you know? No more secrets."

"Of course. No more secrets." He puts a hand on her cheek.

She pulls back and looks straight into his eyes. "Craig—you won't leave me, right?"

He holds her gaze. Waits a long moment. Thinks of the packed luggage that's still sitting in the trunk of the car.

Then he says: "Of course not. I'd never leave you. I promise."

She offers up a small smile, looking relieved. She unbuckles her seat belt and lets it slide free. "Thank you. Come on. Let's go inside."

She shuts off the headlights. He opens the passenger door.

As he steps out of the car, she looks up at the house through the windshield and says, "Did you leave the door open when we left?"

15

They approach together in the dark up the porch steps in silence, watching the vertical sliver between the door and the jamb.

Their front door. Ajar.

The interior of the cabin cast in darkness.

"Didn't you lock the door?" she whispers.

"It's the country. You said no one locks their doors," he says.

He steps forward, cautious. The porch creaking underfoot. The din of the woods, the tree frogs and crickets, seems cranked up, a rising roar.

"Do you think—" she says, and leaves unsaid the notion that the men from the bar somehow followed them home to finish the fight.

"No way. How?"

"They know these woods. We don't."

"They could never have gotten back here faster than we did."

"Are you sure? Maybe there's another route back here. A faster route."

Craig doesn't answer, just nudges the door open and pauses in the doorway.

"Hello?" he says into the dark.

"Should we call someone?" Daisy whispers.

"Who?"

"Call Shep. You have his number."

"He was at the bar, remember? It would take him forty minutes to get here."

"What about Kit and Bridget? They said they live just up the road."

"Yeah, 'just up the road' could be five miles. And what are they going to do? Hug them to death?"

"We can call that hotline on the phone inside," she says. "They said to use that phone if there's an emergency. Maybe they have someone close by."

"Sure. But that phone's inside."

Craig looks around on the porch for—something. He wants something heavy to hold in his hands. There's a cord of chopped wood piled up by the door. Next to the pile, a small hand axe.

He picks it up.

"What are you going to do with that?" says Daisy, but Craig just proceeds into the cabin.

He hits the light switch and the living room blazes to life.

Empty.

He exhales.

Daisy joins him.

"All clear," he says.

"Did you hear that?" says Daisy.

"What?"

"Upstairs."

Craig heads up the stairs slowly, step by tentative step, axe in hand. Now he's wondering what exactly he intends to do with this axe. If he had this axe at the bar, then maybe—*well, maybe what, Craig?* What would he have done? Split that man's head open in the bar? He wanted to. But would he have done that? He'd be in jail right now if he had.

So no.

But maybe?

And what if that man is here now?

What if Blaze Orange did manage to hightail it here on the back roads? What if he's here with that crazy psycho who jumped up beside him at the bar, the one with the swastika tattoo?

Okay, thinks Craig, it was *maybe* a swastika. You didn't really get a good look.

But still, if there's someone here, if it's a person, someone hostile—
Well, just start swinging, Craig thinks. You've got an axe. It's self-defense.

They're in his cabin, right? He could probably split that kid's head in half and not do a day of jail time.

He takes another step up the stairs, listening.

He hasn't been in many fights, most of them when he was a kid. Rolling-around-in-the-dirt kind of stuff, slapping and pushing and yelling. He's never in his life hit anyone with anything heavy and certainly never with anything sharp. He's never hit anyone with the intent of disabling them or—*say it, Craig*—the intent to kill.

He wishes he had a gun.

For the first time in his life, he'd like to have a gun in his hand.

But would he actually shoot someone?

Either way, he doesn't have a gun, he thinks.

He has an axe.

"Hello," he says again to no one.

He arrives on the second-floor landing.

Dark.

Then he spots them.

Eyes.

Maybe knee-height.

Shining in the dark.

His hand sweaty on the axe handle, Craig gets ready to swing it, and that's when the raccoon charges past him, scurrying, its little claws skittering on the plank floor as it slides in a panic past his feet, then tumbles headfirst down the stairs in a furry ball.

"Did you see it?" Craig stands mid-staircase, axe poised.

"It ran out the front door," says Daisy. She shuts the door and locks it. "How did that thing get in?"

"Have you ever looked at a raccoon? They have little hands," says Craig. "Like, actual little hands."

"They do not."

"They do!" Craig laughs, an exhalation of tension. "They can open doorknobs, you know."

"They do look like little burglars," says Daisy. "Did you see his little masked face?"

"I can't believe we got burgled by a raccoon." Craig descends to the foot of the stairs. "God, we *are* citiots."

"Mugged by wildlife," she says. "Are there any more up there? Do they travel in packs?" Her voice is jumpy but light, the ironic alarm of a crisis averted.

"All clear. The rooms are empty. And either way, I have my trusty axe." He gazes at the weapon in his hand like some mythical warrior.

"Holy shit," she says, laughing, leaning over, hands on her knees, still breathing hard. She laughs again, a laugh unhinged by the rush of relief. "Holy *shit*!"

"I know! I thought we were dead. I thought those guys had come to kill us."

"And what if they had?" she says.

"I don't know."

"You do have your trusty axe."

Craig looks at it, alien in his hand. "Um, yeah." He takes a few swipes at the air. "En garde, motherfuckers!"

"You were going to axe-murder that poor little raccoon." She beckons him forward. "It's kind of sexy. You were going to axe-murder his little burgling ass."

He grabs her around the waist, the axe still gripped in his hand. "Yes, I was, fair maiden. I was gonna go all Jason Voorhees on that little varmint." He hefts the axe, looks at it. "I guess I should put this back outside."

"Wait."

"What?"

She whispers, "Let's keep it with us. In the bedroom. Just in case."

"Okay, Al Bundy," he says. "Wow. I did not take you for a serial killer."

She tips up on her toes, puts her mouth close to his ear. "It's Ted Bundy." She pulls back and looks at him, playful. "Ted Bundy is the serial killer. Al Bundy was the dad on *Married . . . with Children*."

He sets the axe down gently on the dining table and pulls her close.

She mock-squirms, mock-squeals. "I'm so glad," he says, "that you went to three years at the best graduate drama school in America so you can constantly correct me on the names of sitcom characters."

She looks him square in the eye, their faces nearly touching. "I went to three years at the best graduate drama school in America so I could become the best fucking actor in New York City. Which I am."

"Which you are."

"It's just that nobody knows it."

"Nobody knows it *yet*."

She smiles. "And you're the best novelist."

"Which is an amazing accomplishment, given I've never written a novel."

"Never written a novel *yet*." She grabs his button-down shirt by the collar. They're both still pulsing, still fearful, still exhilarated, now relieved to be together, their mouths an inch apart and heart rates high.

"Come here," she says. She kisses him.

In an unfamiliar way. Or long forgotten.

It occurs to him mid-kiss that they haven't kissed like this since their first few months together, or maybe their first date, or maybe ever.

After that, she's out of her dress quickly.

The dress pools on the floor and she tugs his shirt off and starts to wrestle with the buckle on his belt.

He pulls back, pauses.

She reads his face in the cabin's dim light. He's surprised, delighted, gratified by this long-lost spontaneity, smiling at her, bewildered, handsome, beaming, happy, and, for the first time in a long time, fully flushed with love.

She returns the look, then gets back to solving that buckle.

They never even make it to the bed upstairs.

16

She lies in the dark of the bedroom and looks at the axe that's poised on a chair in the corner.

Red-painted blade, curved wooden handle. Like an art object.

Like something from a fairy tale about a woodsman and a maiden in distress.

After the breathless rush, the teenage fumbling, the mutual hunger, the slippery heat—after they were done and they realized, giggling, that they were both naked, their bodies slick and sprawled entangled on the bare cabin floor—they lay there like that for a long while, then gathered up their clothes in bundles, and she asked Craig to get the axe and bring it upstairs.

For protection. Just in case.

You never know, she said.

She nestles now against his chest. He's asleep, of course, his astonished look of satisfaction practically frozen on his face. He seems so happy, so contented. She fiddles with her own stack of pillows. The pillows at this cabin haven't felt right all week. Old lumpy cabin pillows, unearthed from a cedar closet. She grapples with them, their misshapen pliancy, and tries to settle in for the night.

She'd never told Craig about what happened to her in grad school, it's true. Why she dropped out and left early. The boyfriend who followed her there. It was eight years ago. Another lifetime. And she refuses to let it be the defining chapter in her life.

Plus, the grad school chapter is not the first chapter in that story.

And she hasn't told Craig the rest of the story, either.

All in good time, she thinks.

As a girl, she loved *The Wizard of Oz*. Watched it endlessly. Dressed up as Dorothy. Fantasized about tornadoes whirling her away to faraway lands. It was set in Kansas, she was in Wisconsin, but close enough, she thought.

The words of the Wicked Witch always haunted her, echoing. *All in good time, my little pretty.*

Which she always took to mean: Never relax, never exhale. Somewhere evil is always scheming, biding its time, waiting to strike, whether you're aware of it or not.

And now? she thinks. Is evil waiting to strike?

Almost certainly.

All in good time.

She thinks back to her very last night at graduate school, the night of the senior-class showcase, eight years ago. The night that was supposed to be the culmination of three years of training, of dreaming, of hope.

The night she imagined would launch her into the rest of her life.

The night she wound up running instead.

Senior showcase: an evening of monologues and scene studies, the best of the best, agents and scouts packing the house. *This is the night that will make you*—that's what the teachers all said, not publicly, not officially; in class it was all about The Craft, there was never any mention of the sordid subjects of fame or success—but in private, in passing, during closed-door office hours, the teachers would regale you with stories, the lore of showcases past; they'd drop the names of famous alumni, this Tony winner or that Oscar-nominated star, and say, *Showcase, that was the night when everyone knew.* The hush, the buzz afterward, it was palpable, the jostling scrum of agents and suitors lined up at the dressing room door. *A star is born, right there on our stage,* et cetera. The rest is just contracts and opportunity.

Normally in grad school the students performed in anonymity; their shows were simple workshops, open to locals occasionally but not advertised to the wider world. Showcase was different. You could read all about it online. The graduating class, a night of future stars. *Please congratulate the class of.* Here they come.

The teachers would run through monologue choices with you after class, informally advising and confidentially telling you to play to your strengths, show your range but take no risks, you can't afford to flub this one, you've done three years of training and now's the time to stick the landing, center stage, in the spotlight. The showcase made or broke careers, they said. It's not impossible to flub the showcase and still be successful, they assured you.

But if you nail the showcase.

If you shine.

Doors open.

That's what they all said.

And she shone.

A Doll's House, by Henrik Ibsen. Of course. The final scene. Her go-to monologue. A trusty showstopper since high school.

So much so that when she needed a new name to register for graduate school, a new identity, that's the name she chose.

Nora.

Seemed fitting.

And it would be Nora on showcase night, in the spotlight, center stage.

She disappeared and Ibsen's Nora took her place.

The audience was silent. Rapt. Nora's words resonating through the theater.

You have never loved me. You have only thought it pleasant to be in love with me.

And in that illuminated moment, nothing had ever happened in the whole wide world and nothing would ever happen again; there was only this character, a conjuring, a plain feat of sorcery, everyone in attendance could see it, could sense it, this transfiguration.

There was only her, Nora, unstoppable, sublime.

When she finished, there was a long, excruciating silence.

Then came the ecstatic applause.

Flushed, triumphant, she bowed demurely and retreated. She hurried through the wings toward the dressing rooms. She ran a gauntlet of classmates congratulating her as she passed.

In the dressing room, other students who were yet to perform were still getting ready, still warming up, running vocal exercises, making last-minute costume adjustments, getting their five-minute calls—*five minutes, please* came the voice at the dressing room door; *thank you, five,* came the reply—but for her it was over, she'd done it, nailed it, she shone, they might as well have halted the evening right there. She sat down in front of the mirror ringed with lights, suspended for a breath in that kind of happiness that seems to stretch backward and forward in time, magically touching every moment in your life, everything now makes sense, everything you've done and everything you will do is now irrevocably changed, transformed.

That rare moment of happiness in life that, like a lit torch, shows you a new path forward.

She lived in that moment, for a moment.

A giddy classmate approached her from behind and put a hand on her shoulder, warmly, offering a hum of congratulations.

Let her know about the flowers.

While you were onstage, a bouquet arrived for you.

Her classmate set down the vase with the bouquet.

At the sight of them, her heart seized.

Even as she reached out and picked up the little envelope on the flowers—

Even as she slid out the card inside—

Even as she opened the card and read the words—

She knew.

There was only one person in the world, she thought, who would think to send her flowers on a night like this.

But that person didn't know where she was.

So, of course, the card was from him.

Nora, congratulations. Welcome back to the spotlight—

And it was signed—

Your Forever Fan.

Within an hour she'd packed up the few things in her apartment and disappeared, skipping the showcase-night party, never showing up for another class or finishing her final courses, never taking meetings with agents or calls from managers, never even telling her teachers or classmates why she'd left and where she'd gone.

Her email address obliterated. Her phone number disconnected.

Messages left by anxious agents at the registrar's office continued for weeks, persistently seeking that woman who played Nora, please have her call, but these messages went unreturned and they eventually petered out, as the school year ended and the summer passed and the next class, the new stars, began their preparations to take the stage and step into the spotlight.

In later years, classmates would comment among themselves, on social media or while reminiscing in person, about how infrequently that classmate had let herself be photographed and how, come to think of it, like some kind of digital Puritan, she avoided setting up profiles online, never had a social media account, even as they were all so busy raising their visibility, building their brands, and getting their faces out into the world. She was very strict about it, actually. They all assumed it was an upbringing thing. Just thought she was super private, or maybe religious.

Rumors swirled. Some heard she'd up and moved to New York. Or LA. Maybe London.

In any case, they'd recall, she was an odd one. Charming, witty, even warm, but withdrawn.

Hard to really get to know.

But what a talent.

She never made it, though.

Such a shame, because honestly she was the best of them all.

That showcase night—it had seemed like a coming-out party, thrown just for her. They could all feel it. Instead, she just kind of vanished.

Whatever happened to her?

On the night of the showcase she sat in the dressing room with the swirl of activity behind her and stared at the card that she held in her fingers.

Your Forever Fan.

It had been three years since she fled Boston.

Since he started leaving messages for her at the restaurant where she worked.

She wasn't called Nora then. Not yet.

She had a different fake name back then.

She'd arrived for a shift and a coworker told her: "Someone called for you. But it was weird. He kept insisting your name was—" And she said a different name.

A name she hadn't heard, or used, in a year.

Her real name.

"He said you'd understand," the coworker said.

She asked the coworker to cover for her while she ran a quick errand and, within an hour, bag packed, she was on a train.

When she arrived at grad school in the college town in the fall with a new name, she hoped to be safe, shrouded in the cloistered community of school. No one knew her there, no one knew about her past, and everyone at grad school was busy dreaming of stardom, of future fame. Everyone but her. She just dreamt of escaping herself for a few hours onstage every night.

She dreamt of transfiguration.

New name. New personality.

She had plenty of practice.

And it all went well, for a while.

It's not that she hadn't been thinking of him.

She thought of him every day.

She thought of him when she arrived home at night to the dark apartment, slightly afraid to turn on the lights. She thought of him while in line at the coffee shop, spotting a head, a face turned away, thinking, startled, Wait, no, it can't be. Then the head turns and it isn't, but the fear remained. She thought of him every time someone at school called her by the name that wasn't really her name, because then she thought of her real name, the name she'd left behind, and why.

But for some reason, on showcase night, she gave herself a night off from thinking about him. She let herself think instead about the future that might be coming and not the past that trailed behind her like a lengthening shadow.

And, of course, she thought in the dressing room, staring at the card, her struck lamp of hope now extinguished, the showcase night wasn't widely publicized, but it was publicized enough. It was online. It was a big deal. Of course it was.

You couldn't Google her, but if you happened to be, say, combing the rolls of graduate theater programs across the country every single spring, knowing it's the time of year when acting programs do their graduate performances, wondering if maybe that's where she'd disappeared to, a college town somewhere, a stage, you can't keep her off a stage, she needs that nightly escape like a fix, then you might happen to be scrolling through headshots on a website. Looking for graduates. Year after year. Until you find her.

He'd found her.

After that, it must have been easy.

Call a florist. Arrange a delivery.

Dictate the note over the phone.

Why would the school turn away a congratulatory bouquet?

In the dressing room, she knew he'd show up shortly.

That this time the face would turn and it would actually be him.

She gripped the card in her fingers. Paralyzed.

It was in his nature to warn her. She knew that. He wanted to let her know he was watching. That seemed to be important to him.

That she know.

But he would follow. He always did.

Which meant she had the tiniest sliver of a window to escape.

She shed her costume, slipped away from the showcase, dodging the last few congratulatory greetings from raucous classmates, ran out to the parking lot where she fully expected to see him, got on her bicycle, the one she rode to campus to avoid public transit and the claustrophobic captivity of cabs, and headed back to her apartment, the one where she paid her share of the rent in cash every month to her roommate so that her name never appeared on the lease.

Found her prepacked bag in the closet.

Just clothes enough to get by for a week or so.

Grabbed the fake IDs she'd collected. Some more convincing than others.

It took her about twenty minutes to wrap up her life, or at least the parts of it she felt were worth keeping.

It took another thirty minutes to get to the train station. Her classmate Christian picked her up, no questions asked. He drove her to the station and booked the train ticket for her in his name and paid with his credit card so there'd be no trail of her.

It was an hour's wait on the platform before the next train departed. Christian waited with her there, too. He insisted. He was a good guy. He didn't even know why she was leaving. Just that it was an emergency.

She'd picked the train that was leaving soonest.

But she'd always known where she would go next.

The one place where she could be swallowed up.

Christian stayed by her side until the train came. A true friend. Granted, a true friend who didn't even know her real name or where she'd come from or why she was running.

Still, they'd grown close in three years of grad school. Sort of—and despite her best efforts. As much as she'd tried to keep him at bay, he doggedly insisted on sticking by her. Christian was very attractive, her classmates all thought so, with his close-cropped hair and disarming smile—there were certainly plenty of women in their program who pursued him, some flagrantly. But she and he were never involved. She needed him in a different way. He was her stalwart, a trusted ally, even if she never told him what they were allied against. He was the person she could call for a ride to the train station, no questions asked. The person who would wait with her for the train and make sure she got on safely. Christian—handsome Christian, faithful Christian, reliable Christian, persistent Christian—had always been there to help her. She just tried not to dwell too much on *why*. She knew he was interested—that was obvious, he made no secret of it—but she wasn't in a place for that and, frankly, he wasn't the person for her. Too dogged. Too concerned. Too intrigued by the notion of *cracking her open, unearthing her secrets,* truly *getting to know her*.

And she didn't want to be known.

She did, however, need a ride to the train station.

Sure, okay, she sometimes thought that maybe, under different circumstances, in a different life—

But this wasn't a different life.

When the train pulled in, she thanked him. Gave him a kiss on his cheek. He held her shoulders for a moment in his hands and made her promise to keep in touch. To let him know when she'd arrived safely. She assured him she would.

She boarded the train, one last wave as he waited, and then he didn't hear from her again.

Not for years, anyway.

Not until recently.

But by that time she was already married.

On the train ride, she found an empty two-seater, took the window seat, and put her bag on the seat next to her. She wore a ballcap tugged low, not because it would do anything but because it made her feel slightly better.

Sheltered.

She sat huddled in the train seat and gave herself a moment, one moment, a gift to herself, to linger on the sound of that applause.

Sometimes there's a pause right after you finish a performance and right before the applause begins. A long, swelling moment of saturated silence.

The better the performance, the longer that silence.

The moment before the moment.

That night, on the showcase stage, that moment seemed to stretch forever. She almost felt like she could live inside it.

Then she tugged her cap down lower, pulled her one bag close, and decided on her new name.

The indistinct landscape rushed past outside the train window.

She'd already thought of it.

Simple. Unassuming.

Her New York name.

Daisy.

She dozed on the train, then woke, and there it was: beautiful, over-crowded, anonymous New York, rising majestic, uncaring, on the horizon.

Just another aspiring actor arriving in New York.

You couldn't be more unknown if you tried.

In New York, you can act for years, for an entire career, without ever becoming famous or even that well known. Stick to downtown black boxes with half-empty houses. No movies. No TV, of course. You can still make a living. Maybe.

But most of all, you can spend as much time as possible, every night if you choose to, suspended in that moment before the moment, shel-tered between performance and applause, pretending to be someone else.

They talk about actors who aren't yet famous as "undiscovered."

Perfect, she thought, as she watched the skyline approaching.

Let her be that.

Undiscovered.

At Penn Station she disembarked the train in a comforting crowd of strangers. She found a spot in a hostel she'd checked out in advance online. It took her less than a week in the city to find a place to live, renting a room in a two-bedroom apartment with two other women, also artists, deep in Brooklyn, several subway stops past the last safe place to live, on a block where gunshots weren't uncommon in the early-morning hours. Her name wasn't on the lease, and she paid each month's rent up front in cash. She got a job as a bartender, lived mostly on tips, and started volunteering at downtown theaters, working box office or manning concessions at intermission or pitching in to strike sets. Downtown theaters are always grateful for free labor. She met people. Made a few connections. Introducing herself to everyone as Daisy. Within a month or so, she'd landed a couple of roles. Because she was good. Those roles led to more roles.

On her off days, she'd occasionally visit her local library to check the social media pages of her fellow grad school students, making sure to always use public terminals, just to see if there was any word of her, just to make sure she hadn't left a trail. To see if anyone was speculating about her vanishing. Only one person knew where she went, only one, Christian, that friend who'd escorted her to the station, but she thought she could trust him and, besides, she'd lied to him and said that New York was just a hub and she'd hop on another train from there. Maybe Philadelphia, maybe Chicago, maybe, ultimately, LA.

As for everyone else in their class, those students were quickly caught up once again in their own dramas, their own lives. Actors love to romanticize eccentrics, they love grand mythic *stories,* she knew that, so a person dropping out unexpectedly wasn't the subject of gossip for long. She herself had never been on social media, and if anyone asked her about it, she shrugged it off as a personal quirk. So as best she could tell, whatever thin vapor trail that might have remained of her in her former life had quickly dissipated into the air.

She'd almost given up her library visits when she stumbled on the story.

It was maybe two weeks old at that point. She only found it because it was linked to by a few of her frightened ex-classmates with appended warnings: *Scary!* or *Let's be careful out there.* Her onetime roommate, back in the college town, an older woman she'd lived with for almost three years but who she knew very little about and who definitely knew very little about her, had been put in the hospital. She'd been beaten. The victim of an apparently random home invasion, on the same night that Daisy left town.

Never caught the guy.

She sat in the library reading the short clip from the local news website and felt her chest hollowing out. She thought for a moment about trying to reach out, to send a note of solace to her ex-roommate, but knew she absolutely could not do that. She felt herself crying, first softly, then racking sobs, sitting there alone in the library's silence. When a stranger came up behind her and laid a hand on her shoulder, a female librarian asking if she was okay, she startled at the touch, recoiled, and nearly fell from her chair at this small exhibition of kindness. Later, she thought about that reaction, her instinctive flinching, the way her body clutched at a stranger's approach, and she cried about that, too.

After that, she stopped going to the library.

According to the last news report she read, the mystery intruder didn't take anything from the apartment. Which didn't surprise Daisy.

Everything he was looking for was already gone.

The night scratches at the cabin window. She settles against her stubborn pillows again.

Day three.

Here we are.

Her and him.

Daisy and Craig.

Her sleeping husband's chest rising and falling, unwitting, in the bed beside her.

This man who's only ever known her as Daisy.

Who doesn't know anything about what happened in her life before.

Let alone what's about to happen.

No wonder he can sleep so well.

She's restless. She shifts again. He lies stone-still and sprawling. She read once that people who always sleep on their sides, like she does, are curling up, protecting themselves from the world, while people who sleep on their backs, like he does, splayed out, are fearless and carefree.

Makes sense.

She shifts again.

Still not right.

Chasing sleep, she thinks once more of that night in grad school, that train ride, then puts the night expertly out of her mind, as she learned to do, or mostly do, in the subsequent years.

She finally finds a posture she likes and feels herself slipping into a slumber.

She slides her hand deeper under the bundle of pillows and feels something lumpy and slick and warm.

She pulls her hand out as quick as she can and looks at her hand, which is covered in blood, and she sits up straight in the bed and she screams.

17

He's up with a start.

What's happening?

She's got slick dark blood on her hand.

He's disoriented, confused. Is she cut? Hurt?

She grabs her pillow with the bloodied hand and tosses it aside, leaving a handprint on the white linen. She yanks away the second pillow. Revealing a handful of mangled dead something on the bed.

A sodden, slick, leathery coil of black that lies on the white sheet in a stain of soaked red.

She's still screaming.

He looks closer.

It takes a minute to register. To find and recognize the body and make sense of the missing head.

"It's a snake," he says finally. "A dead snake," as if this information is supposed to reassure her.

A coiled black snake, maybe two feet long, the head cut clean off or bitten off neatly. She's sobbing in a way that borders on hyperventilation. He gets up and heads downstairs and hits the lights and fumbles bleary-eyed through the pantry cupboard in the kitchen until he finds an old metal dustpan and a hand broom. When he gets back to the bedroom she's in the exact same position as when he left, her back heaving rhythmically, staring at the mangled carcass.

He tips the snake carefully onto the dustpan with the hand broom and carries the whole thing out of the room. He walks straight down the stairs and to the front door, then opens it and walks out and across the porch, and using the dustpan as a catapult, he flings the dead snake into the woods, its body uncoiling as it flies, hurtling into the dark. Craig knows it's dead, but he can't help but startle at the sight of the snake jerking in the air, as though rousing, headless, to mount one final attack. It lands unseen in the brush with a rustle. He looks down at the gore-smeared dustpan in his hand. He leaves it propped against the porch to deal with later and sets the hand broom beside it. Only once he's back safe inside the cabin with the dead bolt locked again does he wonder if maybe the bloodied snake in the woods will attract larger creatures, like bait.

They strip the sheets. The fitted white sheet is clean except for one irregular crimson stain. She balls the sheets and the pillowcases up and carries the whole load downstairs and leaves them in the corner of the bathroom and immediately and almost without thinking she starts drawing a hot bath.

When she gets back up to the room, he's already got a fresh pair of sheets on the bed.

"It must have been the raccoon," he says.

"The raccoon left a dead snake under my pillow?"

"We had a cat when I was a kid in Michigan who liked to leave dead birds on our doorstep, like a present. It left one on my pillow once."

"Some present." She says it like a joke, but her face is puffy and tear-swollen and drained of anything save exhaustion and fear.

"I'm sorry that happened," he says.

"That was terrible."

"We'll make sure it doesn't happen again." He means it. She's not sure how he intends to deliver on the promise, but she hears that he means it.

She smiles. "Thank you," she says, and stands. She looks down at her palm, at the hand that was bloodied, which still seems stained to her. "Now if you'll excuse me, I'm going to go take a very long, very hot bath."

IIII

She disappears to the bathroom and he finishes making the bed. The story he told her was true, about the cat. It really happened. He was six. The cat left a dead bird on his bed. Not on the pillow, that was an embellishment, a small lie to calm Daisy down, the cat had left the bird smack in the middle of the blanket. He cried about it for hours. The blanket was feather-flecked and bloodied. The next day his mother set the cat on the doorstep and declared that the cat would live outside full-time from now on. A few days later he noticed he hadn't seen the cat around. He asked his mother and she said the cat had won a prize and was taken to live on a huge farm with other prizewinning cats.

When he got older, he figured either his mother had given the cat away or, more likely, it got hit by a car or killed by some fiercer animal. He'd always meant to ask his mother for the truth about the cat, but he didn't, and then she died.

His mother had lied to him, though, of that he was certain, a small lie, and now he'd lied to Daisy, just a little bit, and he was sure that both he and his mother, in their lies, had done the right thing, given the circumstances.

As to whether any animal, even a conniving raccoon with creepy little person hands, could wrestle a snake and bite its head off, then slip its carcass under a pillow, he's really not certain. It's a plausible enough explanation for now and, frankly, the best, most reassuring one he can come up with.

He tries not to entertain the thought that maybe this special gift was left for them by someone else as some sort of warning. He tries not to imagine that somehow this is a carryover from the incident at the bar. That somehow someone got in before they got home and left this as a promise to them of some retribution to come.

As he smooths the white sheets to a satisfying crispness, he tries not to wonder who would go out of their way to do such a thing, and what else that person might be capable of.

18

He's asleep again upstairs and she's in the bath, alone.

It's the middle of the night. Steam whispers over the water. The vapor rising from the rippled surface reminds her of cauldrons, of potions, of spells. She thinks of *Macbeth*. Of toil and trouble.

She's spooked, her heart still hammering. For the first time this week, she wants to run back to the city. She misses the clamorous noises, the soothing anonymity, the swallowing crowds. She never feels safer than when she's hidden among eight million strangers. Out here, they're alone, exposed, just her and him. She has only him to rely on, her famously unreliable husband. Maybe that's part of the test, too. Either way, she feels endangered, panicked. Maybe it was a mistake to come out here, she thinks. This whole thing. This whole week. This whole test.

But it's too late now. It's happening.

She breathes. Watches the steam on the water. Tries to calm herself.

We're halfway there, she thinks.

Four more days. Four more questions.

And then we finish it. All of it. We finally see what we're capable of.

She settles further into the near-scalding bath.

She takes another deep breath, holds it, then dunks her head under, releasing herself to the warm amniotic rush in her ears, the feeling of her hair floating free, the sudden weightlessness of water, the enfolding comfort of being totally submerged.

There's a baby inside me, she thinks. The baby is also in water. Bodies within bodies. Like Russian dolls. And a crazy thing about babies is how they live in the womb for nine months, submerged in amniotic fluid, aquatic, and then, once they're born, they come bursting out into the open air, wailing, gasping, and somehow, miraculously, they know how to breathe.

She lingers under the water a moment longer and lets the day's tension dissipate. The warm throb welcomes her, welcomes her body, welcomes her baby's body, the two of them together, alone, nested, and for an instant she feels like the world can never touch her, never touch them, which means, just for this moment, that she's free.

She surfaces.

Feels better now.

She looks at her left hand, the one she stuck under the pillow, the one that made the grisly discovery, and rubs her left palm with the fingers of her right hand, scrubbing the spot where her hand got smeared with blood. Checking for some permanent stain.

Nothing.

Clean.

Okay. No city. Not yet. You're right where you need to be, she thinks. You're doing what you need to do.

Exactly as planned.

As if on cue, the flip phone that's sitting on the small wooden table by the side of the tub, the phone she brought up here with her and kept hidden all week, starts to buzz, its little window sparking to life.

She checks the clock on the phone. Right on time. A good sign.

It's a cheap disposable phone that she plucked from a spinner rack in a discount store weeks ago. The kind that comes in a blister pack. Bought with cash. Untraceable.

Craig doesn't know about this phone, of course.

There's so much that Craig doesn't know about.

She flips open the phone and reads the text that just arrived.

where are you

She taps a reply.

in the woods

She pauses. Then taps.

in the bathtub actually

The phone buzzes in her hand.

lol don't drop the phone

She taps.

i'll be careful. where are you?

Phone buzzes.

on my way

She taps.

you tell anyone?

Phone buzzes.

of course not. who would i tell. besides you

She smiles. Taps.

our little secret then

Phone buzzes.

of course. can't wait

She taps.

me too

Then she flips the phone closed, sets it aside, and sinks back into the water.

Our phones and our secrets, she thinks.

Would you change for me?

   Would you sacrifice for me?

   Would you fight for me?

   Would you . . . ?

Four more days. Four more questions.

She lowers her jaw to the surface of the water and feels the last of the steam lick her face. Then she dunks herself under the water again and disappears, the surface swallowing her, the rush of the water, like the loudest ovation, roaring in her ears.

Underwater, she thinks of witches.

She thinks of witches being dunked back in Salem.

She played a role onstage in *The Crucible* once.

She thinks of the stories of witches and how in the Salem witch trials they'd tied women accused of evil to wooden chairs and dunked them underwater. She thinks of the practice of "swimming" the witches, of binding women's hands and throwing them into a river. If the women floated, they were proved to be witches and condemned to burn at the stake. If they sank to the bottom, they weren't witches, they weren't evil after all, they were innocent, absolved.

But they were often drowned.

She closes her eyes and holds her breath under the water and she waits.

Waits.

Waits.

Waits.

To see if she is evil. Or to see if she will drown.

The Fourth Day

||||

SEASONS

19

Lying in bed, Craig takes a drowsy moment to realize what he's hearing: a clatter, a commotion, coming from downstairs, someone knocking at the front door insistently. He sweeps a hand beside him—the bed's empty, Daisy's already up—so he swings out of bed, grabs a bathrobe, then hurries down the stairs. He spots Daisy tucked into the doorway to the kitchen, cradling a coffee, watching the front door, and when she sees him, she gestures toward the source of the noise, pantomimes a shrug, and mouths the words *I don't know.*

Craig treads over in bare feet to the door.

Who drops by unannounced? he thinks, running a hand through his sleep-mussed hair. Who pounds on your door at first light? No one would do this in the city. You text, you DM, maybe you call, but you don't just—

He opens the door a crack to find two figures looming.

"Good morning!" the first one booms. It's Dr. Kit Arden, he of the voluminous beard, clad—despite the morning's evident heat—in a turtleneck and corduroy trousers. Behind him, an old man loiters, wearing gray coveralls and a bent ballcap, with a white dust mask hanging around his neck, bulging like an untreated goiter.

Craig squints.

He recognizes this old man.

It's the same guy he bumped into at the bar last night, the one wearing a musty flannel shirt, the one who warned him cryptically to be careful, to "watch yourself."

"Sorry to rouse you," Kit declares brightly, his huge smile peeking through his thick beard like an intrepid explorer emerging from the bush.

"Normally, I promise, you wouldn't see my face all week. However"—and here he steps aside dramatically and swings an arm back toward the old man, like a magician introducing his talented assistant—"I'm afraid today there's going to be a slight disruption."

The old man gives Craig a little crooked-fingered wave.

"I assume you're here about last night," Craig says.

Kit regards him quizzically. "Why? What happened last night?"

What did happen last night? Craig plays the images back in his mind: the man in the bar, the standoff, the churn of the hostile crowd, Shep stepping in, punches thrown, their retreat, the silent drive home, Daisy's story in the driveway, the door ajar, the scampering raccoon, their frantic naked grapple on the floor, the pillows, the bed, the blood, the severed snake. These last parts—everything that happened at the cabin—seem like fragments of a disjointed dream.

"We had a little run-in at the bar in town," says Daisy, stepping up in the doorway to stand dutifully at Craig's side. "Some trouble with the locals."

The old man shakes his head and intones, as though contemplating the weather, "I told you to watch yourselves."

"I'm so sorry to hear that," says Kit, his face clouded now in a grand show of concern. "I've always found the people up here to be nothing but welcoming, though I understand things have changed somewhat since the halcyon hippie days." He grips Craig's shoulders. "Honestly, I recommend that couples stay close to the cabin, on our land. That way, you can stay focused on each other and the purpose of the week and avoid any undue distractions."

"That makes sense," says Craig, his hands thrust in his bathrobe pockets, feeling like a teenager being chastised by his dad. He decides not to mention the part about the break-in—if that's even what it was. He doesn't want to sound even more like a city slicker, spooked by the wildlife.

"So what brings you by this morning?" asks Daisy, all business.

Kit claps once. "Yes! The task at hand. I wanted to introduce you to my trusted arborist and local miracle worker, Mr. Alwyn. He's going to be fumigating the orchard this morning to deal with a bothersome blight."

"You mean the orchard we're not supposed to go to?" says Craig.

"Yes, exactly," says Kit. "Normally, we'd simply sneak in the back way and visit the orchard via the access road, but the fungicide we'll be using is sulfur-based—it's got a bit of a fire-and-brimstone stink to it. I didn't want you to come out here for your morning coffee and get concerned if that hellish odor started wafting your way."

"It won't take but an hour," says Alwyn.

Craig sighs, already resigned to this intrusion. "It's your property."

Daisy shoots him a pointed glance, then turns to Alwyn. "I was hoping to paint out on the porch this morning. Can I do that?"

"If you can stand the stench, then sure," says Alwyn.

"Also," she says, and she gives Craig another nudge here, hoping to recruit his support, "I'm very—sensitive to chemicals right now."

"That's right," says Craig, clueing in. "She can't be near anything toxic. This fumigation can't wait until after we're gone?"

Kit glances back at Alwyn, who says matter-of-factly, "We've already lost this entire season's crop. Another week and we'll lose the trees for good."

Kit turns to them and shakes his head with what he telegraphs as a kind of fathomless empathy. "I'm so sorry, but it has to be today. However, the fungicide, while fragrant, is absolutely harmless—unless you're a fungus, of course!" He brightens and chortles, the shift from his previous show of concern so abrupt as to be disarming.

Alwyn nods toward Daisy. "Why don't you lend me your husband a spell so he can inspect the materials? Warning labels and whatnot. And maybe I can give him some pointers from a longtime resident on dealing with the local rowdies."

Craig looks at her. She shrugs.

"Excellent!" says Kit, clapping his hands again with what can only be described as cruise-director energy. He takes Daisy's hands in his.

"Thank you so much for your indulgence. And I promise—you won't see me again until week's end, when I'll bring Bridget by and we can all check in about your progress."

Craig pulls his robe tighter, this day already off to an unexpected and unwelcome start. "Let me just throw on some shoes."

"Flip-flops'll be fine," says Alwyn, beckoning Craig to follow. "I promise, I'll keep the critters at bay."

At the edge of the orchard, Alwyn stoops to unlock a padlock on the low gate, then swings the gate open. It's weird, Craig thinks as he trails behind, to make such a big show of a padlocked gate, especially when it's easy enough—as he and Daisy already discovered—to simply hop the waist-high wooden fence.

Humming softly, Alwyn ambles ahead and proceeds to prowl the rows of tangled trees. He pauses every so often to inspect a mottled branch or cradle a rotting fruit in his palm. "What I suspected," he says, pulling one deformed specimen clean from its stem. "Fire blight." He holds the fruit out for Craig, like he's seeking Craig's confirmation. Sure enough, the apple looks spotted, soft, diseased.

Alwyn tosses the fruit and continues his rounds.

"So how long have you worked with the Ardens?" Craig asks.

"Going on twenty years. Though I've known them even longer than that, since they first came up here as visitors."

"And you take care of all this?"

"In my experience, you get these gentleman farmers up from the city, and they typically turn out to be neither—they're not gentlemen and they sure aren't farmers." Alwyn turns back to Craig and flashes a smile. "Sometimes they need a little hand-holding."

Alwyn continues through the trees as Craig trails. "And what can you tell me about those guys at the bar last night?" Craig asks tentatively.

"People want to tell you that things have changed up here," says Alwyn. "As though once it was a pristine Paradise and now it's all gone to hell. But there's always been troublemakers, like anywhere. Bad seeds—and bad seeds grow up to be bad trees, then release their own bad seeds into the world."

"When you warned me in the bar," says Craig, "it's like you knew something would happen."

Alwyn stops and pulls heavy gardening gloves from his coverall pockets. "Just a hunch. I didn't even recognize those boys you tussled with and I don't suspect they're from around here. But when you see a pile of dry kindling on the ground and a gas can sitting nearby, you expect you might soon see a fire." He tugs the gloves on. "Shall we get to work?"

Craig looks around, confused. "Where's the sprayer?"

"You think I'm going to lug that apparatus all over Creation? I store all that on-site." Alwyn turns and heads toward the edge of the orchard. By the far fence line, buried in the underbrush and obscured by a tangle of weeds, sits a rusted metal footlocker, also padlocked.

"You keep it under lock and key, all the way out here?" says Craig. "You worried about fungicide pirates?"

Alwyn chuckles—a hard-won laugh that leaves Craig feeling a little proud of himself—and kneels and takes the padlock in a gloved hand. "It's purely ornamental. I lost the key years ago." He jams the padlock with the heel of his hand and it pops clean open. He pulls the lock free and opens the lid, which lets loose an oil-starved squeal.

From inside the locker, Alwyn hefts a large tank with a hose attached. On the hose, a nozzle. He pumps a handle on the top of the sprayer a few times, priming it. Then he reaches into the locker and retrieves a large plastic jug of sloshing liquid. He holds it out, label forward, for Craig to inspect. "Don't mind the skull and crossbones. That just means don't drink it. Fumes-wise, it won't harm a pregnant lady."

Craig looks at him, surprised. "How do you know my wife's pregnant?"

"A skittish woman has no secrets." Alwyn unscrews the cap on the jug and tips the liquid into the open sprayer. As he does, Craig glances at the contents of the footlocker: gardening spades, pruning shears, extra gloves, extra dust masks, and something else, something unmistakable, wrapped in oilcloth.

Craig knows exactly what it is even as it takes a moment for it to fully register.

A .45-caliber handgun.

Craig asks—he can't help himself: "You keep a gun out here?"

Alwyn glances over, unperturbed. "What, that? That's my snake-shooter. Old souvenir from my time spent in service to Uncle Sam, running up and down dunes in the desert. I told you I'd keep the critters at bay." He raises a gloved finger to his lips. "Don't tell the good doctor. They're hippie pacifists from way back, so I think they'd frown on this."

"Is this orchard really so dangerous that you need a gun for protection?"

Alwyn chuckles again, this time not as indulgently, and it leaves Craig feeling abashed. "This is what the city folk never understand," says Alwyn. "A gun is just a tool. Like a hammer. Like a spade. It has its uses, like any tool. Sometimes I need shears to prune a branch, so I get my hands on some shears. Sometimes I need a pistol to scare something off or stop something wild that needs stopping, so I get my hands on a gun. No more thorny than that."

"Is it loaded?" asks Craig.

"Do I look to you like a country dumbass?" says Alwyn, standing and brushing his hands on his coveralls. He bends and lifts the gun from the locker and pulls away the oilcloth. "This is the gun"—and then he reaches back into the locker and retrieves a rattling coffee can—"and these are the shells. Some assembly required."

He replaces the coffee can and wraps the gun back in the cloth, returns it to the locker, then plucks an extra dust mask from his stash. He closes the locker and replaces the padlock, then holds the dust mask out to Craig. "For the stink, mostly."

Craig pulls the mask on, then follows as Alwyn pulls up his own mask and lugs the sprayer back toward the first row of trees. He primes the pump a few more times—then stops.

Alwyn reaches up to a branch. Then he says, his voice muffled by the mask, "Well, would you look at that? Like the blight skipped right over it."

He plucks a piece of perfect fruit and holds it out to Craig.

"A gift, for your expecting wife," he says.

Craig takes the apple and pockets it.

His mind still fixed on that gun.

Then Alwyn works meticulously through the rows, wielding the sprayer like a symphony maestro, until the sulfur spray is so thick in the air that it wafts back over them both in pungent, otherworldly clouds.

20

Craig expects that Alwyn will return with him to the cabin, but after an hour or so, Alwyn simply packs his tools away in the footlocker and moves to exit the woods via the access road, a small, obscured dirt trail that leads them both back to the main road. Alwyn's battered truck sits parked askew at the head of the trail. He tosses his gloves in the open driver's-side window, then points Craig back in the direction of the cabin—"It's easy to lose your way up here, but just head back past the dented black mailbox on the broken post," he says—before climbing into his truck and trundling off, tires coughing up dust.

Craig walks the road back in his bathrobe and flip-flops, the dust mask slung around his neck. He thinks of the orchard and his inadvertent discovery in the footlocker, of the knowledge he now has and cannot shake. He thinks of the gun, the fact of it, and how it changes the calculus of everything. He thinks of the man in the blaze orange cap—that smear of bright orange when he first spied him in the woods, then, later, at the bar, looming over him, sneering, his wiry friend coiled at his side. Craig's so lost in these thoughts that when he finally arrives at the mouth of their driveway, he almost passes it, unnoticed.

Approaching the cabin, he spies Daisy sitting splay-legged in her overalls, painting on the porch, her decorative rocks displayed before her in a colorful coterie.

She looks up, surprised. "Where'd you come from?"

"We took a different way back."

"Come here," she says. "I want to ask you something."

He mounts the porch. "What is it?"

She looks up at him. In her hand, she holds a stone festooned with the letters *D + C 4Evah.* "Sit down."

He sits next to her, cross-legged.

"I've been thinking," she says. "Maybe we should leave, like you said."

"No," he says. "We're staying."

"But what about last night at the bar? And what we found when we got home? I mean—it all feels a bit crazy, no?" She puts the stone down carefully, turns her full attention to him. "Maybe you were right. We're *not* prisoners. Plus, I think we're really doing well. This has been useful already. Maybe we don't need the rest of the test."

"No," he says calmly, conclusively. "We're not running. Not now. Especially not now." He thinks again of the gun. He won't touch it, he won't retrieve it, he'll leave it exactly where it is, of course he will. She never even needs to know about it at all. *Unless . . .* If they need it, if it comes to that, he knows exactly where to find it.

He takes her hands in his, the matter settled in his mind. "You're the one who was right. This week is important for us. We're staying."

"Are you sure?"

"Absolutely." He pulls her close. "We'll be fine. I promise. I'll protect you."

"My hero."

"Just your husband," he says and stands. "You paint. I'm going to change and go for a run. Clear my head." He reaches into his bathrobe pocket. The apple—he almost forgot. "Here—" He holds it out for her. "A present from the orchard."

She takes it. Inspects it. "It's . . . okay to eat?"

"Yes. It's fine. Trust me."

She smiles. Takes a bite. "It's good." She stops. "Wait—aren't I the one who's supposed to be offering *you* the apple in the Eden Test?"

"What?" he says, distracted, his mind now on the run, the day, the task before him, now that he knows exactly what he needs to do next.

"Never mind," she says, and takes another bite.

He appears again a few minutes later in a ratty old T-shirt, the swimming trunks that she packed for him, and a pair of Converse she threw in the bag.

"Sorry I didn't pack your jogging clothes," she says sheepishly, still seated on the porch. "It was hard packing all that stuff for you in secret."

"No worries." He jogs lightly on the spot, knowing that he's got a full set of exercise clothes and a pair of $250 jogging shoes in one of the suitcases he packed for Cabo that's still hidden in the trunk of the car. "You'll be all right here by yourself?"

"Don't worry about me." She looks up. "I'm going to wash those sheets today. I think I can get that stain out. You take your time. I'll be fine." She holds up the rock that she's been working on. *D + C* again, this time with a rainbow. "What do you think?"

"A masterpiece."

When she turns back to the rock, he feels for his smartphone in the loose pocket of the swimsuit to make sure it's still there. Then he gives a last wave and heads off up the driveway. When he reaches the road, he takes a right and starts running at a good clip.

As the cabin recedes behind him, he recalls the three questions so far.

Would you change for me?

Would you sacrifice for me?

Would you fight for me?

He wonders about the next questions. Wonders what they might be.

Would you . . . ?

To be honest, he can't wait to find out. As he runs, he thinks that maybe this crazy program is starting to work.

21

Craig's feet drum the dirt as he wends his way along the winding road. It's a warm day, sunny. He starts to sweat. Brow damp. Heart chugging.

Feels good.

He hits a T in the road, turns right on instinct, keeps jogging, the dirt lane turning to gravel underfoot. The road takes him up over a hill where he approaches a fork and veers right again, thinking, If I just always turn right, I can find my way back. Right? Wait, is that true? Because suddenly he realizes that finding his way back may be a slight concern, given he's been jogging for a good twenty minutes and he doesn't really know these roads at all.

Another bend. Another fork.

He turns right again.

This is far enough, he thinks. He pulls up, sweating, panting lightly. He's put plenty of space between himself and the cabin to do what he needs to do next.

He pulls the phone that's been jostling in his shorts out of his pocket and wipes the screen on his shirt. This feels fortifying, he thinks. This feels like a fresh start. This feels like a chance to do the right thing.

To be worthy.

He lifts the phone to check for a signal.

Three bars. Bingo.

Here we go.

He dials Lilith's number.

Holds the phone to his sweaty ear and waits.

Feels nervous. Like someone's watching. Like he's doing something wrong.

Well, technically, he's calling his mistress in secret. So he *is* doing something wrong.

Except he's doing it in order to do something right.

That has to count for something.

He listens as it rings.

They met at a playground, of all places.

His work friend Kyle—the haggard father of two relentless toddlers who climb all over Kyle like attacking predators, like lion cubs felling an elk—had been over to their apartment in Brooklyn one weekend afternoon with his two kids, and he left behind a toy scooter. Which child exactly the scooter belonged to, Craig couldn't possibly say. He just stood agape in the calm of his apartment, staring resentfully at the remnants of the double-kid-orchestrated mayhem: a carnage of torn paper and overturned containers and spilled juice and strewn kitchen utensils and crayon masterpieces scribbled on every accessible inch of white paint on the walls. ("Don't worry. It's washable," Kyle said, exasperated, exhausted.) The stray scooter, once Craig spotted it, was just another piece of kid-detritus left behind by the good ship *Parenthood*, a party cruise that had temporarily docked and disembarked its rowdy passengers at the port of Craig and Daisy's normally quiet and orderly adult Brooklyn life.

As such, Craig wanted to get that scooter out of the apartment as quickly as possible. So Craig texted Kyle, and Kyle told him to meet him at a faraway playground the next day.

Which is how Craig found himself, alone, in a distant neighborhood at an unfamiliar playground, a place he'd never normally be, watching a bunch of parents play with their kids while holding a child-sized purple scooter in his hand.

Watching one parent in particular.

She wore a long black coat and chic black leather boots and a knit black cap.

She stood out against the backdrop of shrieking and scampering children, of wailing and whining offspring and their dutifully attendant guardians, the makeup-free moms in hassle-free haircuts and sensible puffy coats and the Weezer dads in their interesting glasses and carefully curated sneakers. These parents, Craig noticed with some element of pity, stood immersed in their phones and burdened like Sherpas with overstuffed bags of provisions for their toddler masters, diaper bags stuffed to bursting with wet wipes and Goldfish crackers and bubble wands and sticker books and snot-encrusted stuffy toys, all the supplies they apparently required to survive a trip that takes them just a few hours and a few blocks from home.

She, however, was sexy.

Black coat, chic boots, knit cap.

While he had strayed habitually in his three years with Daisy, he had never considered a dalliance with a mom, who by definition was (a) likely married herself and (b) tethered to a kid. But Craig considered himself an innovator in the field of adultery, a forward thinker in philandering, a *disruptor,* and as he watched this woman, he might have thought, consciously or unconsciously, that a woman with a kid would necessarily never scrutinize him too closely, would absolutely be divided in her attention, would unquestionably have a person in her life who she valued far more than Craig, and thus promised an enticing combination of fortifying affection and active disinterest. This was a proposal that Craig—someone who craved attention and affection but also lived in perpetual fear of being exposed as a ridiculous fraud— suddenly found deliriously appealing.

Hot moms, he thought in the playground. Who knew?

Especially this one.

Black coat, chic boots, knit cap.

Deep black curls stuffed up under the cap, with only a few stray tendrils hanging free.

Red lipstick, hastily applied.

Obviously expensive black leather boots, salt-stained from last winter and never cleaned.

Nail polish chipped and not refreshed.

Scrolling through her phone while keeping one eye on whichever of these roving hellions belonged to her.

Then the hot mom looked up at him.

Caught him staring.

And she spoke.

"Looks like you forgot something," she said, pocketing her phone and giving him a tentative, even flirty, grin.

He gazed at her dumbly.

"The scooter," she said. "I assume it comes with a kid? It looks a bit small for you." She nodded toward the teeming play structures. "So which one is yours?"

"Which what?"

"Which kid."

"Oh—I don't have a kid."

She regarded him, as if trying to assess whether or not he was making a feeble joke, eyeing him with that particularly urban combination of wariness and intrigue. "So you're just a lone guy who likes to spend his Sundays hanging out at playgrounds?"

"Why? Is that weird?" Having regained his footing, Craig shifted intuitively into flirtation mode, his favorite mode, peppering his response with an expert dash of playfulness.

"Yes. It's very weird."

"I'm an emissary from a childless world on an anthropological mission," he said. "I'm here to observe your rituals."

"Ah, the childless world," she said, nodding. "I lived on that world once, too. How are you finding us so far?"

"Curious. But not without your charms." He grinned. "Actually, I'm meeting a friend. The scooter belongs to him. To his kid."

"Welcome," she said. "Enjoy your visit to our planet." She glanced back toward the mob of tiny revelers. "The funny thing about parenthood is that, before you have a kid, you almost never spend any time in playgrounds. Then, after you have a kid, all you do is go to playgrounds. It's like you can never leave."

Craig sensed in her jaded statement a kind of wistful longing, which he interpreted, in his way, as an opening.

They stood like that for a moment longer, side by side, amid the ambient joyous screeching of the children.

After a calculated beat and delivered with the timing he'd honed his entire adult life to great effect, he said: "I'm Craig, by the way."

22

Daisy crouches by the water's edge and rinses the bloody sheet in the lake. Dip and scrub, dip and scrub, kneading at the rust-colored stain.

She likes this kind of work, work with her hands, work that feels connected to a previous, simpler time. Manual labor is one of the parts of doing theater that she loves the most. Before a show begins, before opening night, before the crowds and reviews and applause, there's all the physical work to be done: building sets, lugging props to the theater, sewing costumes, mending seams, erecting bleachers, laying down flooring on the stage. In a Broadway or even an off-Broadway show, the actors never get to do any of that; it's all delegated, unionized, cordoned off. As an actor, you just arrive one day to a fully realized world.

But in her downtown shows, the off-off-off-Broadway shows in black-box theaters for no money, it's all hands on deck, everyone chips in, and she absolutely loves it. Grab a hammer, paint a wall, stitch a costume. She loves to watch a whole world rise out of nothingness. And she's always amazed that a set built late at night, just a flimsy plywood approximation of life, with its painted facades and trompe l'oeil effects, can still become, to her, once the lights come up, once she's onstage in full costume, deep in character, an entirely new reality. That she and her colleagues can conjure a whole world out of planks and particleboard and paint, then say to an audience full of strangers: *Join us. We are who we say we are. And if we do our job, you'll never question it because you'll believe in our world as well. And in the end you'll stumble back out into the night air and wonder how we pulled it off.*

Honestly, if that's not magic, what is?

She stoops by the lakeside, scrubbing idly at the stain on the sheet.

When she looks down, she sees, to her relief, that the stain is entirely gone.

She stands, with the sodden white sheet in her hands, and she's so lost in thought that it isn't until she turns to leave that she notices the lanky man in red at the edge of the woods, silently watching her.

She startles. Then recognizes him.

Shep. Of course. In his red SECURITY windbreaker. He stands about ten yards from her, knee-deep in tall grass.

"You snuck up on me," she says.

"I didn't mean to scare you."

"What are you doing here?" Her voice wheezes slightly, the breath chased out of her.

"I'm doing what I'm supposed to be doing," he says calmly. "I'm watching you."

23

Voicemail.

Craig hangs up, waves away a persistent mosquito, hits redial, and listens again.

Still sweating in the hot sun, heart only now settling down.

Lilith keeps her phone on her, always. She has a kid, after all. So she's probably just ignoring his call. Screening him.

She's probably furious at him.

She's no doubt furious at him.

She has every right to be furious at him.

But he's doing the right thing. He believes that.

Still ringing.

Voicemail again.

He hangs up.

Dials again.

They wound up getting a drink that day, on the first day they met at the playground. Daisy was in rehearsal for a play all weekend, which meant Daisy would be incommunicado until well into the early-morning hours, which meant Craig was on his own in the city: a dangerous state of affairs. The woman brought her daughter, who was three, and whose name Craig could never remember—it was an old-fashioned name like Olivia or Marguerite, the kind borrowed from an ancient novel about marriage and manners—to the bar, and her daughter sat transfixed by a smartphone while the two of them sat side by side on stools and drank cocktails in the early afternoon. As for the scooter, Craig just left it propped against the fence for Kyle to find.

Her name was Lilith.

She was in an open marriage, she said.

It had been her idea, she explained, fingering the stem of the cocktail glass, but her husband hastily agreed. He'd agreed, she said, not out of some enthusiasm for new carnal possibilities, God knows, but because it felt like one less thing on his overstuffed agenda that he'd have to worry about. *Keep wife happy*—check. Her husband's only rule for their arrangement, she said, was leave no trace and make no mention. Don't ask, don't tell—which ironically robbed it of all the excitement for her. Because, she only realized later, she was really just trying to get his attention, but she had only managed to introduce yet another thing into their lives for him to ignore.

Craig nodded throughout, sipping his drink.

So that was four months ago.

They'd meet in the evenings while Daisy was in rehearsals and otherwise find time to hook up in Lilith's king-size bed in her toy-strewn brownstone in Boerum Hill. Craig would take the subway in to Brooklyn from Manhattan over his lunch hour, these afternoon absences easily explainable to his colleagues as "work lunches" taken in pursuit of increased productivity. Of late, his manager had taken note of his frequent truancy, and his standing in the company was declining, but after a certain point, what did he care?

He was going to Cabo.

She was the one who suggested it, one afternoon as they lay in the king-size bed. Even then, he could tell that her proposition had less to do with some transformative love for him than with her own realization that an open marriage and an ongoing affair weren't nearly enough to numb her to the fundamental dissatisfactions of her life: brownstone, toddler, hard-driving husband in finance, cartoons blaring in the background at all hours. She had a law degree, never used. Back in law school, she'd escaped the boredom of lectures with daydreams about months-long treks to Patagonia and fantastic sex with strange men on the beaches of Peru. Now she didn't even practice law. Cabo wasn't Peru, she figured, but it wasn't Boerum Hill, either.

As for him, the Cabo plan would represent a crisis point with Daisy, but maybe that's exactly what they needed—a crisis. They'd lapsed into an aggravating routine of arguments and absence, fighting about her lack of a career and his perpetual job-related misery. Daisy away at rehearsals half the time, Craig prowling the bars of Brooklyn, both of them, it seemed, struggling to recall the initial electric spark that drew them together.

Once the Cabo idea was introduced, it felt suddenly inevitable to him. It would be hard to break with Daisy but probably for the best— she was, after all, the woman he was apparently put on this earth to disappoint. This impetuous act of marital demolition seemed, if not appealing, then inescapable. He'd learned in his three years with Daisy that she was funny and smart and fantastic, true, but also sporadically sullen and stubborn and exceptionally difficult to unravel, and honestly, in their time together, he had never shaken that initial doubt that he didn't really deserve her. That he could never truly be worthy of her. He wasn't sure he deserved Lilith or that he was worthy of her, either, but in her case, he didn't much care.

So of course they should run off together.

That had been his previous thinking, at least.

But now Craig is in the woods, in the clean country air, away from the city and asking the tough questions about love and sacrifice and change. And he isn't so sure anymore that what he'd be giving up by losing Daisy isn't much more valuable than what he'd gain.

He isn't so sure that he can't be a different man.

A better man.

Worthy.

Why not?

And, besides, that stupid question keeps nagging at him.

Question Three.

Would you fight for me?

Seriously, would he *fight* for Lilith?

He left her stranded at a gate at JFK, so he already knows the answer.

And if she told him today she was breaking it off, he would simply shrug and say, *Okay.*

But Daisy—

Daisy he would fight for.

Daisy he would axe-chop a raccoon for.

Or scoop up a dead, mangled snake.

Or sweep protectively out of a barroom about to explode into a brawl, which is how he chooses to remember the events of that particular night.

In fact, let those hayseed assholes come, he thinks, let them start some shit now, as he envisions the .45-caliber surprise he'd spotted in Alwyn's footlocker.

Because he'll change for Daisy. He'll sacrifice for Daisy. And, goddammit, he'll fight for Daisy.

Look at you, he thinks as the phone keeps ringing in his ear by the side of the gravel road. I believe this is what they call personal growth.

Still ringing.

Then Lilith picks up.

24

Shep doesn't look at all like a security guard, she thinks. He's tall and lean with shaggy hair that falls occasionally in his face. He looks more like a roadie or a guy who plays bass in a band that never quite made it. He stands watching her in his red windbreaker with one hand stuck casually in the back pocket of his jeans and the other hand holding a small festive paper gift bag, its sides shiny and striped. For a second, she thinks stupidly that he's brought her a present.

Then she recognizes the bag.

"Oh my God," she says, her hand drifting to her mouth.

He holds it out to her. "You left this at the bar last night."

She grabs the bag and checks the contents, fumbling around in the white tissue paper. Her fingers find the cigar box, and she pulls it free and opens it, letting the bag flutter to the ground.

And there it is inside: the bone-handled pocketknife, worn to the touch, its contours familiar.

Her grandfather's knife. Her anniversary gift to her husband. They must have forgotten it as they rushed out of the bar.

She looks up at Shep. "Thank you so much."

He sticks both hands in his back pockets and shrugs. "The bartender's the one who spotted it. She knew you were doing the Eden Test, and I said I'd return it to you."

Daisy clutches the knife. "It's very important to me. I can't believe we almost lost it."

"There was a lot going on last night." Shep glances toward the cabin. "Is he here?"

"Craig? He went for a run." She shows him the white sheet she's been scrubbing. "I just came down here to take care of some chores."

"Looks pristine to me," says Shep.

She looks him over, remembering all the improv classes from her graduate theater school days. The ones where you'd stand opposite a partner and feel each other out, give little clues as to the situation, a cautious give-and-take. *It's all about listening*, the teachers said, *and you must always be willing to say yes*—that's an essential rule of improv. Never deny, never refute, never say no, never block, always say yes. If someone says, *I can't believe we're on the moon*, you can't say, *No, we're not, we're in Cleveland*. You have to say, *Yes, and—let's find ourselves a lunar restaurant because I'm starving.*

Say *Yes, and*— then push the scene forward. That's the only way it works. It's one of the most important rules of improv.

That, and never break character.

"Someone entered our cabin last night," she says. "When we got home, our front door was open. Then I found something under my pillow—a dead snake. My husband thinks an animal did it. Like a raccoon or something."

"What do you think?" says Shep.

"I think I know that raccoons don't leave dead snakes under pillows. I think someone wanted to scare me and has maybe seen *The Godfather* one too many times."

"I'm so sorry that happened," he says. "You want me to come up and stay at the house for a few nights? Keep an eye on things?"

"I don't think that's necessary. We'll be fine. We've only got—what? Three more days? And it seems like you're doing a perfectly good job keeping a watch on us."

Shep smiles. "I just happened to be in the neighborhood."

Her heart's still drumming from the recovery of the knife, from the fact that she could have forgotten it. Everything this week has been planned to the letter, perfect, so a careless slip like that—

She bundles the wet sheet up in her arms. "Shep. That's an unusual name," she says.

"Short for Shepherd. It's an old family name."

"You can call me Daisy. Short for Daisy. It's not an old family any-thing," she says. "You look like you could use a drink. Can I offer you something up at the house? Glass of water? Early cocktail?"

He eyes her. "Do you think that would be okay?"

Say yes, she thinks. *Yes, and—*

"I think it would be fine. You can take a little break. We both can. You're supposed to be protecting me. There's no better place to protect me than up at the cabin." She holds up the pocketknife. "Let me at least say thank you for getting this back to me."

He looks down at his feet. Then back up, bashful. Brushes his hair back. "Maybe just for a moment."

"Exactly. Just for a moment."

"Until your husband gets back," he says.

25

It's kind of funny, Craig thinks later, because the first thing Lilith says to him after she finally picks up, after three separate attempts and thirty rings, after he says hello, then says hello again, after a pause, a very, very long pause—the first thing she says, very quietly, in hushed tones, like she's telling him a secret, is "I'm at the grocery store."

After that, it's just incomprehensible yelling.

Rage and anguish. Pain and tears. So much so that Craig actually holds the phone away from his ear like he's in a cartoon, while her frantic voice *wah-wah-wah*s out of the tiny earhole. He catches snippets—*hours in the airport, left my husband, you fucking asshole, I have a* kid—but a lot of it just sounds like static, like a white-noise machine turned to a setting called Betrayed.

Every so often he brings the phone gingerly back toward his face—*Lilith, I know, but it's different, you have to understand*—but his interjections do nothing to deter the torrent of tear-soaked abuse.

Which he deserves. He gets that.

The path to being a better man is not without discomfort.

He holds the phone away from his head and looks around at the calm of the woods. So peaceful. Disturbed only by the very, very faraway sound, a wailing anger.

He's sorry. He is.

I'm sorry, Lilith, he thinks.

Humans are stupid and they hurt each other. They have since the beginning of time. That's exactly what he's trying to work past.

He even thinks to say it out loud—*I'm sorry, Lilith*—but when he looks at the screen of the phone, he sees the little round red disconnect button. Just floating there.

So red.

So tempting.

Like an old friend. An eject button. An exit sign.

He could just hang up. He could.

But he's trying to be a better person.

He brings the phone's microphone close to his mouth, while keeping the phone itself angled in such a way that the speaker is far from his ear.

He says it. "I'm sorry, Lilith."

Then he does it.

He presses the button.

Silence.

The quiet of the woods.

Well, that's done, he thinks.

Then he turns off the ringer, just in case, and pockets the phone with some self-satisfaction. It wasn't easy, but he made the right decision, he knows that. He did the right thing—didn't just say the right thing to Daisy, or hide the details of his wrongdoing, but made things right, despite the pain. And, suddenly, he feels good. He feels *great*. This is the day it starts, he thinks. This is the day everything gets better, that *he* gets better. He dodged an enormous bullet, and Daisy is none the wiser. A few days ago, he was ready to leave her forever. But today—today is the beginning of something new.

No more secrets. No more lies. No more excuses, no more ducking out, no more running around, ashamed and anxious.

Just him and her.

Perfect.

He can't wait.

He looks around, takes note of his surroundings. Remember this feeling, he thinks. Because on this fine, sunny late-summer day in the country, he started his journey toward being a better man.

He's excited to get back to the cabin, back to Daisy. He'll hurry back and surprise her. She'll be happy to see him, no doubt. Maybe they can recapture the passion of the cabin floor last night.

Then get started on their new life together.

Honest. Devoted. The two of them.

The three of them.

He shakes his head. A baby! Can this be possible?

It is. It's happening.

Fortified by a sense of wonder and a sudden surge of paternal resolve, having made the hard choices and feeling encouraged now by his hard-won and frankly unfamiliar rectitude, Craig savors this moment, so eager to get started, then tries to figure out which is the fastest way to get back home and surprise his waiting wife.

26

Daisy invites Shep to sit on the porch. It's become her favorite spot. The damp white sheet hangs over the railing, drying lazily in the sun. Shep's perched, polite as a suitor, in the wicker chair across from her, one large hand wrapped around a glass of water, drinking. She lounges on the wicker settee with her bare legs curled up beneath her, shoes off, relaxed, her fingers encircling her own sweaty glass, the ice cubes lightly jingling, watching him.

He sits perfectly straight. He gulps the water deeply, his bare throat exposed, his Adam's apple pulsing rhythmically. She remembers a game they used to play in theater school that her teacher called Postures. You'd partner up with another student and your partner would write down different scenarios, then call them out, and you'd have to convey each character simply through how you seated yourself in a chair. *Rebellious high school kid caught with weed, waiting to meet the vice principal—go!* Or: *Anxious single mom on the bus on her way to a job interview.* Or: *Devout teenager seated in an abortion-clinic waiting room.* The challenge was to communicate an entire emotional backstory simply through posture and body language: how you drape yourself, how you hold your head, how you flutter your hands. Each gesture carefully calculated, each glance contrived.

She loved that game.

She regards Shep and thinks: Earnest farmer, courting an urbane lady above his station. Then she considers herself, with her legs folded up under her and her hands cupped around her glass, the wet rim held close to her lips, her lips self-consciously brushing against it, eyes held intent on her guest, and thinks: Lonely wife entertaining a hot security guard at her empty cabin while her husband goes for a jog so he can secretly call the woman he's been fucking for the past four months.

Shep finishes his water in one long sustained swallow and sets the glass aside, wiping his mouth with the back of his hand. He looks over his shoulder toward the lake. "The view from here is magnificent. Tell me again—how'd you happen to find this place?"

"Just discovered it online. I was looking for a getaway. For my husband and me."

"So what did you search for? Did you just type in 'isolated cabin'? 'Beautiful lakefront view'?"

"Actually," she says, "I searched for 'couple in trouble.' I just typed that phrase in and this place came up. This whole program. The Eden Test. All of it. *Seven days. Seven questions. Forever changed.*"

"Which question are you on now?"

"Number three: *Would you fight for me?*"

Shep smiles at her. "I hope the answer is yes."

She flushes. She can't help it. "Speaking of fights, I saw you at the bar last night. Just as we were leaving. I saw you step in and stand up to that guy."

Shep glances away, his hair again falling alluringly over his face. "I didn't like the way he was acting. I thought he should reconsider his choices."

"I'm pretty confident he's doing that right now."

Shep grins. He seems to like this banter, too, the back-and-forth, like playacting. "You certainly looked ready to tussle, if I recall correctly. Before your husband dragged you away. You got right in that guy's face."

"I don't like that kind of man. I've met his kind before."

"I'm so sorry to hear that," says Shep. "So what do you do back in New York?"

"I'm an actor."

"Very cool. Are you successful?"

"Have you ever heard of me?"

"No, but that's not how I would measure success."

"Good," she says. "Neither would I."

"So how do you measure success?" asks Shep.

"By how convincing you are."

"And how convincing are you?"

"Completely," she says.

She likes this kind of conversation, the kind that happens on parallel tracks: There's what is said and then there's what is implied, and both participants have knowledge beyond what they're willing to reveal. Each of them is playing their assigned role, waiting to see who will break character first. Who'll violate that cardinal stage rule: Don't break.

This is the kind of exchange you always have onstage, of course: The dialogue is rote, the lines already known, so the challenge is to find surprise and spontaneity and electricity in a pause, an inflection, a glance. It's all about the moments *around* the words, *between* them, the crackle of implied meaning, the feint and parry of unspoken intent. People call it acting, but isn't this just what we all do every day? Play a role, be who we know someone needs us to be, recite our expected lines, all while searching for some clue as to the other person's real meaning, their honest motivations?

Onstage or off, she finds it thrilling. She's very good at it. She has to be.

Feint, she thinks—that's almost an antagonym. Two opposite meanings, though the spellings are different. Faint can mean to weaken, to lose consciousness, or lacking courage, like faint of heart. And a feint is a mock blow or advance, a trick intended to disguise the true point of attack.

"So how long did you say your husband will be gone for?" says Shep.

"I don't know," she says, smiling. "But I think we have some time." Then she adds, "We're all alone up here, you know."

He leans in. "So we can talk freely?" He seems ready to spill something, make a confession.

"Be my guest," she says.

Shep exhales. "Do you think he suspects?"

Daisy rubs a hand over her knees and considers the question.

"No," she says finally. "He doesn't have a clue."

"None of it?"

"None of it," she says.

27

Change for me.

Sacrifice for me.

Fight for me.

Soon I'll be back at the cabin, Craig thinks, his feet finding a steady stride, a pleasing, pounding rhythm. And they've still got half a week and four questions to figure everything out.

They can do the next question tonight. He can't wait.

Question Four. *Would you...?*

He wonders what the next *Would you...?* will be.

Move away with me? Cut your hair for me? Quit your job for me? Dump a friend for me?

Right now, flush from his moral triumph, he's having a hard time imagining something he *wouldn't* do for Daisy.

What else can you do for someone, he thinks, besides change for them, sacrifice for them, fight for them? He's already done all three of those, and he feels satisfied, like their relationship is salvaged and saved.

Would you...?

What more can you possibly do for someone?

I guess we'll find out tonight, he thinks.

He keeps jogging. Savors the scent of pine, admires the endless tree line, the forest like a crowd of onlookers gathered roadside at a marathon to cheer on his progress.

And, for the first time, he wonders whether he's seen these trees before.

I mean, how would I know, he thinks. They're trees.

But this path doesn't look familiar.

He pulls up, panting. Hands on hips.

Takes a moment to assess.

Where was the sun? he thinks. Now it's just high overhead, so it's impossible to tell which way is east or west. Not that he really remembers what direction he came from or what direction the cabin is in.

He's been jogging back the way he came from, he thinks, so obviously it's going to look different. Because all of this was at his back when he was running before, right?

Either that or he's going in exactly the wrong direction.

In his mind, he tries to be rational, soothe himself, but his stomach sends up the first sour flare of unease. That first tight, queasy suspicion that he may be totally lost.

He looks around for landmarks. He spots a large boulder a few yards back beyond the trees, obscured and scribbled with red graffiti. It looks like some kind of arcane altar. There's a scatter of beer bottles in the underbrush. Okay, I definitely don't remember that, he thinks.

That settles it, he determines. You made a wrong turn. No big deal. Just retrace your steps.

He starts jogging back in the direction that he came from. The hot sun even higher now.

See? Nothing you can't handle, he thinks. He lets his mind roam once again, back to his celebratory accounting of his new prospects. Where was he? Oh, yeah—no more hiding, no more secrets, no more sneaking around, no more lies. He had the opportunity to leave, he came right to the precipice, but he didn't: He stepped back, he *stayed*, and good for him. Now he's ended things with Lilith. From here on out he and Daisy will be fully open with each other, fully honest, finally, which is maybe all they've needed all along. Maybe that's all they've been missing, maybe that's the secret— He halts again.

Okay, he thinks. I'm totally lost.

Don't panic. Time to admit your shortcomings, he thinks, and fall back on the comforts of modern technology. You don't have to be Daniel Boone; there's a reason God invented smartphones.

He reaches into the mesh pocket of his skimpy swim shorts and pulls out the phone he brought with him—its screen, he sees now, smeared with sweat from where it's been bouncing and rubbing lightly against his thigh.

He taps the phone alive. It lights up brightly, eager to be of service.

He swipes.

No bars. Of course.

He turns around and around in a tight little circle, back and forth like a malfunctioning toy, searching, shaking the phone hopelessly, trying to activate a signal, awaken the gods, but he knows, he knows. He's in a dead zone.

He pauses another moment, thinking, searching for that one smart revelation he's certain is just waiting to alight, but when it doesn't, when he finds he's stuck on the same dumb options—*run this way, run that way, hope for the best*—he stows the contraband phone back in his swimming trunks pocket and finally admits to himself that he has no idea where in the world he is or the first clue how to get back home.

28

On the porch, Shep looks at her, serious. His question lingering between them.

Do you think he suspects?

No. He doesn't have a clue.

None of it?

None of it.

Shep speaks: "Are you sure about that?"

Daisy knows they're alone and that there's no one else within miles, but now that they're actually talking about it out loud, she wants to pull him in closer, to keep their voices low, to properly conspire. She's worked so hard to plan it all out, to keep it all a secret, to recruit the players and assemble the pieces and set it all in motion that, even though she knows there's no one else around, it feels unnatural, reckless even, to voice it out loud.

"Yes, I'm sure," she says. "He doesn't suspect anything. Not yet."

Shep leans back in his chair, a wry smile spreading. "Goddamn. I really shouldn't be surprised. You always were the very best actor in our class."

She returns the smile. "You're pretty good yourself. As this week has proved."

Shep's posture has changed now, the rigidity of the anxious suitor replaced by an actor's backstage ease. He shakes his head in admiration. "I have to say—you don't look a day older than when I last saw you, waving goodbye from that train to New York."

"Now you're just flattering me. It's been eight years. And New York takes a toll on a girl."

"No, you look exactly the same. Better, even. Why would I flatter you?"

"Because I'm paying you?"

"You're paying me to act, you're not paying me to lie," he says, grinning. "And honestly, you're not paying me enough to do either."

He hasn't changed much himself, she thinks, even though it's been eight years. She remembers how his cockeyed grin was the envy of her graduate school class. How notorious he was for the charisma he had onstage. Offstage, in civilian clothes, he was always handsome, sure, but Christian—his real name, the one she knew him by back then—absolutely sizzled onstage, you couldn't tear your eyes from him. Back in school, that enviable, ephemeral quality—that *sizzle*—seemed like his stamped passport to the promised land. He had *it*, whatever "it" was—they both did, her and him, that's what everyone said. That's why a lot of people back in school assumed they were a couple, or thought they should be. Christian certainly did. He could have had anyone in their class—and he had plenty, as she recalls—but she always kept him at arm's length. She played the role of the Girl Who Doesn't Talk About Her Past, the Girl Who Is Impossible to Know, and he played the Dutiful Friend, the Chaste Champion, despite the fact that he clearly wanted more. And when she truly needed him, on the night of the showcase, the night he drove her to the train station and waited on the platform to make sure she was safe—that meant a lot to her. That was everything.

And now he's here. After all these years. Because she knows she can count on Christian.

Look at us, she thinks, we could be right back in theater school. It could be showcase night all over again: lights, costumes, showtime.

"I really appreciate your help with this," she says.

"I always loved acting with you, you know that." He rubs his hands over his thighs, relaxing now, like he's happy to shrug off the pretense.

"I just never suspected that the next time I'd be doing it, it would be in the middle of nowhere for no audience."

She corrects him: "For an audience of one."

"Audience of one—that's right." He chuckles. "Look at you—you went and got married! Of all the people in our class, I thought you'd be the *last* one to get hitched."

"Why's that?"

"Back in school you just always seemed—a bit enigmatic. You certainly didn't come off like the type to settle down," he says. "More like the type to disappear at the drop of a hat without a word. Which is exactly what you did."

"Yeah, well—" She offers him a tight, polite smile. Clutching her glass of water, she thinks of the wide gulf of years since they last spent time together. How fitting it is that they both are calling themselves by different names now: She's Daisy, her New York name, a name he never knew her by, and he's Shep, a name he dreamt up and adopted just for this character and this week. When you meet in theater school, as they did a lifetime ago, you're always trying on and discarding different identities. It's all part of your training, slipping in and out of costumes, onstage and off. "Once I was in New York for a while," she says finally, "it felt okay to get married. It felt good. It was a new life. I needed that. I needed things to feel different. To feel *new.*"

"So that's what Craig is, huh?" says Shep. "New?"

"He's a good man."

"Oh, really?" Shep laughs. "Is he? Is that why we're out here in the woods, doing all this?"

She sips her water. "He can be. He will be." She thinks of the first question. *Would you change for me?*

"If you say so," Shep says. "Look, I get it. Everyone wants to start a new life after school. But not everyone's as extreme as you. Changing your name? Dropping off the face of the earth? Everyone wondered what happened to you."

"I had to do it, you know that."

"And I guess that's why I never heard from you for eight years?"

"No one's heard from me," she says curtly, cutting off this line of questioning.

"I don't mean— I'm sorry," he says. "I know all that stuff was hard. When you left school."

Hard, she thinks. Sure, that's the word for it.

When you're running to save your life. When you have to leave everything and start over. Then do it again. Then again.

It's *hard.*

This is the part people never understand, she thinks, especially the few people she's left behind—it's not personal; it's more primal than that. It's not a *choice* and it never was.

You run. Because you have to.

You don't look back. Because you can't.

Because if you do, he's right there, always, one half step behind you.

"You're being careful, right?" she asks him, eager to talk about anything else. "Don't wear that windbreaker except around us."

"Of course." He tugs at the windbreaker. "Was it hard to get this made?"

"You know me and costumes. I can be very resourceful. I just want to make sure no one from the actual foundation spots you and starts asking questions."

"But I thought they leave you alone."

"I thought so, too, but then the founders dropped in on us unannounced the other day. We were skinny-dipping." She smiles at the improbable memory: the two of them splashing about, naked, giddy.

"What were they like?" says Shep. "I've only seen them on TV."

"The Ardens? Honestly? Happy," she says. "Like they've figured something out. And they're eager to help us figure it out, too."

Shep looks her over, as if he can't really believe it's her, after all these years. "So the Edenic people don't have any idea what you've got planned for this week?"

"As far as they know, we're just another couple in trouble from the

"That was just Mother Nature!" says Shep, delighted. "That raccoon just snuck in through the open door after we left." Shep rubs his chin, excited for what's next. "Of course, none of it matters until we see how Craig acts at the moment of truth."

She thinks of all she's put Craig through so far: the diner, the bar, the cabin. And all she'll put him through before the week's done. "He did say something the other day about the program feeling weird," she says. "Like they were watching us. But he thinks it's the people running Edenic who are doing it."

"What tipped him off? Not me, I hope."

"No," she says. "I think it was the waitress. Which surprised me. Craig's not usually suspicious if a waitress flirts with him. Quite the opposite, actually."

"And she's so good."

"Paulette? Yeah, she's great, right?" says Daisy. "We were in a show together, long before I met Craig. Way downtown. Total flop. But I always remembered her. I was so happy she agreed to do this."

"What's she calling herself?"

"Lorelei, like the mythological siren. Her choice. It's a little on the nose for my tastes."

"What did the temptress Lorelei tell the owners of that diner to get them to play along?"

"She said it was her friends' wedding anniversary. And that we were planning a big surprise. All of which happens to be true. It's definitely going to be a surprise."

Shep leans back, considers another question, then asks it. "Do you think she's rooting for you two to survive? As a couple?"

"Me and Craig? I hope so," says Daisy.

Shep pushes, probing. "Because it's just, you know—"

"Just what?"

"Some of us might be hoping for a different outcome to the week."

She eyes him. "What do you mean?"

Shep intertwines his fingers and tilts toward her, resting his elbows on his knees. "Why do you think I dropped everything and came out here on a moment's notice? You think I haven't been thinking about you for the last eight years, stuck up in the Berkshires?"

"I've been thinking about you, too," she says cautiously. "Of everything you did for me and how grateful I am."

"Sure, but this week there's one big difference between you and me," says Shep.

"What's that?"

"You're hoping that Craig passes this test. And I'm hoping he fails."

She clutches the cold exterior of her water glass. "And what do you think will happen if he fails?"

"Then maybe the rest of us get another chance." He lets that linger, then leans back. "Mostly, it's just so great to see you again."

"I'm really thankful for your help," she says. "You, Paulette— everyone."

"Speaking of our temptress waitress, where is she right now?"

Daisy sets down her glass. "She should be driving in the woods, looking for Craig."

"She's going to offer little lost Craig a ride home?" says Shep.

Daisy smiles. "She's going to offer him a whole lot more than that."

"You think he can resist temptation?"

"It's supposed to be a test," she says. "So let's find out."

29

Craig jogs half-heartedly down the road in one direction, hoping a route will reveal itself, but there's nothing. No route. Just trees. He looks in the other direction.

More trees.

He stands with his hands on his hips, unsure, cursing himself that he wasn't more diligent in marking a trail, looking for landmarks, but what's he supposed to do now? Maybe if he just starts running he'll see a landmark soon, something familiar, though what that would be, he can't imagine. Every tree looks exactly like the last one and together they all make up the forest, which looks to him like every other forest he's ever been in. You know—he searches for the right word.

Wooded.

He glances around. Didn't that old couple who run the place say they lived somewhere nearby? But he has no idea in which direction they live, any more than he knows the way home. And he has a sinking and unshakable feeling that, whichever way he decides to go, he'll only get more lost.

As he ponders this dilemma, head bent, he hears it.

Faint at first, then louder and, increasingly, unmistakable.

The cough and bang of an approaching car.

Sure enough, a dusty cloud appears just beyond a bend.

Then he sees it: a dented brown Chevette.

A rush of relief engulfs him. He waves his arms above his head, like a castaway frantically signaling a passing vessel on the horizon.

The car approaches and pulls up slowly beside him, halting in a whine of ancient brakes.

Behind the wheel, the driver leans over. Assesses him.

Cranks down the passenger window.

It's that hot waitress. Lorelei.

"What are the chances," she says.

They trundle along the gravel road in silence. Craig shifts, uncomfortable, in his seat. He's sweaty and his bare thighs are sticking to the car's hot vinyl interior. The whole car is ripe with the sickly smell of fake apples, thanks to the cardboard-apple air freshener that dances and dangles from the rearview mirror.

Lorelei glances over at him, brows arched provocatively. "Dude, you've got to stop stalking me."

"What do you mean?" he says, with a tone of mock indignation. A little bit flirty. Just a little. He can't help it.

"Look at us—here we are again. Alone. *In my car.*" She pops her eyebrows at him, like, *Fill in the blanks, dude.*

Craig twists toward her. "Hey, I was lost. You picked *me* up."

"Yes. But somehow you've been up here all of—what—four days? And you've managed to run into me twice."

Craig smiles at her and notices only now that she must be on her way to work, since she's wearing that same baby-blue waitress uniform, low-cut with white lace trim at the neckline. Her serpent tattoo blazes on her breastbone.

"I appreciate the ride," he says.

"Right place, right time." She glances over. "Call me a Good Samaritan. I can be nice when I want to be. Just don't take it for granted."

"I won't." He lets his eyes linger on her.

"You've got to be careful," she says. "Not everyone's so fond of strangers up here."

"Tell me about it. Someone broke into our cabin last night."

"Really?"

"By the time we got home, they were gone. But it was—unsettling."

"We definitely have people in these parts who get bored and like to fuck shit up," she says. "Put on their camo pants and play army out in the woods. And they don't like citiots, as a rule."

"I met two of those guys at the bar. Same assholes I saw at the diner the other day. They tried to pick a fight with us."

"What happened?"

"We didn't take the bait. We left." He shifts, a bit embarrassed. "Discretion is the better part of valor, right?"

"What?" she says. "Running away?" She looks over at him in mock concern and adopts a baby voice. "Did you have a bad experience at the townie bar?"

He's peeved by her derisive tone. "Where are you headed anyway?"

"Off to work. Hence the outfit. Where are *you* headed?"

"I was going for a jog."

"And a little secret phone call?"

He glances at her. She shrugs. "Hey, most people don't stop in the middle of a run to have a long argument on the phone unless they're trying to be, you know, discreet," she says.

"We don't get service at the cabin."

"That's bullshit, but whatever. Don't worry. Your secret is safe with me."

"Wait—how do you know I was having an argument?"

"Maybe *I'm* stalking *you*." She turns her eyes back to the road. "You missed a hell of a show the other night. Blaise Orange rocked the house."

"Who's Blaise Orange?"

"My band? The flyer? Jesus." Now she sounds genuinely hurt.

"Of course. I'm sorry. I couldn't make it. You know. I'm stuck up here with my wife."

"Stuck, huh?"

"You know what I mean."

"Too bad, because I would have given you a VIP backstage pass," she says finally, sullen. She glances over at him. "Hell of an after-party, too."

He looks at her. With her blunt black bangs, her choppy black hair piled up, her black lipstick, her bow-shaped lips, she's so much his type it feels painful.

"I'm sure it was fun," he says, his throat feeling a little tight. "I just couldn't get away."

"That's what people always tell themselves when they're too chicken-shit to do something naughty." Her expression, he thinks, says, *Prove me wrong.*

Then she brakes. The car halts. He jerks forward against the shoulder strap. "What the hell," he says.

"Now would you look at this."

"What?"

She nods out the windshield. "We seem to have come to a fork in the road."

He looks up. Sure enough, the road splits ahead into two branches. "Well, I have no idea which is the right way to go. That's why I'm lost."

"Don't worry, I know the way." She turns to him, shifting in her seat, her short skirt sliding up as she twists, revealing her bare thigh, where he spots a tattoo, newly exposed: a mermaid, singing on a rock, a myth-ological siren.

Lorelei.

"If you know the way, then what are we stopped for?" he says, a bit of a croak audible in his voice.

"You've got to choose." She extends her arm languorously and rests her wrist on the steering wheel, carnival tattoos ribboning her pale skin. "To the right is the road back to your cabin."

"And to the left?"

"The after-party," she says.

He looks her over. His palms are clammy. The car seems very small. The two of them seem very close together, like they're two astronauts alone in a space capsule, circling a distant Earth.

"To the right," he says, almost inaudibly, like a forced confession.

"What's that?" she purrs.

Old Craig would be half out of his pants by now, he thinks. Old Craig would— He knows exactly what Old Craig would do.

But not this Craig. Not New Craig.

"I want to go to the *right*," he says, his voice clearer now, more reso-lute. "I want to go home. To my *wife*."

She keeps looking at him, then giggles—she can't help it. She shakes her head, like she's contemplating an incomprehensible mistake. "To the right it is."

She hits the gas again and steers the sputtering car forward, toward the branch in the fork that will take Craig back to Daisy.

30

"And what exactly have you put your good friend Lorelei up to?" says Shep.

"Don't worry. Nothing will happen."

"Because you trust Craig?"

Daisy almost laughs. Does she trust Craig? Not exactly. "Because she knows when to cut the scene. She just needs to find out for me if he *would*. It's like attempted murder—sometimes you just have to establish intent."

They both hear the bleat of a wheezing car horn approaching up the road, once, twice. Two horn honks, Daisy thinks. That's the signal they established.

Daisy smiles to herself. Then she looks up at Shep. "He chose right."

"So far," says Shep. "The week's barely half over."

"You should get going," she says.

"Don't worry, you're not the only one who knows how to disappear." He stands. Grins. "See you in Act Three."

In the claustrophobic heat of the Chevette, Craig turns to Lorelei. "What are you honking at?"

"Animals," she says.

He's about to reply when he spies the shimmer of the lake through a stand of trees, the silhouette of the cabin. He points. "There!"

Lorelei turns the wheel and pulls into the driveway. "This is you," she says.

He unbuckles the belt, steps out of the car, then walks around and taps on the driver's-side window. She cranks it down.

He leans in. "I love my wife."

Lorelei nods toward the porch. "Don't tell me. Tell her."

Craig looks up and there she is: Daisy, alone, standing with her arms crossed in the cabin's open doorway. He waves.

"See you around," says Lorelei, then puts the car into gear. "And do try to avoid the townies. I hear they bite."

The Chevette backs up in a rumble of gravel, then drives off with one last friendly toot of the horn.

Craig bounds up the stairs to the porch.

"Old friend?" Daisy says from the doorway, her eyebrow arched.

"Very funny. I got lost on my jog. She happened by and offered me a ride. I swear."

Her eyes soften. "I believe you. I just got worried, is all."

"I'm really sorry. I missed you. And you know what? I think I'm starting to figure things out." He puts a hand on her face, then pulls her toward him and hugs her, unexpectedly tight. He pulls back. "How was *your* day?"

"Uneventful. I cleaned that sheet."

"How'd that go?"

"Spotless," she says.

31

They sit side by side together on the couch, looking at the white envelope on the coffee table with the gold letters on the front: *Q4*.

They're eating bowls of Frosted Flakes for dinner, an old beloved ritual from their past, from weekends spent holed up together when they didn't want to leave the bed, let alone the apartment, for groceries, because they had each other, and that was enough. Long afternoons telling jokes under the covers, among other activities.

He points a spoon at the envelope. "You read it," he says.

She sets her bowl aside, grabs the envelope, and rips it open. "And the Oscar goes to—" she says, a joke she makes pretty much every time she opens any envelope for any reason. Craig dutifully makes the sound of a drumroll, happy to play the straight man in this recurring bit.

She unfolds the paper, and he looks at her as she sits cross-legged facing him on the couch. She's changed into comfort clothes, an old T-shirt and sweatpants, the pair with the name of her prestigious drama school printed down one leg in block letters. *The hundred-thousand-dollar sweatpants,* that's her trusty joke. He's the only person in the world who knows this joke—it's for them alone. To be honest, the pedigree of her graduate school embarrasses her, she almost never mentions it, and she always avoids telling people where she went if they ask. And she never wears those pants outside the house, *would* never wear them, Craig knows, around anyone else but him.

And all of a sudden he realizes, he knows for certain, sitting there with her, holding his bowl of Frosted Flakes, that he wants to be with

Daisy forever. He wants inside jokes and fake drumrolls and hundred-thousand-dollar sweatpants and secrets and good news and arguments and joy. He wants to be a better person and a better husband and a better man, for her. He wants to be here, now, with someone he knows, really knows, and who knows him, too. He wants to be understood and to understand. He wants to be loved and to love. He wants to feel worthy. He's starting to feel worthy. Worthy of this.

Worthy of her.

"I will change for you," he says to her suddenly, with the solemnity of a wedding vow. "I will sacrifice for you. I will fight for you."

She laughs; she can't help it, she's taken aback by his jarring sincerity. "Thank you. Me, too."

"And whatever the next questions bring," he says. "I'll do it. I'm ready."

"Good," she says. "Me, too."

He looks at her, adoring.

"I love you, Daisy."

"I love you, too," she says.

And it occurs to them both, right then, that tonight is the first time this week that either of them have said those words out loud.

She unfolds the paper. "You ready?"

"Let's do this."

She reads the question aloud. "*Question Four. Would you lie for me?*"

"Daisy, I told you, I won't lie to you. Not anymore. Not ever. I promise—"

She stops him. "No. Listen. That's not what the question says."

Question Four.

Would you lie for me?

Do you lie to your partner? Probably. We all do, in large and little ways. Do you say he still looks just as handsome as when you met even though he's put on a few pounds? Do you tell her you love her new haircut even when you both know it was a terrible mistake? Our relationships consist of these tiny lies; they are the web that holds us together. They are harmless. They are how we get through the day.

Now here's the real question: Would you lie for *your partner?*

If so, how big of a lie would you be willing to tell?

In the military, there is a concept called unit cohesion—the notion that people engaged in a life-or-death fight must have total trust in one another and be able to depend on one another beyond all doubt.

Do you and your partner have unit cohesion?

Do you trust *each other, above all else? Not just in the sense that you believe what your partner says to you, but in the sense that you believe they would do* anything *for you.*

Even lie.

Even more.

Imagine you did a terrible thing. Imagine you had a secret so awful that it would ruin your life if it ever got out.

Would you tell each other about it?

If not, then you aren't together, not really. You are alone. And you always were.

Love demands a loyalty beyond morality. Beyond "yes" and "no," or "good" and "bad," or "truth" and "lies." The greatest love stories in history and myth are defined by a couple's absolute fidelity to each other. Romeo and Juliet. Orpheus and Eurydice. Macbeth and Lady Macbeth. Adam and Eve.

They were willing to do anything *for each other. Drink a potion. Travel to Hell and back. Cover up the most heinous stain. Turn their backs on Paradise.*

Anything.

Change for. Sacrifice for. Fight for.

Lie for.

They were willing to do that.

More than willing.
Are you?

She folds the paper and looks up at him.
He's crying.
"There's something I need to show you," he says.

32

He leads her out the front door of the cabin and she follows him in silence. His flip-flops slap the gravel as he approaches the trunk of the car. He stands over it, waiting as she catches up to him.

The air is colder now, the light waning. As she walks, she looks up at the transitioning sky, where she can already see the faint stars. There are a million stars in the night sky out here, she's noticed, a startling abundance. It seems impossible to her that this sky overhead, so full of possibility, is the same sickly one that arches pale all night over Brooklyn, starless, bleached empty by the city's bleeding light.

Once she joins him at the car, he says nothing but simply pops the trunk.

Points inside.

She sees two large suitcases, packed.

"Are we going somewhere?" she says, with a dry laugh.

"I had an affair," he says. "I just ended it today. We were supposed to run away together. I had these suitcases packed and ready. I was going to tell you about it and then go."

"How long has it been going on for?"

"Four months."

"Where were you planning to go?"

"Cabo San Lucas."

"Did you pack sunscreen? You know how pale you are."

"I'm sorry," he says.

"It's okay. I'm kind of relieved."

"Why?"

"When you opened the trunk, I thought for sure you were going to show me a dead body."

He laughs through tears. "I'm really sorry, Daisy. I love you."

"I love you, too. Come here."

She takes him into her arms. He folds into her. Why *she's* comforting *him*, she's not entirely sure. But that's okay.

He's confessed.

That's a step.

Step one, but a step.

Now this week has started for real, she thinks.

Everything needs to come out now. She needs to tell him all of it. The full story. If they're going to be able to handle what's coming next.

Poor Craig. He has so much more ahead of him. She cradles his head, strokes his hair. She thinks of their baby, on the way.

"I just want to do the right thing," he says, a hoarse whisper.

"I know," she says.

"No more secrets. No more lies," he says.

"Of course," she says, and pulls him in close, and kisses him on the head, and thinks of the texts on her secret phone.

where are you

on my way

you tell anyone?

of course not. who would i tell. besides you

our little secret then

The climactic act of the week, set in motion.

The final surprise.

The real test.

Intermission

The gas-tank needle bounces just above the red, but if the driver is feeling anxious, he shows no sign of nerves. He pulls his dirt-streaked SUV into a filling station that's just over the border of western Pennsylvania, slowing to a stop by the one pump that's cast in darkness under a flickering light pole.

He's been a day on the road and has a day more at least. Heading east.

He gets out of the truck and readjusts his black fingerless gloves, mostly from restless habit. He's dressed all in black, with a black goatee, and a black down vest despite the summer season. He fiddles for a moment with the pump display, though he already knows he wants to pay in cash, which means he'll have to interact with the attendant, who, at this very late hour, is half dozing in a booth inside the station kiosk.

He approaches the kiosk. The attendant's booth, he notes, is highly secure, the kind you only find in crime-ridden areas, where employees are hidden behind thick, scratched-up Plexiglas. The booth has one of those security compartments, a pass-through hopper on a swivel that the attendant has to open out to you so you can place your money or credit card inside; then he swivels the compartment back open toward him so that you two never have to interact.

What is this world coming to, the man thinks as he approaches the booth, where this kind of thing is necessary? People just don't trust each other anymore. And it gets worse the closer you get to the coast. Cities burning. Lawless looting. Hell in a handbasket, he thinks.

He taps on the Plexiglas and startles the attendant, who looks up with hooded eyes.

"I want to pay cash," he says, and holds up a fat wad of bills as proof.

The attendant nods, and looks to flip some switch or other to activate the pump remotely, but he seems to be thwarted because finally he hoists himself with a sigh from the stool with the duct-taped padding and says loudly, "I'll have to come out."

The man walks back to his truck. The attendant follows, in no rush. The attendant, he notes, is a young guy of some foreign origin, Middle Eastern or Indian or something, and he thinks again of how, as he makes his journey eastward, the farther he gets from where he's coming from and the closer he gets to where he's going, the more different kinds of people he can expect to encounter, an aspect of his travels that does not fill him with delight.

Even so. A necessary journey. With an indisputable reward.

The attendant pulls a swipe card that's attached to a tether clipped to his belt and swipes it on the pump, then punches in some kind of code, then says, "I got you. What do you want?" and unholsters the pump nozzle.

"Fill it up, regular." He stows the wad of cash back in one of the many pockets in his tactical black pants. He leans against the front of the truck and crosses his arms and watches the road, where at this lonely hour no cars pass.

He wonders again, as he has many times on this solitary drive, what would have happened if he hadn't seen it.

He was keeping his eyes open, of course. But still.

He doesn't even watch that show. Stupid cop-and-lawyer soap opera. But he was scrolling online, searching cast lists, fan forums, publicity stills. And then—

He could hardly believe it.

He can hardly believe it now.

The attendant holds the trigger of the nozzle steady as the pump dings to mark the gallons. The attendant catches his own reflection in the truck's tinted glass, then glances through the dark window into the back of the SUV, where he sees what's recognizable to him as a long-gun case and, next to that, a smaller gun case that holds several handguns, and next to that a large black duffel bag. None of which, at least on their own, are particularly rare or noteworthy in these parts.

"You going hunting?" the attendant asks, to be friendly.

The man looks over. "I am."

"I do some hunting myself. Where you headed? Allegheny?"

"New York State."

"All the way there? Gun laws are tight as a tick in New York and the deer are no different from here."

"I'm meeting up with an old friend," he says.

"Hell of a long drive for a deer hunt," says the attendant, then adds, "I noticed your Wisconsin plates."

When the man says nothing in return, the attendant looks again into the back of the SUV and thinks about what he doesn't see in there, which are grocery bags bursting with provisions or coolers of food and beer or rolled-up foul-weather fluorescent gear and muddy rain boots or any of the other things you might expect to pack for a long hunting trip that necessitates a drive across five states. Maybe he'll go shopping when he meets his friend, the attendant tells himself—then the nozzle trigger jumps under his fingers, the tank full. The attendant reads from the pump aloud. "That'll be $42.66."

The man nods back toward the kiosk. "Let me pay at the register. I'm going to need some change and I can save you the walk back."

"No problem," the attendant says, slightly relieved to be retreating to the safety of his station. The attendant reenters his booth, secures the door, and, once seated, flips the pass-through hopper open toward the man, who now stands just outside the kiosk; the compartment gapes up at the man like the open mouth of a hungry fish.

The man reaches a fingerless-gloved hand into the pocket of his black down vest—not, the attendant notes, the same pocket in his pants where he conspicuously stowed the wad of cash.

As the attendant contemplates this turn of events, the man pulls from his vest a small, round hand grenade, about the size of an apple, pulls the pin with his middle finger, and drops the grenade with a heavy thunk into the pass-through compartment, then jams the compartment hard with his elbow so that it slams open on the other side, the attendant's side. From outside the booth, the man hears the attendant's muffled frightened shrieks even through the thick Plexiglas, and he takes his finger in the fingerless glove, with the ring of the pulled grenade pin still dangling, and slams his raised middle finger against the window and says, "Keep the change," then laughs and walks away.

He still hears the attendant's muted shouts of panic as he heads back to the SUV, climbs in, and starts up the refueled engine. The grenade is a dummy, a fake, the kind you can buy online at any army surplus store—he bought a case of them for fun while he was searching online for other, more practical items. It won't go off, but by the time the attendant figures that out, his SUV will be long gone, and if the attendant tries to note his license plate, only then will the attendant notice the strategically disconnected license plate lights or the fact that the numbers have been subtly but unmistakably altered or obscured with small tabs of black electrical tape.

He pulls the SUV quickly onto the empty highway.

Half his journey behind him, half still ahead.

The Fifth Day

||||

EVERY LIVING CREATURE
IN THE OCEANS AND THE AIR

33

She sits alone on the porch in her flannel nightgown, clutching a coffee against the early-morning chill, and watches the new day unfold.

Herons skim the surface of the lake. Chipmunks dart and vanish in the underbrush.

Daisy blows across her coffee to cool it and thinks of just how bestial they've both become.

Two years into marriage, three years into being a couple, they're just two creatures now, sharing a pen. He snores, farts, snuffles in his sleep, emitting animal noises and animal smells. He's got wild hairs unfurling from his nose, his ears, his eyebrows. The scent of his sneakers left by the door, after a jog in the rain, their tongues pulled down like two panting dogs, fills the apartment with a fetid tang. She fights it off with baking soda, scented candles, essential oil diffusers, unsuccessfully. Pry open the windows and the city leaks in, with its own inescapable feral smells. It's a hothouse they live in. A petting zoo of two.

It's not just him, she knows that. It's her, too. It's the clogs of hair she pulls from the shower drain, like some tiny, twisted sea creature, a baby kraken hanging limp and damp from her fingertips. Not to mention all her own stray hairs in surprising places, her collection of razors, tweezers, and creams, to burn and blanch and bleach her body, like scorched-earth warfare waged daily on herself.

Like animals, they live together. They curl together in their lair. No longer ashamed of their noises, their scents, their growths, their selves.

They're like the first two humans, she thinks, like Adam and Eve discovering their bodies in the garden.

Imagine what that was like, she thinks.

The first and only humans on the planet.

Left alone to roam, to live in Paradise, under a watchful eye. The two of them, in love, without even having a word yet to describe it. Without the knowledge of the difference between good and evil.

Not yet. Not unless they chose to defy God and discover it.

She thinks of the moment she fell for him, the real moment. It was on their third date, and they were walking together in late autumn in New York. Leaves crackling underfoot, hand in hand like young lovers, strolling in the West Village, both in thick scarves, looking like an LP album cover. He'd talked to her often about his ambitions, about the great novel he would one day write. He described what the cover would look like, the epigraph he'd already chosen, the influences he'd cite in his interviews, how he had the guest list for the launch party already started. At the time they barely knew each other, so she couldn't yet tell if he actually had it in him to write anything, but she liked that he had dreams and optimism about the future, two things she'd given up long ago.

As they walked, they came upon a bookstore. One of those picture-perfect shops you find tucked away in certain cities on certain streets. The light was perfect, the air trembling with possibility. And there, in the window display, piled high, were all the latest bestsellers, their covers practically glowing, the window like a warehouse of fulfilled dreams.

They halted, hand in hand. They could see themselves reflected in the shop window.

We look just like a real couple, she remembers thinking.

Happy.

What would that feel like? she thought.

Then he turned to her after a long moment and said with great put-on bravado: "One day."

But she saw it then, clearly in his face: the doubt.

The doubt that he would ever accomplish anything. The doubt that he would ever be worthy of anything at all. Let alone her.

Imagine that.

Someone who wanted to be worthy of her. Who believed that she was someone who was worth being worthy of.

And that was it. She couldn't help it.

She fell.

She suddenly, involuntarily, standing there on the leaf-strewn street, let herself believe that the two of them together might actually have a chance at something.

She hadn't let herself believe in that for a very long time. And she'd thought she'd never believe in it again.

She looked back at the window, at their ghostly doppelgängers in the reflection, the couple haunted by the prospect of happiness.

Right then and there, for all his obvious flaws and undeniable drawbacks, his complications and dealbreakers, she decided to believe in him. To believe in them.

She hadn't let herself do that in a long time, either.

Believe the best about anyone.

She couldn't.

She thought that part of herself was broken or buried.

But maybe.

Maybe, she thought, standing on that street corner.

One word. But it was life-changing. It was alien to her. It was everything.

Was this feeling hope? No, because she didn't allow herself hope.

But *maybe* was the next best thing.

Maybe, she thought then, watching him, watching them, their reflections in the shop glass, hand in hand.

Maybe, she thinks now, cupping her mug and gazing out over the tranquil view from the cabin's porch.

It's time, she thinks. To tell him. All the things she's never told him before.

Never told anyone. Not in school. Not in New York.

It's time to tell him what happened to the woman she was before she became Daisy.

||||

He finds her on the porch. He's still achy from all that happened last night, their post-confession reconciliation. Still sore. Still smiling, too.

"Morning," he says.

"Morning."

"What should we do today?"

"Sit down," she says.

He sits.

"I haven't been totally honest with you. About what happened before we met," she says.

"Okay."

"This was before New York. That guy I told you about, the one who followed me to grad school."

"Okay."

"I want to tell you what happened. I want to tell you everything."

He leans forward. Girding himself, perhaps, for some confession of a whirlwind romance, a sordid affair. "You can tell me."

And then, for the first time, she does.

34

She was in high school. She did theater. She had a boyfriend. He worked on stage crew.

In all her years with Craig, she's never talked about any of this.

All he knows, all he's cared to know, is that she grew up in Wisconsin, in a suburb of Milwaukee. Fox Point, Bay Point, Cedar Point, something like that, some Point somewhere. Nice parents, big house, cul-de-sac, both parents gone now, he's never met them. When she tells her life story, it usually starts at the moment she arrives at the big fancy East Coast graduate school for theater. It's a dramatic moment, full of portent, fresh-faced girl, bags in hand, poised in a doorway, so it seems like a natural beginning. She was twenty-one. Everything else was prologue. Childhood. High school. Normal stuff. She'd gone to the University of Wisconsin as an undergrad in Madison, then dropped out, he knows that much.

At their wedding, she'd had her New York theater friends there and all the friends they'd made together, of course, but no childhood friends, no college friends, no grad school friends, and no family. She told him she hadn't kept in touch with many school friends, and as for family, she said they didn't get along; her parents were religious, judgmental, and she and they had drifted apart long ago. He noticed but didn't think much of it.

After all, he was happy. They were happy.

This was the extent of what he knew about her life.

On the fifth day, on the porch, she tells him the rest.

She had a boyfriend. Call him a high school sweetheart. They met on a school show in high school when both of them were seniors. *The Crucible.* She played Goody Proctor. The good wife. He was in charge of lights, sound, tech. Most of the students on stage crew were straight weirdos, the kind of kids who wear Columbine trench coats and ride unicycles and learn to do yo-yo tricks. He was different. Tall, lean, muscular. Looked five years older than seventeen. Looked older than everyone else at school. Had a shaved head and a goatee. Cheekbones like razor blades. Dark eyes. Long lashes. When in rehearsal she said something that made everyone laugh, he never laughed. Maybe smiled a little, then went back to adjusting a light. And she could make anyone laugh. That was her thing. She was the life of every party. So when she finally said something that made him chuckle despite himself, she noticed that. It stuck with her. It felt *earned.*

She wanted to feel that feeling again.

In rehearsals for a school show, everyone stays late, always. It's mostly seniors, upperclassmen, so nobody's parents really care. You end up staying until eleven, midnight, sometimes later, smoking up after rehearsal in the schoolyard; then the few people in the cast with their own cars drive everyone else home. He had his own car. A beater. Not like the kids whose parents bought them Audi convertibles when they turned sixteen. He'd bought his own car with his own money and fixed it up himself. He drove her home, often. And he always dropped her off last.

She noticed that, too.

The first time he dropped her off, when it was just her and him, she expected him to make a move as they sat in the dark at the foot of her parents' circular driveway. He didn't. He seemed—uncrackable. Gentlemanly. Chivalrous, even. She was disappointed.

He became a project for her.

When they did finally fuck for the first time in the backseat of that car in the darkest corner of the high school parking lot at 2:30 in the morning after a particularly stressful tech rehearsal, with her keeping one eye open just in case the night janitor happened by, him on top of her, serious, working hard, their pants tangled, she felt good; she felt like she'd unlocked an accomplishment in a video game.

It was good. He was good. It was not hard, in her experience, to convince high school boys to fuck you. But he wasn't like a high school boy. Which made him feel like a prize.

There were rumors about him. That he was older than everyone, lying about his age, already twenty, maybe twenty-two, that he'd been to community college already, dropped out, reenrolled in high school for extra credits. That rumor, she learned, wasn't true. But he did live alone, like everyone whispered, in his own small apartment over a consignment store for children's clothes. His apartment as neat as a pin. Everything just so. It took a month of hookups in that car with him before he invited her back to his apartment and four more months of dating until he opened up and told her about his parents, what had happened. Both dead in a car crash. He was ten. Left him some money. No siblings.

An only child. Same with her. She could relate.

He had some family, an uncle and aunt who took him in and raised him until he was sixteen, but they didn't get along, not with each other and not with him, so he moved out, he still had that money in a trust, and his aunt was a bitch and his uncle was a prick, so he said.

Besides, he preferred to be on his own.

Loner type.

Sexy. Mysterious.

They became a thing.

She loved how it felt to show up to places with him. Like an alternate prom king and queen. Theater royalty. It made her downright giddy. She knew people talked about what an unlikely couple they were, her so garrulous, funny, him so quiet and withdrawn, and she liked that, too. She liked to be surprising. She liked to be unlikely. To let people know they hadn't quite figured her out, this loudmouth theater kid.

She liked the notion of her onstage, under the lights, soaking up the applause, and him up in the rafters, on the catwalk, in the darkness, aiming the follow spot on her, always making sure she was well lit. Stay "on zero," he'd tell her, the technical lighting term for center stage. He felt supportive, in all the right ways, and she knew all his secrets, too, or so she thought, how he was wounded under that hard shell, and she felt protective of him.

She felt more than wanted by him by now. She felt *needed*.

He didn't drink or do drugs, he was straight-edge, which made cast parties tough. She'd always have one too many, gather a crowd; she just liked the sound of laughter all around her, encircling her. She should be a stand-up comedian, everyone told her that. Meanwhile he sat in the corner and nursed a seltzer, checking his phone. His dark face lit by that little light. On the drive home, he'd rant about actors, and how self-centered they all were, and how much attention they needed, and how without the tech crew they'd be nothing but a bunch of assholes spouting nonsense in the dark, and she'd sit in the passenger seat and listen and look out the window and wonder if he remembered that she was an actor, too.

She got into college. Madison. Theater. He didn't. But they stayed together. He moved to Madison with her.

It seemed romantic.

Her parents told her to live on campus in a dorm, but instead she got an apartment with him. On a commercial street, over a store, just like his place back home, and he set it up to look identical to the one he'd left behind. Every poster in the same place on the walls—he measured it out exactly with his tape measure and a pencil. Every book in the same order on the bookshelves. Her stuff went into closets. She wanted to hang posters, too, of the high school shows she'd done, but he wouldn't allow it. He let her tack those posters up in the bathroom with masking tape. And only shows they'd worked on together.

He was jealous. His moods would change in an instant. The feeling of

She had the lead role, always. She was the best actor in the school. Everyone knew it. Everyone said it.

She was the star.

Then the curtains closed, the applause trailed off, and she went home.

Cracked the door.

Soft steps.

Lights on.

Quiet hello.

Black ink.

Every time.

She was thinking of leaving him.

Knew she had to.

Of course she would.

Planning to.

Then she got pregnant.

An accident.

Surprise.

35

"You had an abortion?" says Craig quietly, on the porch, his first interjection.

The morning is in full flush now. Birds serenading the sun. Both their coffee mugs long since drained.

"No," she says quietly. "I didn't."

36

She'd been thinking of leaving him, knew she had to, had been planning on doing it for months, and then she missed her period. She sat in the bathroom alone and stared at the stick. She tried to ignore it for weeks, told herself she got a faulty test, kept putting off buying another one, but she knew. She knew.

Then she took another test with her best friend, Ada, in the theater dressing room one night right before a show. In costume, twenty minutes to curtain, hiking up her crinolines. She lied to Ada and said it was the first test she'd taken.

Acted surprised at the result.

Convincing.

She was the best actor in the school, after all.

"I'll go with you," Ada said, and held her hand while she cried. "To get one."

"He'll never let me go," she said.

Knock at the dressing room door.

"Five minutes, please," the stage manager called out.

"Thank you, five," Ada said.

The stage manager moved on.

"We won't tell him," Ada whispered. "Of course we won't."

She nodded and, five minutes later, she was someone else.

For a couple of hours, at least.

Maybe we will have a baby together and it will be better, she thought.

She'd only just turned nineteen.

She didn't want to have a baby, she wanted to be an actor, but maybe a baby would make her a better actor, she told herself. Open her up to a broader spectrum of human experience.

This was all just a distraction, she realized later, from making the choice she didn't want to make, which was telling him or not telling him. Which itself was a distraction from the other choice she couldn't make, was unable to make, which was leaving him or not leaving him.

She loved him.

She thought she loved him.

She felt a connection to him.

He was wounded.

He'd lost his family so early. He had no one.

Just her.

If she left, it would destroy him.

That's what she told herself.

He'd threatened suicide and everything else when she'd even hinted at moving out. One time she said maybe they needed a break and he swore he'd burn the apartment to the ground.

Wounded.

And he needs me.

She told herself that, too.

So she decided to tell him.

She shouldn't have done that. She knew the minute she did it.

The words still hanging in the air.

His face blank.

But once it was done, it was done.

No way to untell him.

She thought it would make him happy. She thought that he would change. For some reason she still thought that.

He looked at her, silent.

No ink.

No anger.

Just a question.

"How do you know that it's mine?"

It got bad after that.

She couldn't get an abortion now, she knew that, too, he would kill her.

So as the baby grew inside her for weeks, she considered her means of escape. She imagined a million scenarios, each one like a small, one-act play. She even gave them titles. *I Tell My Parents.*

She imagined how it would go.

Lights up. Onstage we see: an elderly couple in a comfortable suburban home. The father is reading a newspaper. The mother reads a Daily Devotional booklet.

Enter Daisy.

Except her name wasn't Daisy back then.

Not yet.

Enter Daisy.

Daisy: Mom, Dad, I have something to tell you.

But the play just had blank pages after that.

She loved her parents, but they did not approve of him and they did not approve of her choices and they did not approve of them living together and she'd honestly never had the kind of relationship with them where she could show up one day and say, *Mom, Dad, I'm pregnant and my boyfriend hits me and I'm scared and I need help.*

She knew what that would get her. A door closed in her face.

So: play number two.

A double bill. This one a thriller.

The Getaway.

Lights up on: Daisy, packing a bag. She leaves a note and sneaks out an open window.

She is on her way to—where?

Milwaukee?

New York?

To do—what?

Waitress? With a baby?

It's hard to explain now, she says to Craig, how easy it is to convince yourself, how badly you want to believe, against all evidence, that one day everything will change. To believe that you're just one conversation, one breakthrough, one moment of clarity away from escaping the pattern that traps you. To believe that even though one of you is, yes, hitting and the other is, yes, being hit, that you're both still in this together somehow, drowning, clinging to each other, and the most important thing is that you don't let go, that somehow together you will survive. And, okay, maybe today was horrible and, yes, yesterday was definitely shit, and the yesterday before that, and the one before that, but tomorrow—

Tomorrow will be different.

We'll be different.

It was so easy to believe that.

After all, it's what he promised every single time.

And while she was plotting and planning and stalling and rehearsing, the baby was growing and he was becoming angrier. Sullen and angry and withdrawn. Convinced that this baby was proof of what he'd suspected all along. She'd been cheating. This was what he accused her of every time. She'd been fucking every golden-boy actor in the wings, all the leads, the supporting actors, too, the extras, the spear carriers, during dress, during tech, in the changerooms, in the bathrooms, in the lighting booth, in the wings while waiting for her cue, skirt hiked, legs up, getting fucked, that's what he said, on her knees, sucking cock, all those late nights, all those fucking pretty actors with their orthodontically perfected smiles, pants around their ankles, the understudies, too, probably lining up to get their go at her when the leads were done, probably taking photos of the whole thing on their phones, probably sharing them online. He knew actors. He knew fucking *actors*. He'd watched them for years from the booth. Barely able to stop himself from slamming all the switches on the lighting board down with an open hand and plunging the stage into darkness. Or turning all the stage mikes way up and swallowing their reedy voices in squealing feedback. These happy-faced fucking *actors* learning lines and *pretending* and having cast parties and getting shit-faced while he watched with a seltzer in the corner. Watching them flirting with his girlfriend. Thinking about fucking her. And her in the center of it, the circle, laughing, loving it, and then fucking them and them fucking each other and them fucking his girlfriend and getting his girlfriend pregnant.

Getting his fucking girlfriend pregnant.

What a joke.

What a joke on him.

To have to raise their fucking kid.

To see it in that kid's face every day. That he'd been fucking cuckolded like that.

He spent a lot of time online.

He spent way too much time online.

She always told him that.

She was at class all day. He worked. The rest of the time, he sat at the computer.

You need more friends, she always said. But what did she think he was doing online?

Maybe he spent too much time in forums, on message boards, maybe she was right, but as a result he knew the way the world works. He knew how the happy-faced people of the world work, how they will just laugh at you, just laugh with each other while you watch, just rig the game with their complaints about this injustice and that injustice when what do they know about injustice, what do they know about disadvantage, what do they know about loss, what do they know about being alone, these fucking people, smiling.

And he was online that night in the pale sickly throb of the screen when she came in the door.

Late from rehearsal again and it was nothing but black ink that greeted her.

He'd hit her before but never like this.

He hit her and he hit her and she stumbled to the ground and from behind he hooked his arm around her neck in a choke hold and choked her out.

Blackness.

The next thing she remembers is waking up on the floor and coughing and him curled over her, crying, on his knees, begging forgiveness.

She went back to class.

Back to normal.

Voice hoarse for a few days. Laryngitis, she said.

Later that week, during a late-morning rehearsal, she doubled over with crippling cramps.

Couldn't stand. Classmates steadied her.

Some friends convinced her to let them take her to the emergency room.

Nobody said anything about him, but they all knew enough not to call him to let him know where she was going.

She watches the lake from the porch, dry-eyed, with Craig at her side listening.

"I lost the baby," she says finally.

She remembers it.

She allows herself to remember it.

It's always there, always. She just doesn't always allow herself to acknowledge that it's there.

But now she does.

Goddamn her fucking baby died her fucking baby died.

||||

On a gurney at the hospital, while she waited for the doctor to return, a woman came to visit her.

The woman pulled aside the curtain that hung in a semicircle around the gurney for privacy and sat down in a chair beside her.

The woman introduced herself and explained why she was there.

The loss of oxygen from strangulation, the woman said, can cause a miscarriage.

Which seems to be what had happened here.

The difficulty with strangulation, the woman said, is that much of the time the act itself leaves very little physical evidence. Especially days later.

Which can make it very hard to prosecute.

As the woman spoke, she listened and lay in the bed and stared at a stained tile in the ceiling of the hospital.

Strangulation, the woman said, is often the last escalation before homicide. A woman who is choked by an intimate partner is seven times more likely to be killed. The woman listed off the known escalations: slap, punch, kick, attack with a weapon, then strangulation.

"And after that?" she asked the woman from the bed.

"There is no after that," the woman said. "After that, he kills you. That's why I'm here."

She lay in the hospital bed and looked at the stained tile ceiling and thought of the baby that was no longer inside her. She remembers how the noises of the hospital sounded so loud, the beeps, the wheels of the passing gurneys, the nurses' voices beyond the curtain, barking with urgency.

She asked the woman about the police.

The woman explained that they could certainly file criminal charges. They could absolutely do that. What would follow, the woman said, is that it would play out over weeks and months, over which time she'd be answering questions and, assuming her abuser denied her account, which abusers typically did, she'd be spending that time trying to prove that what had happened to her had actually happened to her.

Weeks and months.

The woman held her hand as she lay in the bed and took this all in.

The woman assured her she wasn't alone. The woman explained to her the options and then communicated the urgency.

Then the woman asked her if she already kept a bag packed, just in case.

She went home. He was there.

She told him rehearsal went late.

The woman waited in a car outside, parked just down the street.

He cried and begged forgiveness again and she held him and said she forgave him.

Then she told him she had to get back to the theater. That she'd just popped in to grab something she'd forgotten. They were running a tech rehearsal that night. Could be a late one, she said.

Packed what few things she cared about quickly.

As for the rehearsal, she never showed and no one ever heard from her again.

She spent that night at a shelter run by the woman.

By that same time the next day, she was in Boston.

She spent a week at a new shelter, arranged by the woman, and eventually the women at that shelter helped her find an apartment.

She told no one where she was. Not her parents. Not Ada. Not him, of course. No one.

She was nineteen.

She had a little money saved.

She'd left everything of hers behind, save for the small bag she packed, at the apartment. All her clothes, all her plays, all the posters of the shows she'd done tacked up with masking tape in the bathroom.

She called her parents from a blocked number at the shelter in Boston to tell them she was okay, then hung up.

She and the woman chose Boston together because she didn't know a single soul in Boston. No reason for her to go there. So no way to find her there.

She spent weeks alone in her room at the shelter.

She didn't want to face anyone.

Not her parents. Not her teachers. Not her friends.

Not anyone.

Because she felt ashamed.

She couldn't say why. She knew she shouldn't. But she did.

She felt ashamed. Of what she'd allowed to happen.

She knew she shouldn't feel that way. But that's how she thought about it then.

"That's why I thought I couldn't have a baby," she says to Craig. "Nothing genetic. Just—the doctors, that's what they told me after. The injuries were bad. I'm sorry I lied about it. I just couldn't get into it."

"It's okay," he says. "Of course. I'm so sorry that happened."

"It just never seemed possible," she says.

She waitressed for a while in Boston and got an apartment with a pleasant-enough roommate who didn't pry. The women at the shelter checked in on her regularly. She attended group meetings for support.

Eventually, almost a year later, at the urging of one of her counselors, she got in touch with a teacher who she trusted back at school in Madison. Even then, out of habit, she called from a restaurant, and not the one she worked at.

Her teacher, she knew, had a colleague at a prestigious graduate school on the East Coast, an old friend, and the teacher was happy to hear from her, and happy to hear she was okay (she told the teacher she was okay), and happy to hear she wanted to continue acting, she had always been so good, so very good, and the teacher agreed to recommend her to the graduate school and help explain the special circumstances.

She traveled alone on the train to the town where the school was and did an audition in person. Afterward, she met with an admissions officer.

They admitted her under an assumed name on a need-based scholarship.

Just like that.

A new life.

It hardly seemed possible.

It's not that she had some aching desire to resume acting, she thought on the train ride back to Boston after the audition.

To be honest, she didn't have an aching desire to do anything back then.

She just couldn't be herself anymore.

And she only knew of one place in the world where she could reliably escape herself.

One night, a few weeks before she was scheduled to leave for grad school, she came in to work at the restaurant. Her coworker told her someone had called for her repeatedly, leaving messages.

Claiming she had a different name.

Said she'd understand.

She stared at her coworker for a second, then explained it was a silly private joke, and then she thanked her coworker for relaying the message and asked the coworker to cover for her for ten minutes while she ran a quick errand. Then she went home, grabbed her prepacked bag, left the next month's rent in an envelope on the kitchen table for her roommate, took a taxi to the train station, and got on a train.

She spent the next few weeks in seclusion at a hostel in the grad school town, waiting for the semester, and another new life, to begin.

Started calling herself Nora.

Managed to make it through three years of graduate school.

Hiding. Acting.

Disappearing into roles.

She was the best in the class, everyone said so.

Then she got a bouquet of flowers in the dressing room on showcase night and she ran again, and the next morning she woke up in New York and she was Daisy.

They sit and watch the lake.

She hasn't spoken to or seen him since, she tells Craig.

She does have a restraining order against him, filed in a court somewhere.

Apparently, after she first left Madison, he harassed her parents so much that they got a restraining order, too.

Apparently, he also cornered Ada one night, late, after a rehearsal, outside the theater in Madison, not long after she'd disappeared. Luckily, two other actors, two guys, a couple, gym-buff, happened by at the same time and asked if she was okay and walked her home.

She assumes he still lives in Wisconsin. As far as she knows.

He's forbidden by law from ever contacting her, of course.

Hasn't stopped him from tracking her down. Twice.

On the first day after she left him in college, her phone filled up with his texts, apologies, pleadings, confessions, self-flagellations, suicide threats.

Tactics.

She bricked that phone and got a new one in Boston.

How he found her in Boston, she doesn't know.

And then the showcase. That time, she knew she had slipped. Allowed a photo of herself to show up online. But she thought it would be okay. It had been three years, after all. The whole class had their photos online. She wanted to be part of the class.

Then New York. And since New York—nothing, she says.

Not a word.

Eight years.

She doesn't think about him anymore, not really, or at least that's what she tells Craig.

Only when she's onstage, to this day, she still imagines he's up there in the booth, or on the catwalk, watching, ready to turn off the lights at any moment and plunge her into darkness again.

In the weeks after she arrived in Boston, she says, she thought about getting a tattoo. She wanted so badly to get a tattoo. She wanted so badly to get something to memorialize the baby she'd lost. But she didn't. Because people ask questions about tattoos. Tattoos are conversation starters. No matter how oblique or obscure the reference someone will eventually ask, *So what's the story?*

Her story.

She couldn't handle that question.

She thought about getting it somewhere hidden on her body, some protected place, but she knew that if you bury the tattoo on your body where no one would normally see it, that just means that someone will glimpse it eventually, in an intimate moment, and by virtue of being in that moment of intimacy that person will feel emboldened to ask about it.

Especially then.

It's like a booby trap you set for yourself. To sabotage you when you're at your most vulnerable.

So you can't show your tattoo. And you can't hide your tattoo.

And you can't put a tattoo on the inside.

That's where the scars are.

So she sat in that chair in the tattoo parlor in Boston with the tattoo artist's needle buzzing just above her skin.

Just above.

Close enough to feel it but not close enough to leave a mark.

She'd even had him draw it out for her on a piece of paper, a sketch, the tattoo she would have gotten, of the name she'd had in mind for the baby she never had.

And, yes, she had to assure the tattoo artist three times that, yes, this was what she wanted, just hold it above her skin but leave no mark.

Hold steady.

And of course he thought it was fucked up, but hey, it's her sixty bucks.

And it was hard to hold his hand steady like that, but he did.

He held steady.

And she cried and cried and cried and cried, and then she got up and paid him and left.

She tells Craig all this without getting emotional.

Her voice never wavers.

She lays it out calmly. Dry-eyed.

After all, this all happened to someone else.

Not Daisy.

She shows Craig where the tattoo would have gone.

The one in Boston.

Right over her heart.

She pulls the collar of her nightgown aside.

Taps the skin with her finger. Drums her breastbone. Bare skin.

Unblemished.

"Right here," she says.

37

He's not sure what to say. He holds her.
Birds trouble the lake. The woods whisper.
The morning passes.
They sit like that together for a while.

38

When she breaks from his embrace, she hands him an envelope. It has
_Q5_ embossed on the front.

"I found this on the porch this morning," she says.

"Should we read it?"

"I read it already. I'm sorry. I know it's still morning, but technically
it's the fifth day, so I peeked. I couldn't wait. Take a look."

He pulls the sheet of paper out. Unfolds it and reads it aloud for both
of them to hear.

39

Question Five.

Would you die for me?

Would you lay down your life for your partner?
  Would you jump in front of a bullet?
  Would you run into a burning building to pull your loved one out?
  You'll probably say "Yes, of course," solely as a matter of reflex. And maybe you would. But these are instantaneous decisions. Automatic. Instinct.
  But what if your spouse was kidnapped? Would you trade your life for theirs?
  What if your partner was on the other side of a chasm, beckoning you to jump, and you did not believe you'd survive?
  Would you jump?

What quality of love do you aspire to? Is it the disposable love promised to us by this world of hookups and dating apps, in which partners are taken, then discarded at the first difficulty like ill-fitting shoes or out-of-season outfits? Where you pledge till-death-do-us-part loyalty at the wedding altar and then years later move on and split your belongings and unfollow each other on social media and decide to be cordial and send each other holiday cards once a year?

Look at Adam and Eve, the very first love story. Traditionally, the story goes like this: Adam and Eve lived together in Paradise. Tempted by a serpent,

Eve disobeyed God. She ate of an apple from the Tree of the Knowledge of Good and Evil, then convinced Adam to do the same. Both of them were punished by being cast out of Paradise. They forever lost their claim to eternal life.

That's one way of reading the story.

But there's another way, too.

What if Adam did not eat the apple? What if he had resisted temptation and rebuked Eve's offer? What if only she *was cast out of Paradise and he was left to live forever in Eden, righteous, unspoiled—and alone?*

Would that have been a happier ending?

Adam chose to eat the apple, which means he chose to die for Eve. That's the simple truth. He chose to die with her in an imperfect world rather than live forever in Paradise without her.

Why? Because he loved her. Because she was a part of him.

They didn't choose wickedness.

They chose each other.

Now that's *a love story. That's a happy ending.*

Isn't that the kind of love you want?

No one's suggesting you have to die for love.

Of course not.

Just be honest with yourself. And with your partner.

And know whether or not you're willing to.

40

He folds the sheet of paper carefully and replaces it in the envelope. He turns to her.

"I would," he says.

She smiles. She kisses him. She doesn't answer. He doesn't press.

"Let's stay in today," he says instead. "Just you and me. We've only got two more days up here."

"And then what?"

"Then we go home and we have ourselves a baby."

"Are we ready?" she says.

"Honestly? I don't know." He rubs her arms, reassuring. "But whatever happens, we'll do it together."

"I'm sorry I kept all this from you for so long."

"Maybe I didn't deserve to hear it."

"I felt like it was mine," she says. "Mine alone to carry. I didn't want to burden you. I just know that with this baby I can't have secrets anymore."

"You're going to be okay. We'll be okay." He believes it. They will be. They say nothing more. They watch the lake.

Then he says, hoping to cheer her, "I'm hungry. Are you hungry? You must be starving. You should eat. You're having a baby!"

"We're having a baby," she says. Finally she's crying. But laughing, too. Pent-up sobs.

"It's going to be good, I promise." He kisses her on the forehead. He's being kind. He likes this feeling. He could get used to it. The feeling of being—what's the word?

Loving.

||||

"Are you sure we don't have anything?" He's flummoxed now, thwarted, his head bent into the open refrigerator.

"We had Frosted Flakes for dinner last night," she says, leaning in the kitchen doorway. "That should tell you where we are on supplies."

He closes the fridge. "No worries. Let's go into town and get groceries. We could visit that bookstore I saw earlier. Maybe go for a hike this afternoon."

"You go. I have things I want to finish up here."

"Are you sure?" He steps toward her and puts his hands on her shoulders. "I don't want to leave you alone."

"I'll be fine," she says. "I have my stones to paint. And I'd enjoy a few quiet hours to clear my head."

He gets dressed, and when he comes back downstairs, she's changed into her overalls and she's sitting outside on the porch. She's got a paint-splattered newspaper spread out before her and she sits in the sunshine, painting her rocks, a smudge of color smeared across her cheek. There are at least two dozen of these painted rocks by now, scattered in every corner of the porch.

When she notices him, she stands and hoists the stone in her hand. "*Alas, poor Yorick! I knew him, Horatio,*" she intones, a *Hamlet* joke. Then she says, "It's a beautiful day. When you get back, you should sit out here and whittle with me."

She unsnaps the pocket on the front of her overalls and pulls out the pocketknife she gave him and deftly opens the blade with one thumb, her impressive trick. She brandishes the blade in a grand theatrical flourish like a saber, channeling Mercutio. "*Men's eyes were made to look, and let them gaze! I will not budge for no man's pleasure, I.*"

She holds the knife out to him. He takes it. "What am I supposed to do with it?" he says.

She grabs a stray branch from the porch and snaps the twigs off.

"Whittle me a marshmallow-roasting stick," she says. "That seems like a good first project."

He sits down in a chair with the knife in one hand and the branch in the other. He looks at them both like he's never seen either object before in his life. He places the knife's blade on the stick and pushes it away from himself slowly. The blade's sharp. A fine layer of bark curls easily. The fresh wood is green underneath. He has to admit, the motion is pleasing. "What kind of stuff did your grandfather like to whittle?"

"Small wooden boats. Little ducks. He could even whittle a whistle."

Craig looks up. "Whittle a whistle? Weally?"

"Weally!" she says, and laughs. "A widdle working whistle, for weal."

He laughs, too, and in that moment the blade hops free from the branch and clips his thumb pad. "Fuck!" he exclaims, and shakes his thumb, like putting out a struck match. A fat drop of bright blood appears.

She holds out an open palm. "Let me have a look."

He rests his hand in hers. She inspects his thumb, then places the end of it in her mouth and sucks on it lightly. It's a strangely comforting gesture, he thinks.

She pulls his thumb out. Inspects it again. "*'Tis not so deep as a well, nor so wide as a church door, but 'tis enough, 'twill serve.*" She smiles and kisses him better. "*Ask for me tomorrow, and you shall find me a grave man.*"

"Hamlet again?" he asks.

"That's Mercutio, from *Romeo and Juliet*. His death scene."

"Well, Mercutio, I need a Band-Aid."

"You'll have to get some when you go into town."

"I won't be long. What should we do when I get back?"

"Anything we want, Romeo," she says, popping her eyebrows with mock lasciviousness.

"Wait—but doesn't Romeo die at the end of the play?"

"They both die," she says. "Yet it's the greatest love story ever told."

His thumb now wrapped dramatically in a knotted white cloth napkin stained red, he blows her one last kiss out the open window of the car, the knotted red bandage making it look like he's holding out a rose. Then he steers up the gravel driveway and out to the road toward town.

She stands and watches him go. She tastes the faint residue of his blood in her mouth. She blows a kiss back to him and waves goodbye.

When he's out of sight, she reaches into her overalls and pulls out her secret phone.

41

In town, his thumb now swaddled in a proper Band-Aid, Craig carries a paper bag from the grocery store full of provisions in his arms
toward his car, parked on an otherwise empty street. The village has
never been bustling exactly, but today, midweek, with all the weekend
visitors gone, it's like a ghost town, with half the stores shuttered and
CLOSED signs dangling askew in their windows. The grocery store was
open, thankfully, but the already sparse shelves had been emptied to
their final offerings. He managed to find everything Daisy had asked
for: eggs, butter, milk, coffee, even the last, lonely pint of chocolate ice
cream, and a roast chicken for good measure, something for them to
feast on together tonight.

As he approaches the car, toting the bag, he fumbles with his free
hand in his pocket for the keys. He props the bag on one knee and
pops the trunk and remembers it's already full with the twin packed
suitcases.

So stupid, he thinks, staring at the suitcases. The notion that he
would have done that.

Left her.

But that was Cabo Craig. Not this Craig.

Not Better Craig.

He wedges the grocery bag in between the luggage and slams the
trunk shut.

Brooklyn, in fact, feels like a different world to him now, like they
haven't been back in years. Dodging his manager to slip out of the office?
That must have been two years ago, at least. Finding her note on the

kitchen table and, with great irritation, driving hours through the night? A decade ago, a fading memory.

He looks up and down the quaint main street. So far from the rest of the world.

I could get use to this, he thinks.

This life.

A cabin. A lake.

A fire in the hearth.

A baby in the cradle.

He walks around to the driver's-side door.

There's a bright orange flyer stuck under the windshield wiper blade. At first he worries it's a traffic ticket—*How the hell did I get a parking ticket?*—then plucks the flyer loose and reads: *Big End-of-Summer Sale Tree of Life Books, Main Street, Plain, NY.*

He looks up and spots the storefront. Sure enough, there's a big sign in the window advertising the sale. He'd noticed the bookstore on their previous visit and made a mental note to check it out sometime. It's an old firehouse turned into a bar, by the looks of it, which also sells books; there's a rack of used novels out front for cheap, a dollar each. They're exactly the kind of books Craig is particularly drawn to, the kind he loved as a kid: thick, weathered, pulpy paperbacks you can stick in a back pocket and devour over a weekend.

He taps the flyer against his palm. He should get back. He knows she's waiting. But then, she seemed happy on the porch, lost in her paints.

Keys in hand, he walks a little closer to the store, just to check out the window display. New novels are featured proudly in the window, each one presented on a little pedestal. The store's hours are posted. It's open today but closed Wednesdays and Thursdays, and then they're leaving, so—last chance to pop in, he thinks.

He spots himself reflected in the glass. He sees an appealing version of Craig standing in the street.

Writer. Family man. Small town. Authentic.

New Craig.

New Craig could also use a notebook, he thinks. Scribble some stray thoughts. Maybe finally start that novel.

A blank page. A fresh start.

He pockets the keys.

Just ten minutes, he thinks.

42

She leans on the railing of the porch with her flip phone open, waiting for the signal to kick in. The view before her is glorious, tranquil, the rippled layers of striated cloud reflected impeccably on the long crescent of the calm green lake. But the view is not what she's thinking about right now.

She thinks about that morning. She'd meant to tell him only the bare bones of her story, but once she started telling it—well, she'd never told all of that to anyone. Not all of it. Certainly not to her parents, who she hasn't spoken to in years—she remembers calling her mother after she landed in Boston just to let her know that she was okay and, after a long, excruciating silence on the phone, her mother's reply came: "Well, I'm sorry you've managed to get yourself into such a mess."

So she never told her parents, and she never told any of her friends at grad school, and she's certainly never told her newly minted New York friends.

Before today, she'd never even told her husband.

Sometimes she could convince herself that there was nothing to tell, that she'd left it all behind like a shed skin. She was Daisy now, a new woman, and everything that had happened before had happened to a different woman, not to her. She didn't realize until she was sitting on the porch, looking at the lake, until her mouth was forming the words to tell him, how badly she'd wanted to speak them aloud all these years.

It felt good. And necessary. And now it's done.

Now she has to think about what's coming next.

Courage, she thinks, to steady herself, and she remembers *The Wizard of Oz.* How she loved it as a kid. Watched it in Technicolor as a little girl, rapt, on weekend afternoons.

Of all the characters, she loved the Cowardly Lion the most.

The Scarecrow sought a brain. The Tin Man sought a heart. Dorothy wanted to find her way home.

But the Cowardly Lion sought courage. Which always seemed funny to her.

Because home was a physical place to return to, and a heart and a brain are both physical organs, bodily vacancies to be filled. But courage—that was not a physical object or a missing piece. It was something you had to conjure inside yourself, right? It was—what? A feeling? An attribute? An attitude?

If you lacked courage, what did that mean, exactly? What part of you was missing?

Then again, what does the Good Witch say to Dorothy at the end? *You've always had the power.*

It was inside you all along.

Let's find out.

She steadies herself and taps out a text.

you close?

Hits send.

Waits. Turns her eyes back to the view. She hears birdsong, a serenade. She thinks for a moment about hurtling her secret phone as far as she can into the water, about letting it sink unseen to the lake's murky bottom and forgetting this whole week, this whole plan. Just stay here forever, she thinks, in this moment, on this porch, living here and never leaving.

In the moment before the moment.

The phone buzzes lightly in her palm.

very close

She taps.

good. can't wait. we're almost there

Then flips the phone closed.

One more day, she thinks.

"Pressing news?" The voice surprises her and she startles, nearly drops the phone, and turns.

It's Shep, mounting the steps with a big smile, wearing his red wind-breaker, giving a friendly wave. "Hope I'm not too early."

She grins, a brave face. "Nope. Right on time."

He nods toward the phone. "Who were you texting?"

"Just checking for news from the city about an audition."

"Any word?"

"Not yet."

Shep nods. "I'm sure you'll get it. You should. Who's better than you, right?" He glances around. "Craig's gone?"

"For now. He should be back in an hour or so."

"It's kind of exciting, isn't it? Like opening night," says Shep. "I confess—I miss this feeling." He knocks on the railing twice, like knocking on a dressing room door. "Knock knock. Five minutes, please."

She answers him reflexively.

"Thank you, five," she says.

43

Craig browses the shelves of the bookstore, running a finger over the spines of the bestsellers. Each of them represent a triumph for someone, he thinks, the fulfillment of a lifelong dream. Maybe, he thinks, he could do that up here in the woods. Find a farmhouse. Write a novel. A little office in the attic with a gooseneck lamp and him banging away on his laptop. With a big beard, too. Definitely. He strokes his stubbled chin. Five days' growth. More scruff than substance. But still.

He could do it, he thinks. Write a book. Have this baby. Be a family. Drink a beer in celebration when he finished the last page.

He glances up at the bar. It's open, even though it's early in the afternoon. The bartender swabs out glasses while a guy with a goatee, wearing fingerless gloves, nurses a glass of something at the other end of the bar, scrolling through his phone.

"What's on tap?" Craig asks the bartender as he climbs onto a stool. The bartender reels off a list of about a dozen microbrews with names like Pinched Urchin and the Grumpy Troubadour, none of which Craig has ever heard of.

Craig nods to the other guy. "What's he drinking?"

The guy at the end of the bar looks up. "Just a seltzer," he says.

"You want another? It's on me. I'm celebrating." Craig's feeling generous, on account of his new life, his baby, his imminent bestseller. He says to the bartender, "Another seltzer for my friend and I'll have that troubadour one."

"Grumpy Troubadour?" says the bartender.

"Sure. Is it hoppy?"

"They're all hoppy." The bartender pulls a clean glass out from under the bar and turns to pull the tap.

Craig gets up, feeling country friendly, expansive—no one locks their doors out here—and slides onto the stool right next to the other guy. "You mind?"

The guy looks up from his phone. "Be my guest."

Craig sizes him up. Crew cut. Goatee. Craig holds out a hand. "I'm Craig."

The guy stashes his phone and they shake hands.

"I'm Frank."

Craig settles in. "Hello, Frank. What brings you to these parts?"

"What else? Eat. Sleep. Hunt."

"Is it good hunting in these parts?" *Parts* being a word Craig would never say in the city and now he's said it twice.

"So I've heard," says Frank. "What about you? What brings you up here?"

"Why? I don't look like a local?"

"Lucky guess."

"I'm here with my wife," says Craig. "For a getaway."

Frank smiles. "Most men I know, when they take a getaway, it's to *get away* from their wife."

The bartender sets the pint down in front of Craig, who hoists it, as though proposing a toast. "Actually, we're about to have a baby."

"A baby," says Frank. "Congratulations."

Craig leans in, conspiratorial. "We're kind of on a marriage-counseling retreat. My wife arranged it. To make sure we work everything out before, you know, the baby arrives."

"How long you two been married?"

"Two years."

"And you love her?"

Craig looks at him, surprised. "Of course."

"And she loves you?" Frank lobs his questions at Craig with the cold calm of a cop at a traffic stop.

"Yes, she does," says Craig. "Isn't that how marriage works?"

"Don't tell that to my parents." Frank raises his glass. "To love—may it never afflict you."

They toast.

"What about you?" says Craig. "You married?"

"No, sir."

"Ever been close?"

"Once. But we separated."

"Well, don't lose hope," says Craig. "If it was meant to be, it will come back to you—isn't that what they say?"

As Craig takes another long swig, the bell over the front door jingles. The three men turn in unison. A figure is backlit in the doorway by the bright afternoon, but it's unmistakable: the silhouette of a woman.

Craig raises his hand to shield his eyes and recognizes her: It's Lorelei, the waitress.

She points at Craig. "There you are. I've been looking all over for you."

"Old friend?" says Frank to Craig.

"Her? No, she's a waitress at the diner," says Craig.

The bartender looks at Craig. "Bro, that woman does not work at the diner."

"Sure she does," says Craig.

"Trust me, I would have noticed," says the bartender.

Lorelei strides toward Craig with some urgency. "Come outside. We need to talk."

Frank looses a low whistle, like *You're in trouble now.*

Craig thinks a moment. "That's weird."

"What's weird?" says Frank.

Craig turns to him. "What you said just now. 'Old friend.' Like we're involved or something."

"What's weird about that?" says Frank.

Craig looks at him, puzzled. "My wife makes that same joke all the time."

Lorelei grabs Craig's arm, her face grave. "Outside. Now."

||||

The two of them stand on the empty sidewalk, Lorelei squinting against the sun. "You need to get home to your wife," she says, her voice fraught with fear.

"I just stopped in for a minute. I was about to go," says Craig.

"She's in danger. You both are. It has to do with the men you tangled with the other night. Just get back to the cabin. That security guy from the company will meet you there—"

"Who—*Shep*?" Craig feels a pang of anger—jealousy, really, a sharp supplement to the knot of concern already twisting in his chest.

"Yes—he'll explain everything when you get there," she says. "There's been some sort of threat against you both. Your wife didn't know how to reach you, so she called the diner and asked me to find you."

Craig glances up and down the sun-bleached street, his concern rising. "Do you have a phone? Can I call her?"

"Just get back as quick as you can." She puts a hand on his arm. "Listen to me. This is serious. Those guys you tangled with? The other night at the bar? They're bad dudes. They've caused trouble up here before. Sent some people to the hospital, is what I heard."

"I thought you said they were harmless."

"I never said they were harmless. I said you should leave them alone."

"Should I call the cops?" he says.

"The local cops aren't going to intercede with these guys. Trust me. They're all buddies." Craig's face falls; she sees it. "Get back to your wife," she says. "She needs you."

Craig reaches in his pocket and pulls out the keys to the car. He looks up once more, hesitant, hoping for one last word of guidance.

"Just go," she says.

He takes the curves home at high speed, the route more familiar to him now. In a rush to get back to her.

Just one stop to make first.

Whatever happens, whatever's coming, he'll be ready, he thinks.

No hand axe this time.

Up ahead, he spots the dented black mailbox on the broken post, the landmark Alwyn used to guide him home from the orchard access road.

Jerking the wheel sideways, he brakes abruptly on the shoulder. He gets out of the car, leaving the driver's door ajar, the car chiming behind him as he jogs a few steps forward, looks around, sure that it's here, it's got to be somewhere—

He spots it.

The mouth to the access road.

He runs down the trail toward the orchard and the footlocker that's overgrown with weeds, toward the padlock he knows he can pop open with the heel of his hand, toward the gun he knows he'll find there, waiting inside.

44

In the cabin, Shep stands at the window, holding the curtain aside. "You think Lorelei found him?"

Daisy's leaning in the doorway to the kitchen, her arms crossed. The empty cabin stretches out between them like a stage. "She should have. It's not a very big town."

"And you're sure he'll come back?"

"Of course he'll come back."

Shep turns to her. "You say that like it's a certainty. But isn't that the whole reason we're here? To see what he'll do at the moment of truth? I mean, his original plan at the beginning of the week was to leave you, wasn't it?"

She shouldn't have told Shep that. She shouldn't have told him any of that.

"Just wait. He'll come," she says.

Shep lets the curtain drop, thrusting his hands in his pockets, a rueful shrug. "And when this is all over, what happens next?"

"What do you mean?"

"We'll still be friends, right?" He glances up through his shaggy hair at her, each move practiced, over years, to appeal.

"We *are* friends," she says.

"Yes, but—I'll hear from you again, right? Before another eight years go by?" He lets the question linger between them, then says, "Because I keep thinking about that night at the train station in school. Standing there, watching you leave. What a mistake that was. Anyway, you deserve better. I just want you to know that."

"Better than what?" she says.

He gestures at the cabin, the window, the woods. "Better than whatever this week has been about."

She watches him from the doorway, feeling the solidity of the frame against her shoulder. She likes doorways, she always has, she escapes into them, they're transitional, like portals, they speak to her of quick getaways. She remembers hearing once as a girl that, in case of a natural disaster, a doorway is the safest place to be. *If the ground starts to buckle, if the earth starts to shake, stand in a doorway,* that's what someone told her. As if the whole world could collapse around you in great thunderous clouds of dust and you'd be left standing safely in the doorway, unscathed.

She doubts it would happen that way in reality. But you have to find someplace in this world to feel safe, she thinks.

"He's my husband," she says, as though that settles it.

"I wonder, though—how can you be married to someone and still feel like you don't really know them?" says Shep.

She smiles. "It's easier than you think."

"I have to confess, marriage is a mystery to me."

"It's not a mystery," she says. "It's not magic. It's just marriage."

Shep looks at her a moment longer, then looses that famous cockeyed smile, the one that *sizzles,* the one he was notorious for in grad school. Like the perfect spiral of a high school quarterback, Shep's smile now seems like an impressive tool with no further purpose in his life. In school, though—she remembers how Shep was someone accustomed to getting his way. She's sure that, with her, the challenge was always part of the appeal. He liked playing the white knight, the Boy Who Will Heal You, and he wanted to be the one to unravel her, to solve her, to *save* her. He never understood how that was the opposite of what she wanted or needed. And it was the opposite of what she eventually found, and clung to, with Craig.

"Do you ever wonder what might have happened for you if you hadn't quit acting," he says offhandedly.

"I didn't quit acting."

"But you know what I mean. You never made it."

I'm alive, she thinks. I made it.

But she doesn't say that.

She's always thought of herself like a pool ball, her life's trajectory continually altered by violent collisions. She considers how she's been forced to ricochet, changing cities, changing names, feeling fearful and helpless, just a random pool ball looking for a pocket to fall into, a dark refuge in which to feel safe.

For a while, grad school was that dark pocket.

Craig felt like a dark pocket, too. For a while.

And the stage—the stage has always been her favorite dark pocket. Her place to feel safe.

The one place where she can reliably disappear.

None of which has anything to do with *making it*.

"I honestly don't think about it," she says.

"Did you ever hear from that guy again? The one from the night of the showcase?" says Shep. Like they're talking about some old mutual friend.

She stands stock-still in her doorway, arms tightly crossed. "No."

"But he's still out there?"

"Yes."

Shep nods. "It's been a while. Maybe he's moved on."

"Men like him don't move on," she says. "I'm the one who has to keep moving."

Shep considers this, then says, "Look—I have to say something. Before your husband gets back."

She tenses, her crossed arms tightening, like the arms of a straitjacket. "What do you have to say to me?"

"Craig is no good for you. And he doesn't deserve you," says Shep. "I'm sorry, but someone has to say it. And I'm your friend."

Is that what you are? she thinks. She says nothing.

"Who knows you better than me?" says Shep. "Look, I know it's hard to hear, but he's no good for you, Nora."

He calls her Nora. Her name in grad school. Stolen from *A Doll's House*, her favorite character in her favorite play. Her go-to monologue.

You have never loved me. You have only thought it pleasant to be in love with me.

She looks at Shep. "Don't call me that. Not now. We're not done with this."

"But it's your name," he says.

It's not even her name. It's just the name she used back then.

He doesn't even know her real name.

"Don't do it, Shep. We're so close to the end. Don't break," she says.

He considers her, like he's weighing the power he has over her in this moment.

She trembles. Clutches herself tighter. Not now, she thinks. Not after she's worked so hard.

He looks about to say something more when they both hear it—the rumble of the car in the driveway, the crunch of tires over stone.

Shep glances out the window. "Guess who!"

He turns to her. Grins.

A cold grin.

"Showtime," he says.

45

Shep lays it out for Daisy and Craig as the two of them sit at the round table, listening.

There's been chatter in town all week, Shep explains, rumors and credible threats. Normally, he says, he wouldn't give it much credence, but these men had apparently already been by the cabin once on the night of the incident at the bar. They'd broken in, tossed the cabin, left something gruesome behind as a shock. When Daisy and Craig didn't leave after that, they apparently decided to escalate.

"But if you know who's doing this," says Daisy, "why can't we just go to the police?"

"And tell them what?" says Shep. "Some harsh words were exchanged at a bar one night? Then you found a raccoon in your cabin?"

"There was the snake," says Craig. "Someone cut its head off."

"But that doesn't prove anything." Shep leans in. "Between you and me, these local cops—everyone knows everyone up here. They'd let these assholes off with a warning, if that." He pushes his chair back from the table and stands, as though wrestling with an impossible dilemma. "Honestly, by the time these guys act, it will be too late for the cops to intervene. So that's why I'm here. To help you act first."

"By doing what exactly?" says Daisy. "You're just one guy."

"Two guys," says Craig, correcting her.

"Two guys, that's right," says Shep.

She turns to Craig. "We should go back to the city tonight. Just pack up and leave."

"No," says Craig, firm. "We're not running."

She pleads. "Don't be stubborn. It's not just about you and me anymore."

"That's exactly why we're *not* leaving," says Craig. "We're starting a new phase of our lives. We're not going to start it by running scared."

Craig thinks again of the gun, Alwyn's .45, now stashed in the glove compartment of their car, with the coffee can of shells stuck under the seat. No one knows about the gun yet except him, and the fact of the gun emboldens him—like it's an edge he holds, a trump card.

He looks at Shep. "I say let them come."

"Good," says Shep. "I agree."

Daisy looks to Shep. "So what do we do?"

Shep leans on the table and beckons them forward. "In my experience, every problem has a proportional solution. But sometimes, if you want to solve a recurring problem, you've got to be willing to be a little—disproportional." He looks to Craig. "Are you willing to do that?"

"Absolutely," says Craig.

"It's like the other night in the bar," says Shep. "You can ask that guy politely to be reasonable. Or you can punch him in the throat."

"So let's punch them in the throat," says Craig.

Shep grabs his windbreaker from the back of a chair. "What I've heard is, these guys are planning to come by first thing in the morning, make some trouble, shout at you a little, try to scare you and send you running off. But we'll have a surprise for them. In the meantime, you two will be safe here tonight. I'll have my people watch the roads and the house and then I'll circle back first thing."

Shep pulls a long white envelope out of his jacket pocket. On the front of the envelope: *Q6*. He drops it in the middle of the table. "They asked me to bring this for you."

Daisy looks at Shep, then at Craig. "For the record, I don't like any of this. I think we should leave. Now I'm going to go and make myself some tea." She stands and heads into the kitchen.

Once she's gone, Craig motions to Shep. He says in hushed tones: "Don't worry. I'm ready."

"That's good," says Shep.

"What you said, the other day—about protection?"

"Yeah?"

"I got some."

Shep looks at him, surprised. "You did? How?"

"Never mind. It's in the car. In the glove compartment. I just want you to know. In case things—escalate."

Shep listens, nodding. "Does Daisy know about it?"

"No. And don't tell her," says Craig. "She doesn't need to know unless we need to use it. At which point she'll be glad we have it."

Shep gives him a manly clap on the shoulder. "Don't worry. Your secret is safe with me."

Shep leaves and they're alone. They prepare a simple dinner. They sit together and eat it on the porch.

They listen as dusk settles in around them and the woodland chatter starts to swell. They clear the plates and wash up, then return to the porch to sit together and watch the day retreat.

The air is filled with portent, it seems to him. His wife, their baby, this night.

As though one day he will look back on this moment as the fork in the road between two lives.

Daisy turns to Craig. "Are you happy?"

He looks over. "I am. Are you?"

"I am." She smiles and holds up the white envelope. "Should we open it?"

"It's not day six yet."

"It's only a few hours away. And it sounds like we might be a little distracted in the morning."

"Okay, then."

She hands the envelope to him. "You do it."

He takes the envelope and rips it open and pulls out the folded paper from inside.

"Question Six," he says.

He unfolds the paper and reads it aloud.

46

Craig finishes reading, folds the paper, and stands. He walks to the railing of the porch.

He fishes in the old clay ashtray on the railing, his fingers digging out the plastic lighter. He sparks the lighter and tips the corner of the sheet of paper into the flame. The paper catches.

He drops it, burning, into the dirt that rings the porch.

He watches the paper curl until it's consumed.

He looks out at the woods.

He looks back at Daisy.

"Yes," he says.

"Yes," she answers, as though repeating a marital vow.

The Sixth Day

IIII

BEASTS

47

She sleeps upstairs.

Craig sits on the porch.

Alwyn's handgun resting heavy in his lap.

Not sure what time it is now. Three, maybe four in the morning.

The forest beyond the porch is just a row of darkness followed by rows of darker darkness. Trees, and then the shadows of trees, and then the shadows of shadows. Like an expectant audience, hushed.

He looks out over at the lake. The moon scatters bright shards on the restless water.

It's quiet.

The night passes.

He thinks of the question.

Question Six.

He can recite it verbatim.

He's been thinking about it all night.

Question Six.

Would you kill for me?

It's an outrageous question.

Forget it.

Throw this paper away.

Fold it up, toss it out, burn it up, and never think of this question again.

Raise your kids. Squabble. Make love. Buy a house. Pick up your dry cleaning. Grow old together. Go on about your lives.

After all, why ask a question you'll never have to answer?

But before you do that, ask yourselves this.

Do you strive for the most intimate, cohesive, and rewarding relationship you can possibly have?

Do you strive for something transcendent? The kind of love you only read about in fairy tales and fables?

The kind of love few people ever get to understand, let alone experience?

If the answer is no, then you're free. No harm done. No shame.

Walk away.

Have a happy life.

But if the answer is yes—then you should at least consider every question.

Including this one.

Would you kill for me?

When you say you would do anything for someone, do you truly mean it?

If not, what is the nature of your love, exactly?

This is the purpose of the Eden Test: to help you find your limits. Together.

And then, once found, to test them.

Transcend them.

Together.

Because let's be honest.

It's easy enough to change.

To care.

To sacrifice.

To fight.

It's even easy enough to die.

But it's hard to kill.

It extracts a cost.

But it rewards you with something priceless in return.
Love without limits.

He sits on the porch and thinks of the burning paper, falling from his fingers. He thinks of their exchanged promises.

He hears a rustling.

He leans forward. Peering into the darkness.

Wraps his hand around the pistol's grip.

Snap of twigs.

Crack, crack.

Louder now.

Crack.

Chased by an echo.

Okay, that was not twigs.

Crack.

A gunshot.

Another.

He sits up straight. Forefinger finds the trigger guard.

Loud reports in the distance like kids setting off firecrackers.

Heart in his mouth now.

A louder rustling.

His eyes struggle to adjust.

He stands.

Tries to call out—*Who's there?*—like they would answer him. But he can't speak. Throat tight. Tongue heavy. Lying limp in his mouth.

He spots figures. Among the shadows of trees. Moving quickly.

He peers again. Eyes straining.

Sees a rush.

The figures emerge from the woods, there's dozens of them, and his finger can't quite find the trigger.

He fumbles with the gun, but the figures charge the porch, nimble and quick, clambering over the railing, they're on the porch now, on top of him, overwhelming him, hands on him in the dark, their faces, he sees now, every one of them has the exact same face—

Daisy.

Daisy Daisy Daisy Daisy Daisy Daisy Daisy—

Hands grasping. Arms reaching. Eyes sparkling.

Full of love.

Shep shakes him awake.

Craig startles. The wicker chair whines under his shifting weight. He sits up quickly.

The dawn gray.

Woods quiet.

"What time is it?" says Craig.

"It's early," says Shep. "What are you doing on the porch?"

"I couldn't sleep," says Craig, his mouth sour. Heart beating hard like he's still in that dream. No gun in his lap. The gun still stashed in the glove compartment. "Did anything—"

"Not yet," says Shep.

Shep's carrying two semiautomatic rifles, one in each hand.

"But they're on their way," says Shep.

The screen door whines, and Daisy walks out on the porch in her overalls, holding two coffee mugs.

Stops dead.

"What the fuck are those," she says sharply, her eyes locked on the long guns in Shep's hands. She doesn't know anything about guns, but these guns she recognizes. They're AR-15s, the ones from TV, the ones you always see on the news, and never because of anything good.

Shep leans one rifle on its butt end against the side of the cabin and hefts the other gun to his shoulder, sighting the gun with a squinted eye. He looks toward the woods, sweeping the muzzle back and forth. Then he lowers the gun.

"I just got a call. My team spotted them," he says. "They're headed here through the woods. Right now."

"I thought you said we're just going to scare them," says Daisy.

"We are."

"So what are you going to do with those?" The anger in Daisy's voice is naked, unmistakable.

"We're going to punch them in the throat," says Shep. He turns to Craig. "You ever handle one of these before?"

Craig takes the rifle gingerly, then looks up at Shep and shakes his head. *No.*

Shep picks up his own rifle to demonstrate. "Once the safety's disengaged, it's straightforward." He hoists the gun to his shoulder. "Relax. Breathe. Point. Pull the trigger." He lowers the rifle and turns to Daisy. "Don't worry. These are a last resort." Then he gives Craig a curt nod. "Keep your finger off the trigger until you're ready to shoot."

Craig just stands there dumbly, considering the weapon in his hands, the weight of it.

Daisy bypasses Shep, grabs Craig's arm, and says firmly, in a whisper, "Craig, listen—" Her voice low and urgent. "Craig, this is *crazy*. Let's just—"

But the sound interrupts her.

They all hear it.

The three of them turn their heads toward the woods.

The same sound comes again.

Crack crack.

Gunshots.

Far off. But not too far off.

"Get inside," says Shep to Daisy.

"I'm not going to hide in the house," she says.

Craig turns to her, the rifle in his hands, resolute. "Shep's right. Get inside. Head upstairs. Until you hear the all clear."

"I'm not going to leave you," she says.

"Daisy, you're pregnant," says Craig, as if that settles it and nothing more need be said.

Shep looks at her. She catches his expression. His surprise. "Congratulations," he manages to say. "I didn't know."

She turns to Craig. "We need to stick together. I want to be out here with you."

"Absolutely not," says Craig, his resolve hardened. "You need to be safe. I'll be fine."

Daisy looks at Shep, then back at Craig. She hates the sight of her husband with that gun. She feels an overwhelming sense that this is all about to go very wrong.

She walks directly to Craig and kisses him, both of her hands on his face. She pulls back. "Be careful," she says. Then she glances at Shep, then heads back inside the cabin.

More shots from the woods.

Crack crack.

Shep says, "You ready?"

Craig nods. "What do you want me to do?"

"We wait for them to show themselves."

"What if they shoot at us?"

"We shoot back."

"We just—shoot them?" says Craig, bewildered.

Shep smiles. "That's what the guns are for."

"And she'll be safe?"

"Yes. If she stays inside."

"Are you sure?"

Shep looks at the woods and lifts his rifle. "If we're still out here, she's safe. And if we're not—"

He doesn't want to finish it. But Craig wants to hear it. "If we're not, then what?"

"She never was," says Shep.

Craig bends on one knee on the porch, bringing the rifle to his shoulder, feeling the rifle's pistol grip. He sights the woods, sees nothing, waits.

He breathes.

"Get down," says Shep.

Craig looks over. Shep's lying prone on the plank-wood porch, propped up on his elbows, legs straight out behind him, rifle at the ready, his muzzle pointed out through the slats of the railing toward the tree line. Craig copies him. Lies flat. Aims the gun again.

The *crack crack crack* from the woods grows louder. Under the erratic crackle of gunfire Craig hears the faint rising of another chilling sound. Like a war whoop. Men hollering.

"Hold steady," says Shep. "That's what this is all about. They expect to send you running back to the city." He nestles his cheek against the gun stock. "They won't expect this."

They wait.

Watch the woods.

A new round of shots sounds and these shots are louder and the shouting comes after and it's louder, too.

Craig listens and now he can hear the approach of feet, of branches snapping underfoot, as men with heavy boots trudge through the brush. The clearing between the cabin and the woods is maybe thirty yards of open ground. Beyond that lies the dark curtain of the tree line.

If they set up and fire from beyond the trees, Craig thinks, we'll never see them. We'll be sitting ducks.

He settles flat on his belly on the splintered boards. Exhales. Steadies himself. Sweaty hand on the rifle's grip.

Out in the woods, beyond the muzzle of his rifle, he spies the flutter of shadows, figures moving.

Then a bright dab of color. Like paint spilled on a drab canvas.

Blaze orange.

At the tree line, branches shudder, then part.

48

They come from the trees, there's two of them, the man in the blaze orange cap and his wiry friend, and they're both armed, lunging forward from the woods, whooping, their long rifles held low, firing again, again, the muzzle flashes sparkling against the tree line as the snap of gunfire shatters the early-morning air.

Shep, prone on the porch, returns fire. The reports from his weapon are deafening, barking in Craig's ears.

Now Craig is sighting the men, steadying the rifle and then pulling the trigger, the rifle jerking in his hands, his shoulder barking at each sharp recoil, the stink of gun smoke as he pulls again, again, again—

Beside him, Shep resettles his body and fires calmly, two shots in quick succession. The wiry one, the man from the bar with the menacing tattoo, he twists now in the sunlight and topples, two great crimson plumes exploding from his chest.

Craig watches in disbelief. His heart pounding hard against the planks of the porch.

The crazed man falls backward to the grass and Shep is yelling now, "Take him! Take the other one!" and Craig pries his eyes from the fallen man and sights his rifle squarely on the one in the blaze orange cap, who's still charging toward him, undeterred.

Twenty yards. Ten. The man runs with his rifle held low. The rifle barks as the man fires and lets loose a rebel yell. Sawdust plumes off the railing of the porch, and Craig squints against the dust and debris and feels the bite of the trigger on his finger pad, and thinks, This is it, this is it, he has the man dead in his sights, and then he pulls, and he pulls, and he pulls.

Once, twice, again—the gun bucking, each shot clapping loud, and the man in the ballcap is hit once, again, blood erupts from his chest as he staggers, then he falls backward, the blaze orange hat loosed from his head, the man toppling to the ground and splayed strangely in the grass, and the hat follows, fluttering, to where he lies.

The woods fall silent after that.

Only the echoes of gunfire haunt the clearing. A haze of gray gun smoke idles over the battlefield.

Craig is sick now, he feels sick, he pulls himself up to kneel, and lurching forward, he retches once, twice, again.

He stays like that, bent, for a moment.

Until he hears Daisy's voice.

"That's enough," she says. Her hand on his back now. Her voice all he can hear. "Craig, I'm so sorry," she says.

Craig turns to her as she calls out to the clearing: "Mike, Dan—it's okay. It's done."

Craig stares at his wife, befuddled. The sharp reports still singing in his ears. Then he looks at Shep, who says nothing. Then he turns toward the clearing, and that's when he sees it, like time reversing, the deed undone.

The two men in the clearing rise, their shirts bloodied and tattered, and they dust themselves off, resurrected and laughing. They give the people on the porch a little wave, like performers acknowledging a crowd.

Despite himself, Craig waves back.

Daisy crouches beside Craig, her hands on his shoulders. "It was just theater," she says, so quietly, soothing, just for him. "Just smoke and noise."

"What?" Craig looks at her. "What just happened?"

"I needed to know what you'd do."

She stands and guides Craig to his feet. He faces her, dumbfounded. He recalls, absurdly, the moment that he and Daisy stood under a tree upstate two years earlier, petals falling all around them, swapping marital vows. He recalls how much fear he felt that day. But also hope.

Seeing her now, on the porch, with the gun smoke hovering and the gunfire still echoing in his ears, he takes her hands again, and it all feels to him, absurdly, like that moment under the tree.

Fear. But also hope.

"It was all fake? This whole week?" he says, tentative.

"I know this sounds strange, but I did it for us," she says. "I did it so we'd know if we can survive."

Craig whispers a reluctant question, barely audible, his eyes now thick with tears. "The baby?"

She's crying now, too. "No, that's true. Of course that's true." She pulls him in close. "That's really happening. That's the reason I did all this."

He says softly in her ear, "But I told you I would stay."

"I know," she answers back, just as softly. "But I couldn't just hear it. I needed to see it. I needed to test it."

"Here I am," he says.

"Yes, you are." She pulls back and takes his hands in hers. "And I'm so thankful. And I'm so sorry for all this." She glares at Shep. "We never talked about *machine guns.*"

"Technically, they're semiautomatic rifles," Shep says. "Look—you said you wanted to test him. So let's test him."

"And all this gore and fake blood—whose idea was that?" she says.

"Blame Mike," says Shep.

Daisy calls out to one of the men who've risen in the clearing, his orange cap now fastened back on his head. "Is that true, Mike?"

"You like those?" says Mike, with a lopsided grin. He seems oblivious to the moment, tickled only by his antics and his prowess with special effects. He nods to the wiry man, the crazed one. "Granted, the squibs were Dan's idea. They don't even let us use those on *Remedies.* Way too gory. I've always wanted to try them out. And Shep said you wanted to make an impression."

"Just smoke and noise, like you said," says Shep. He steps forward, unbidden, and grasps Craig's shoulder. "Hey, man, I know it's a lot to process. But the good news is, you did it. You passed. So congratulations. On everything."

Craig looks at him. "So who the fuck are you?"

Shep laughs. "We went to theater school together," he says, glancing at Daisy. "We're old friends. My name's Christian. I guess she never told you about me."

Daisy says to Craig softly, "Listen to me, okay? I'll tell you everything. I promise." She turns to Shep. "But right now I need you all to go. This has already gone too far. We need time alone."

"I thought maybe we should have a celebratory toast," says Shep. "To the happy couple and their good news." He looks at her, pointed. "To the new *baby*." He turns to Craig. "She never told me that part."

Daisy steps toward Shep, steel in her voice. "No. Just go," she says. "You wanted to test him? You tested him. He passed. I'm sure you're very disappointed."

Shep looks at her, then at Craig, a smile still frozen on his face. A flush of red creeping across his cheeks. "Don't forget, this whole thing wasn't my idea. *You* called *me*."

"I needed your help and you helped me. And I'm grateful. I am," she says. "But please, just go, okay?"

"So that's it then?" says Shep. "Just like before?"

"What happened before?" says Craig.

"I'll explain everything," says Daisy. She turns to Shep. "I need to be alone now. With my husband. Trust me. You need to leave."

Shep looks like he's about to say something more, but he doesn't; he seems to swallow the words and, instead, he gestures to the men in the clearing. "You heard her. Let's give the happy couple some privacy."

Shep hoists the rifles as Mike and Dan mount the porch, their clothes soaked red by the squibs.

Mike holds a hand out to Craig. "Hey, man, no hard feelings. We were just helping out a friend. Putting on a show—that's what we do." Dan, at his side, just gives a bashful nod.

Craig shakes Mike's hand, his eyes fixed on their gore-smeared chests. "What about the gunshots," says Craig. "The puffs of sawdust. On the porch."

"Blanks and squibs." Mike beams, proud of his handiwork. "I planted those on the porch the other day when you were out."

"And that night at the bar?"

"Sorry to get in your face like that. I tried my best to play the heavy. Thankfully, that woman was in on it, too, so I didn't have to carry the scene myself." He glances at Daisy. "She's good. You should put her in touch with the casting agent for *Remedies*." Turns back to Craig. "As for me—there's a reason I quit acting and got into effects work."

"What about the cabin?" says Craig. "The break-in?"

Mike grins, guilty, like a prankster caught. He points an accusing finger at Dan. "Okay, the snake was this psychopath's idea. He caught that thing and prepped it himself. Damned nutjob. Even Daisy didn't know about that. That way you get the honest reaction."

"And the diner?" says Craig. "The waitress?"

"Just part of the show," says Mike.

"You guys need to go," says Daisy. "We need some time. I'll call you when we're back in the city."

"Yeah, of course," says Mike. "Good luck, you two." Silent Dan just nods again.

Daisy points at Shep. "You, too."

"But when will I hear from you?"

"I don't know."

The flush on his face spreads, a wildfire. Whether anger or shame, it's hard to tell. Shep says to the other two men, "Come on, we can take my truck."

And with that, the three of them walk off the porch, leaving the couple alone.

She turns to Craig. "I'm really sorry."

"It's okay. I understand. Why would you trust me?" he says. "When I came here this week, I arrived with my bags packed. I was not a good person to you." Craig laughs, a release, finally, after everything. "This was good! I mean, it was *insane*, but it was *good*." He exhales. "Fuck, that feeling when they were coming from the woods? I thought—my God." He shakes his head. "I'm so glad you did this, Daisy. I am. I'm glad *we* did this. Because now you know for sure, and now I know, too. You can count on me. We know what we're capable of. We know exactly what we're willing to do." He takes Daisy's hands and raises them to his lips.

"I need you to sit down," she says.

He sits next to her on the wicker settee, still holding her hands.

"I don't expect you to understand this right away," she says. "But I needed to see it for myself. If we're going to do this. If we're going to do what comes next."

"I get that," says Craig. "Parenthood—that's *huge*. It's an enormous responsibility. You need to know you can count on me. Of course!"

"That's not what I mean," she says, pulling her hands back from his. "I need you to listen to me."

"This was so important," he says, still working through it. "This— this right here?" He motions to the porch, the aftermath. "*This* is why we came here this week. What a test!"

"It's not why we came here," she says.

Craig looks at her, waiting for more.

A voice interrupts them both.

"Nora."

They turn.

It's Shep, poised at the edge of the porch, holding Alwyn's gun, the one Craig hid in the glove compartment of the car, the one Daisy never knew about until now.

49

Daisy stands.

"Christian, what are you doing? You need to leave. Now. You're in danger."

He strides toward her, holding the gun loose at his side. "I sent those guys home in my truck. But I can't leave you. Not again. You owe me, Nora. I've always been there for you."

She steps toward him. When she speaks, there's something new in her voice. Not steel.

Fear.

"You have to go, Christian. Right now."

He advances, undeterred, thinking the fear he hears in her voice is fear of him, fear of the gun. He holds the pistol up. "Your beloved husband didn't tell you about this, did he? His little third-act surprise."

Daisy looks at Craig. "That's *yours*?"

Craig says nothing.

"Where did you get that?" she says.

"The tree guy," says Craig. "He keeps it at the orchard. I thought it would make us safer."

"You thought we'd be *safer* with a gun?"

"I didn't know what was going on, Daisy," says Craig, his voice tinged now with defensiveness. "Someone threatened us. We had a break-in. Then this threat? There was a lot of weird shit going on."

"Uh-oh," says Shep in a stage whisper, addressing an aside to an unseen crowd. "Trouble in Paradise."

Daisy turns back to him. "I'm serious, Christian. You have to go. Now."

Shep steps toward her, still holding the pistol loose. "I'm not walking away, Nora. Not again. I made that mistake once already."

Craig looks to Daisy. "Why does he keep calling you Nora?"

And now, in a violent jerk, the gun does come up, the dark unblinking eye of the barrel trained directly on Craig. "You need to shut the fuck up, friend, right now," says Shep. "Nora was her name in theater school, back when I first knew her. Years before you two ever even met."

"Christian, please—" says Daisy, her voice still ripe with fear.

Shep turns toward Daisy. "How can you honestly think *he's* the one for you? He doesn't even know you. After everything he's done? The very fact that you even had to *do* this so-called test?"

"This wasn't the test," she says quietly.

"Really?" Shep lowers the gun, looks at Craig, then back at Daisy, like he's waiting for one of them to explain. "If it wasn't the test, then what was it?"

"A rehearsal," she says.

"A rehearsal for what?" Shep waits for an answer that's not forthcoming and, in the resultant lull, they hear it.

A buzz from Daisy's pocket.

She reaches into the pocket of her overalls and pulls out her secret flip phone.

Flips it open. Reads it.

Looks up and says to Shep, "Run. Right now."

Shep regards her, angry, puzzled, the gun still dangling. "What is it? What does it say?"

She hands the phone to him. He reads the text.

tell him to put down the gun

He looks up at her. "What the fuck? Who's this?"

The phone buzzes again in Shep's palm.

He looks down.

Reads the new text.

last chance

Shep scans the tree line, bewildered, newly panicking, and then he does the last thing he should do right now, the very worst thing he could do.

He raises the gun at Daisy.

Shouting, angry.

"I said, who's—"

And they all hear this, too. The gunshot.

A single whistling shot that lands with a soft thud in Shep's chest.

His eyes widen, astonished.

Another shot sounds and hits just below the first one. There's no crimson plume, no explosive squibs, no death-scene soliloquy. Only the startled look on Shep's face at this unexpected turn.

He teeters, unsteady, then slumps to the porch, the dropped pistol skittering away.

Daisy turns to Craig. She's crying. She starts to speak—but Craig's already lunging toward her, Craig's already yanking her to the ground, Craig's already shielding her body with his body, looking up at the woods, scrambling to grab the pistol that Shep dropped.

"No, no, leave the gun," whispers Daisy, frantic, huddled, her eyes now watching the woods.

Craig does. They wait.

The woods quiet.

All the birds and animals startled rudely into silence.

From Craig's low vantage point he can't see anything, just the tree line.

Finally, he says, "Why aren't they shooting at us?"

"Because he's not here to kill me," she says.

Still crouching, she whispers to Craig, "Listen to me. What I'm about to say is very important."

"This is real?"

"This is real."

"Okay."

"Are you listening?"

"I'm listening."

"Daisy plus Craig. Forever," she says. "Don't forget that. No matter what happens."

He's flummoxed. "What?"

"D plus C. Forever," she says again. More urgent. "Repeat it to me."

"D plus C. Forever."

"Good," she says.

From her crouch, she looks back toward the woods.

Then she stands.

She turns toward the trees. Steps forward on the porch.

Puts her hands on the railing.

Like she's taking center stage.

50

He's here, she thinks.

After all these years of running, of hiding, she's conjured him, called him forth out of the past, out of the darkness, and he's here.

He's watching her right now, she knows that.

It's like she's onstage. The trees are the audience. Hushed. Expectant. Waiting for her to begin.

And him, in the catwalk. In the booth. In the wings.

In the woods. In the dark.

Everywhere.

Every time the lights go out. Every nightfall. Every time she closes her eyes.

He's there.

He's always there.

Every time. Ever since.

Watching her.

And now he's here.

She stands on the porch and she says to the woods in a clear, loud voice.

In a stage-trained voice.

"Let me see you," she says.

51

Through a curtain of pale smoke a figure emerges from a split in the trees, dressed in black. Like a stagehand, outfitted so as not to be seen, waiting in the wings.

Black pants, black T-shirt, black body-armor vest strapped over his chest, black fingerless gloves, black hair buzzed to the skull, black goatee, black rifle with a hunting scope held loose in his hands.

Craig watches him approach.

Wait a second.

Craig knows this guy.

Craig's seen this guy before.

It's the guy from the bar in the bookstore.

Frank.

Craig grabs the pistol that's fallen from Shep's hand, stands, raises the gun, and yells, "Stop."

To his surprise, Frank stops.

Frank stands in the clearing between the cabin and the woods, maybe twenty yards away from them both. Haze from the gunfire, all the blanks discharged before, still loiters in a lazy cloud that enshrouds him.

"Drop the rifle," Craig barks, his pistol held steady.

Frank stoops and lays his long gun with the elaborate scope on the ground.

"You know this guy, Daisy?" says Craig loudly, for Frank's benefit as much as for hers.

She says nothing. She looks only at Frank. Who looks only at her.

Finally, Frank speaks.

"Daisy," he says. "So that's what you call yourself now?"

Craig fires.

Fuck it.

For the second time today, Craig pulls a trigger, once, twice, again, again, squeezing, aiming steady, dead center on Frank's chest. He pulls again, again, click, click, click, click, click.

Nothing.

The gun's empty.

Unloaded.

Of course.

Gun in the glove compartment, shells in the coffee can.

Which Shep didn't know.

The gun was empty the whole time.

Craig stares dumbfounded at the impotent pistol, and while he does, Frank starts moving at a brisk jog toward the porch.

By the time Craig looks up again, Frank's mounted the railing, hopping it easily in one smooth motion, he's on the porch now, just a few feet away, and he unclips something from his heavy black belt and with a wrist flick extends a metal baton. He swings it and it whistles in the air and Craig sees a sudden flashbulb of white pain and feels heat spreading in his left leg. Craig crumples, the empty gun skittering away from him. Through starbursts of white he sees Frank tower over him, as though he's whipping a dog, Frank bringing the baton down again and again against Craig's upraised forearms, once, twice, again, each blow announcing a shock of fresh agony until—

"That's enough," says Daisy.

IIII

Frank stands with the baton poised for a moment, then obediently folds it up and hooks it back on his belt. He gestures toward Craig, curled and whimpering on the porch. "I had to. He pulled a gun on me."

"You shot my friend," says Daisy.

Frank glances at Shep's body. "He was your friend?"

"Yes."

"He threatened you. I didn't like that."

"He never should have been here," she says quietly. "I told him to go." She looks at the empty .45 lying discarded on the porch. The tree man's gun. The one she never knew about. The one surprise in a plan she'd spent weeks devising.

Frank holds out his hands to her, palms up, in those fingerless gloves. At this sign of his fond attention, she steps forward, smiling, like he's chosen her from a line of hopeful candidates.

She puts her hands in his.

"Daisy, huh?" he says.

"That's my name." She smiles.

"Not that I remember." He squeezes her hands. "Look at you. You look good. You look the same."

"So do you," she says. "You don't look like you've changed at all."

"I sent flowers. *Your Forever Fan.*"

"I got them."

"But then you ran away."

"What happened with my roommate, Frank?"

Frank is silent. Yes, I know about that, thinks Daisy as she looks him over, her hands still in his. Her roommate in grad school, the one she barely knew and who certainly knew nothing about her, the one Frank put in the hospital.

"I'm not sure I know what you mean," Frank says finally.

"Why are so many people always getting hurt around us?" she says.

"Maybe because they're standing between us."

"I ran because I wasn't ready," she says.

"And now?"

His leather gloves against her fingers feel rough, bestial.

"Now I'm ready," she says.

"You must have thought I'd given up on you," he says.

"No. I never thought that."

Craig watches the scene from his vantage point crumpled at their feet. He tries to rise, but his limbs are useless, his leg still singing in pain.

Daisy slips free of Frank's hands and slides her fingers under his tactical vest. "The body armor seems excessive."

"I didn't know what to expect. So I came prepared. Approached from the woods. Hearing from you like that, out of the blue, after all these years—I didn't know what to think."

"You contacted me, Frank. You found me."

"I know, but I wasn't expecting—an invitation."

She rubs her thumbs on his vest. "Where do you even buy something like this?"

"The Internet." His mouth tilts into a bashful smirk. "What kind of a world is it where you can find body armor on the Internet but you can't find your ex-girlfriend?"

"But the difference is, I didn't want to be found."

"Yet here we are." Frank gestures to the cabin. "What is this place, anyway? Your husband said it was some sort of getaway."

"That's right," she says, then adds calmly, "When did you speak to my husband?"

"We ran into each other in town. Total coincidence. He even bought me a drink." Frank snorts, looks down at Craig, wilted on the porch. "He said this week was going to save your marriage." He prods Craig with the toe of his boot. "How's that working out for you?"

Daisy puts her hands on Frank's face and tilts his gaze back toward her. "Don't think about him. Look at me."

"Do you know how many times I've imagined this moment?" says Frank.

"Me, too."

"I know it's been a while, but it's important to me that you know—" Frank stops himself. He seems uncertain how to continue.

"That I know what?" she says patiently.

He looks up at her. "—that I don't need you to apologize."

She's astonished. Despite herself. Despite everything. "Apologize to you?" she asks. "For what?"

"For how you left me. All that pain you caused me, all those years. Twelve years of my life I spent trying to get you to acknowledge what we have—you wouldn't even contact me. Not to mention how you ran away that first time. No notice, no nothing. That hurt. It wasn't right, what you did to me."

She starts to sense it; she hears it crackling in his words, sees it stirring, uncoiling, always lurking.

The anger underneath.

"You remember what happened the week before I left, don't you?" she says calmly.

"I'm not saying I didn't get out of line." His voice rising. "But I was sorry. I told you that a hundred times. You never gave me a chance to make it right."

She whispers, her voice choked, "I lost the baby, Frank."

"I made mistakes. We both did."

"Tell me," she says. "What was my mistake?"

From the ground, Craig tries again to rise. The pain in his leg like a ringing alarm.

She curls her fingers under Frank's vest, like she's adjusting a groom's tuxedo. "Every time I step onstage, it's like you're always watching me. From the darkness. Just like in the old days."

"And now look at you," he says. "A real actress in New York City. On TV and everything. Man, did I sit up straight when I saw that you were on that show."

She smiles. "I bet you did."

"And you're making a go of it as an actress in New York?"

"I'm doing my best."

"Are you good?"

She pauses. As though seriously considering his question. As though she's never been asked it before or ever thought about the answer.

"I'm fucking fantastic," she says.

Frank nods toward Craig, writhing on the ground. "He told me your news. About—you and him and... what you're expecting." He can't bring himself to say it. He says instead, "It complicates things."

She tugs again on Frank's vest to rotate him slightly so his back is fully to Craig.

"We didn't plan it," she says softly. "It was a surprise. Honestly, I didn't think I could get pregnant, not after what happened. Don't worry, Frank. I'll take care of it."

"Thank you," says Frank, his rising anger dissipating.

She learned in her years with him how to navigate it, the anger, to thwart it, defuse it, fend it off, if only for a while. But it never disappears, only retreats.

Lies in wait.

"To be honest, all this time, I thought you *hated* me," he says.

"I thought so, too."

"So what changed?"

"I guess I realized you can't outrun your past," she says.

"I feel the same," he says. "You try to move on, but you can't. I can't."

"I know," she says. "I know you can't."

"And I would never have stopped looking for you, you know that right? Never." Frank's black eyes glisten as he says this, like it's the truest profession of love, like a vow spoken at the altar, like the romantic speech, with music swelling, at the end of the film.

"I know," she says.

"How do you deal with that feeling?" He sounds honestly pained. "Of not being able to move on?"

"I think you have to make peace with the past."

"But how do you do that?"

From the corner of her eye, she spots Craig finally rising unsteadily to his feet behind Frank. She holds Frank's eyes and puts her hands on his cheeks, cradling his face. Holding it steady.

"You bury it," she says.

She kisses him.

His head held firmly in her hands.

Behind them both, Craig staggers upright.

Which is when Craig spots them.

Scattered all over the porch. Dozens of them.

One within reach. No matter where you look. No matter where you are on the porch.

Her painted rocks. Her plan all along.

Weapons everywhere, in plain sight.

Each one carrying a message.

Repeat it to me, she'd said to him.

D + C.

They're still kissing, and when she opens her eyes, she sees Craig looming behind him and she nods and breaks from the kiss and takes a half step back. She keeps her hands steady on Frank's face and Frank looks lost in the broken kiss, she's still smiling at him, her eyes still shining, holding his gaze, a look of reconciliation, of forgiveness, of devotion, of adoration, as close to a look of true love as anyone in history has ever conjured, real or otherwise.

One hundred percent convincing. Her greatest performance.

She's fucking fantastic, all right.

She holds his head steady for one moment more.

Craig swings the rock, and it lands with a moist crack.

Frank's head lurches forward under the blow, but she holds him steady, unflinching.

Frank's eyes unfocus like someone in the grips of a reverie, his jaw dropping, unhinged, like a snake's.

Craig raises the rock again.

Held gripped in his fist, *D + C* painted in pink, now spattered in red.

Craig eyes the wet wound in the back of Frank's skull.

Rock held high.

Craig hesitates.

It's easy enough to change.

To sacrifice.

To fight.

To lie.

It's even easy enough to die.

But it's hard to kill.

It's hard to kill a person.

Especially with a rock.

And in that brief hesitation Frank extends the baton with a flick of his wrist and swings it blindly backward, catching Craig on his one good knee.

Craig's leg buckles at an unnatural angle.

He drops the rock to the porch with a thud and falls backward against the railing.

He spots the cigar box, close by. The one that holds the whittling knife.

His gift from Daisy.

Craig fumbles for the box. His fingers scramble to open it.

Flips the lid open.

Empty.

And as Craig stares into its emptiness, the second time he's come up short today, Frank turns with blood trailing down his face and swings the baton again and again without restraint and Craig goes down in a heap, in a wail of white-hot helplessness.

Frank stops.

He turns back toward Daisy, skull broken, blood streaming. Baton extended. Eyes swimming. Confused. Betrayed.

His rage, ever at the ready, unleashed.

He snarls. Like a beast.

"I was wrong," says Frank. "You do need to apologize to me."

He tightens his grip on the baton.

She reaches out and puts one hand gently on his cheek. A gesture of comfort. Of consolation.

"Apologize to me," he spits again, sputtering blood.

Half plea. Half command.

She'll get the beating either way, they both know that.

She smiles. Beatific. Like a saint.

Holds his gaze.

With her other hand, she unsnaps the utility pocket on the front of her trusty overalls.

Pulls out the whittling knife with the worn bone handle, the one that her grandfather gave her.

With one hand still on his cheek, she flicks the knife open with her thumb without looking, just like she's practiced a million times before.

Rehearsing.

"I have nothing to be sorry for, Frank," she says. "Except you."

He raises the baton high with a jerk of the arm, and when he does, she sticks the knife deep into his neck.

All the way in, to the worn bone handle.

His eyes gape.

The baton falls with a clatter.

Frank follows, toppling backward to his ass on the porch like a chastised man who's been told to take a seat.

He gurgles. Scrabbles with dirty fingertips at the handle of the knife.

Craig rises behind him.

Craig can't get to his feet, but he can certainly get to his knees.

Craig raises the blood-spattered rock again.

Like Cain did Abel. The invention of murder.

No hesitation this time.

||||

Everything's quiet.

The woods watch without comment.

The trees loom like a hung jury, returning no verdict.

After a long silence, the creatures of the woods, unperturbed, resume their calming choral song.

She helps him up.

He hops on one leg, limping, his arm flung over her shoulders.

They leave Frank sprawled on the porch next to Shep and wobble like that together toward the open cabin door.

His arm around her shoulders. Her arm around his waist.

Supporting each other.

Like one hobbled creature, testing its broken limbs, struggling to stand.

52

Daisy and Craig sit together on the sofa in the cabin, hand in hand, staring in silence at the red phone on the side table.

We need to call the hotline, he said, his one battered leg held straight out before him, still throbbing. There are two dead bodies on the porch. We need to tell someone what happened. We need to call the authorities. What we did was wrong, he said.

No, she said. Frank was wrong. We were right. Right and wrong. Good and evil. She turned to him. We need to remember the difference.

Either way, he said, we have to tell someone what happened here.

She agreed. Absolutely.

We need to tell them what happened here.

Now she sits at his side, staring at the red phone. Thinking back to the beginning of everything.

Okay, Daisy, she thinks, what happened here?

Maybe it began in their bathroom in Brooklyn, months earlier, when Daisy sat alone, staring at the pregnancy test.

Craig was out, of course, Craig was absent, Craig was off gallivanting, and she was home and she was a week late. She never missed her period, ever, so she'd decided to take a test, even though she knew she couldn't get pregnant, even though she'd been told that for years. The doctors had informed her gravely of that fact after what had happened with Frank. It wasn't possible. That's what they told her. So she never used protection and she never worried. Or hoped.

But she was a week late. And she was never late.

Also, she remembered, in her body, how being pregnant felt.

Still, even as she unboxed the test, she cursed herself for being stupid, for entertaining this impossible possibility.

She remembers closing the door to the bathroom, even though no one else was home, a strange ritual of privacy.

She remembers peeing on the stick, then holding it. Waiting.

Then looking at the stick.

Twinned blue lines.

She remembers contemplating this impossible baby. And what it might mean for her life. For their lives.

She remembers the odd feeling that came over her. An alien feeling she had not expected to feel, and one that she had not felt in a very long time. So long that she barely recognized the feeling when it arrived.

A feeling she seemed to now hold in her hand.

Hope.

Or maybe it all began at that opening-night party, a week later, her news still kept secret from Craig. She went out to see her friend's play and she got dragged along under protest to the cast party afterward. She was already feeling a little fatigued and, of course, she wasn't drinking, but she agreed to pop in for a minute before she headed home to bed. At the party, she met that casting agent for *Legal Remedies,* the one who looked her up and down and said to her:

"You'd be perfect."

Imagine that.

The agent basically offered her the small TV role on the spot. "Please say yes, you'd be solving a huge problem for me, we lost our actress and we're shooting in a few days."

Normally, Daisy would refuse outright, demur, make excuses. That was her unbreakable rule: no TV, no movies, not ever. She'd had offers before, but she'd turned them all down and she never auditioned for anything. Because she knew if she did, if she exposed herself to the world in that way, put her face, even for a second, on millions of screens, she knew exactly what would come next.

Who would come next.

If he'd tracked her down in a grad school showcase, he would definitely find her if she appeared on national TV on the country's fourth-rated network drama.

She knew that. It's why she had the rule.

But this time, uncharacteristically, she considered it. She considered the offer, and she thought of her secret, this impossible secret, and she allowed herself, just this once, to look toward the future as well as the past.

To think of an impossible baby and what kind of life that baby might have.

To think of that feeling. Hope.

Then she looked at the casting agent and she said it. The word she never allowed herself to say.

Like the sound of a door opening.

Yes.

Or maybe it all began days later when she stood on that fog-swallowed pier in Red Hook in Brooklyn. She shivered as seagulls bellowed and passing ships blew long, low horns in the fog, in the maritime gloom of a five a.m. call time, the air far too brisk for her flimsy costume, and she got ready to shoot her two scenes for that episode of *Legal Remedies*.

A production assistant wearing thick padded mittens handed her a steaming coffee in a paper cup to hold for warmth. Daisy thanked her and wrapped her bare, trembling hands around the cup. She couldn't drink it. It would smudge her makeup before her scene. But the gesture was kind.

She stood there blowing steam off the coffee, jittery against the biting chill, the sickly sweet smell of the rancid harbor cutting the cold morning air as technicians buzzed around, adjusting cables, repositioning lights. The production assistant appeared again to whisk away the coffee, telling everyone to please take their positions, and Daisy started getting into character, calming herself, *finding her breath*, letting herself become someone else, like it was the most natural thing in the world.

The moment before the moment.

Let another character inhabit this body, with all its scars, just for a while.

The show's stars arrived from whatever warm refuge they'd been sequestered in, and the director started marshaling the crew, and Daisy readied herself, to act tough, to take no bullshit, an honest cop who meets a bad end—she had six lines, only six, but they were her lines, her time to shine.

As Daisy prepared herself among the swirl of blue and red lights on the pretend police cars, the young actress playing the dead body was led out with a blanket over her shoulders. As Daisy watched, the woman shed the blanket and laid herself out motionless on the cold concrete, half naked, covered just enough to suit the standards of network television, this woman's body already bruised and bloodied—how cold she must be, Daisy thought. The woman sprawled herself carefully, and the effects guy squatted over her, daubing her with a few last tasteful splotches of fake blood, and then he retreated and the crowd of extras started murmuring on cue beyond the barrier of yellow police tape, and Daisy took one last look at the broken, dead body of this mute young woman.

Then she heard the crackle of the production assistant's voice on her walkie-talkie calling for quiet, and then she heard the director's voice shouting "Action"—

And then she channeled it.

All the rage, all the dread, all the anxiety, the unease, the exhaustion, and the fear—always the fear.

Fear you wake up with. Fear that follows you home. Fear that bubbles up with every unknown caller on your phone screen, every shadow that trails you as you cross the street at night. Fear you live with like a chronic condition, like an environmental toxin that seeps into your tissue and bones and marrow until it's just as much a part of your body as your blood, your hair, your tendons, your sinews.

Fear like that.

She only had six lines, but still.

The director yelled "Cut" and made a beeline to Daisy, just to tell her how much she loved her performance. *Took my breath away,* the director said. *Tough yet vulnerable. Real emotion. Knocked it out of the park.*

Daisy thanked her.

Later that day, Daisy died.

They filmed her second scene, her death scene, the one in which Daisy got gunned down behind the wheel of a car. *An honest cop who said too much,* which was ironic, she thought, because she had no lines in this scene, she stayed silent, but either way, the crooked cop had to kill her to *shut her up.*

She sat behind the wheel of the squad car, waiting. The effects guy ducked his head in and introduced himself—his name was Mike, he seemed sweet, a bit of a doofus. He squeezed into the front seat, draping over her, apologizing as he fiddled with the squibs he had taped on her skin under her blouse. "Sorry about this," he said, again and again, sheepish; he was very polite. He secured the squibs to her breastbone, to the very spot where she'd once considered getting that tattoo, the one on the night she left Boston when the tattoo artist held the needle just over her skin. She'd left that spot bare, a mute memorial, and now, instead, she would get shot there, a squib of fake blood pluming into the air.

"It's going to look amazing," he said with a smile, then gave her a thumbs-up and retreated from the car, and she settled into the seat.

The director yelled, "Action."

Daisy looked up, surprised, then terrified.

The crooked cop approached, drew his gun, and fired once, twice, again, again. She was trapped in the car, nowhere to run. The snap of gunfire, glass hits peppering the windshield, each glass hit in reality just a small plastic ball filled with Vaseline and glitter, splattering on contact to convincingly simulate bullet holes in the glass.

Vaseline and glitter.

And blood.

Daisy jerked her body in the driver's seat as the squibs popped and the blood bags exploded and crimson arcs splattered the interior of the car.

She died convincingly.

And as she lay there, dead, in the front seat of the car, she suddenly had an idea.

The director yelled, "Cut!"

One take. She'd nailed it.

Everyone said so.

Mike, the effects guy, was giddy.

Daisy smiled and thanked them all sincerely and then she asked Mike if he had a business card.

It will be a kind of play, she thought.

Make-believe. Smoke and noise.

Theater.

She would stage it. Direct it. As a test for him.

But not just a test.

A rehearsal.

The weeks passed and it was getting harder and harder to hide her secret from Craig. She'd stopped drinking, for one, but she just told him she was on some sort of cleanse and, true to form, he didn't press.

A month after she shot it, her episode of *Legal Remedies* aired, and on that night they held a party. They invited a few of her theater friends over to their apartment to watch. She set out bowls of popcorn and fluffed the throw pillows. Craig was beaming, of course, playing host, welcoming everyone to their tiny apartment, so happy that his starving-artist wife had finally broken her vow of poverty and decided to do TV.

Daisy served up the popcorn in big, overflowing bowls, and as their friends arrived, laughing and congratulating her, they all sat on the sofa together, squealing and pointing at the screen during her scenes, everyone drunk but Daisy not drinking, everyone cracking jokes at how serious she seemed onscreen, how very *no bullshit*, this *honest cop with a past*, and Daisy herself cracked the rudest jokes of all, watching herself on the screen, laughing and griping loudly about her brow wrinkles and joking about the inevitability of Botox and the cruelties of high-definition TV. And everyone gasped and hooted when the bullets hit the windshield, as Daisy was cut down in the driver's seat, blood everywhere, and when she died, everyone let out a wild cheer. This magnificent end, this wild death scene. Craig had DVR'd the whole episode, so at the end he rewound it and they all watched her death scene four more times and applauded.

And as everyone said good night with hugs and kisses and congratulations and Craig stood leaning in the doorway flirting brazenly with her last, lingering friend, Daisy watched him from across the apartment—handsome Craig, happy Craig, flirtatious Craig, faithless Craig, unsurprising Craig, oblivious Craig—and thought to herself, This is it.

This is happening.

She wondered how he'd react when she told him everything.

About the baby, yes.

But more than that. All of it.

She knew what he would say, of course. He always said the right things. He was very good at that. He'd promise faithfulness and fidelity. He'd swear to always protect her. He'd vow to be there, to stand by her, through good times and bad, no matter what.

After all, they'd already said all those things to each other before, in front of friends and family under an apple tree in upstate New York.

Vows.

But she wasn't interested in vows.

She wasn't interested in what he'd say.

She had to know, beyond the shadow of a doubt, what he would do.

||||

She had another thought as she stood there, watching him across the room that night—a thought that snuck up on her silently and ambushed her.

She thought: I love him.

For all his flaws, for all his failings, he had allowed her to forget herself. For a few years, at least. To feel distracted, at least a little, at least for a while.

He'd been her dark pocket to fall into as she ricocheted through life.

Her refuge.

That's not nothing, she thought.

Sometimes, it's everything.

And if she pulls this off—if they pull this off—maybe they could be that again.

Maybe they could be something more.

The two of them.

The three of them.

She pictured it.

Happiness.

Why not?

She was letting herself entertain all sorts of unfamiliar feelings these days.

Later that night, Craig long since asleep—he'd garlanded her with praise and encouragement, telling her how proud he was, what a huge step for her this would be, before he headed off to bed—she sat at the kitchen table in the glow of her laptop, scrolling through comments online. It was late now, maybe two in the morning, the episode long over. She scanned the tweets, the posts, the stray digital thoughts floating through the ether; she read every bit of what people had to say about the episode and about her.

After scouring social media, she opened the official *Legal Remedies* show page and started reading through the comments. This was where the most fervent fans always left their thoughts after every episode aired.

Her eyes tracked down through the posts in the forum. Who guessed the guilty character, who saw the twist coming, who liked this actor's suit, that actress's hair. She knew it might be days, weeks, it might even be longer, but still she searched, scrolling, scanning, reading—

And then she saw it.

Unmistakable.

She stared at the screen, the words strobing.

Even though it was exactly what she'd been searching for, even though she'd expected this from the moment she stood at that after-party and said *yes,* a familiar dread still clutched at her when she found it.

Her color-drained face lit paler now by the throb of the screen as she read.

great episode especially loved that new girl what's her name who played the honest cop what an actress so great to see her back in the spotlight though you should have seen her as Nora in A Doll's House now that was a role you never forget—your forever fan

She hadn't played Nora, not once, since the night of the showcase in grad school.

The night she found the card in the bouquet in the dressing room.

The card that was signed *Your Forever Fan.*

She'd already been searching for a couple's getaway, somewhere upstate, somewhere remote, just her and Craig. A place to retreat, to tell Craig everything, about the baby, about her past, and to start over. She'd found rentals but nothing secluded enough, nothing secret enough, and then she typed in a search phrase almost as an afterthought.

"Couple in trouble."

And this site popped up.

The Edenic Foundation.

The Eden Test.

Seven days. Seven questions.

Forever changed.

She clicked on the link.

Just the two of them.

No interruptions. No intrusions.

Just him and her, and seven questions, one per day.

On a private property that extended for miles in all directions.

Sounded perfect.

She emailed the program about cost and available weeks.

She booked the earliest week they had open, which happily coincided with their wedding anniversary.

Cabin secured, the plan was now in motion. She sent out a flurry of messages. First to Paulette, the actress she remembered from the downtown show, who would play the pretty waitress at the diner. She was exactly Craig's type, Daisy knew that, with her curly dark hair and attitude and alluring smirk—or she would be with a few temporary tattoos, the carnival kind that Craig was particularly drawn to, and Daisy also knew a makeup artist whose work was flawless.

Then she texted Maria, who Daisy had bartended with once years ago, a great and very petite actress who would play the cowed woman in the bar, folded frightened over her cocktail.

Then she called Mike, the effects guy on *Legal Remedies*. She'd gotten to chatting with him during the prep for her death scene when he was taping on all those squibs and he'd told her he was a former actor who moved into behind-the-scenes work. He'd play the heavy. He'd be perfect. He even asked if he could bring a friend along, Dan, another effects guy, a kind of prodigy with gore, Mike said, who'd be great just so long as he didn't have to speak.

She agreed.

The more menace, the better.

And she gave Mike a trademark bit of costuming, a blaze orange baseball cap, something conspicuous so he'd be sure to stand out and Craig would spot him whenever he was around.

At the diner. In the woods. In the bar.

Blaze orange. Ideal.

Designed to be seen.

And then, finally, after eight years of no contact, she sent a message to Christian.

She needed someone to play the security guard. This was the most important role. He had to be handsome (which Christian was) and believable in a fight (which Christian could be) and, most of all, someone she could play a scene with and be sure he wouldn't break character, not once, not even a little. Because if he did, the whole thing fell apart.

But she knew him. She knew he wouldn't break.

They'd been the two best actors in the class, after all.

She tracked him down through social media, following a trail of grad school alumni and old friends. He was living in western Massachusetts doing carpentry and had apparently given up acting long ago.

Even better.

She hesitated before she messaged him. He was the only one of the people she was enlisting who knew her from before her New York days. Who knew her before she was Daisy. And they hadn't been in touch for years, not since he'd helped her get to the train station that night.

She also knew they had a history. How he'd always hoped for something more.

But she didn't have anyone else to ask, not anyone she trusted. Because of the fact that she'd run, and run, and run in her life, there were so few people who knew her at all. She needed someone who Craig didn't know, had never met and couldn't possibly recognize, so that eliminated most of her New York acting friends.

And Christian had been there for her when she needed him once before.

Also, he'd quit acting, so he was no longer in the public eye. He'd be perfect for this.

Or so she thought.

She typed up the message and hit send.

It's an anniversary surprise for my husband was how she framed it to all of them—that's how she started each conversation. *Think of it like dinner theater, or a Renaissance faire, or a corporate-retreat fantasy camp—you're each here to play a role. I'll cover all your expenses, plus a generous stipend, you'll get a week in the country, and at the end of the week we'll have the big reveal.*

As the conversations progressed, she laid it out in more detail. The notion that her husband wouldn't be aware of any of it. Not at first.

It was short notice, but to her relief, everyone was game.

They were actors, after all.

Showbiz people.

They loved nothing more than putting on a show.

She'd booked the cabin with the Edenic Foundation—filled out all their forms and signed all their waivers—and she'd arranged the week with all her acting friends.

Still hadn't told Craig about any of it. Not yet. It would be their anniversary surprise.

And there was still one last thing she needed to do.

She bought the burner phone at a discount store.

Found his number. It wasn't hard. After all, he wasn't the one who was hiding.

Thumbs trembling, she tapped the message.

hello

Her thumb hovered over the send button.
No way back after this, she thought.
She hesitated.
Then hit send.
Then waited.

...

...

...

who's this
She texted back.
nora
...

...

...

no way

She typed in their old address in Madison, their wifi password, their pet
names, things only she could know.
Then she wrote:
saw your comment
...
knew you would. ha ha 'daisy' now huh?
...
i've been thinking about us
...
me too
...
but i needed time
...
me too
tho 12 yrs is a lot of time
its ok tho
i forgive you

IIII

That's what he wrote to her.

i forgive you

Like forgiveness might be what she was looking for.

She had to be flawless here, she knew that, no missteps, no slipups, no mistakes.

Because he knew where she was now and, worse, he knew *who* she was. So if this somehow derailed, if she messed up, if she failed to draw him out in exactly the way she had planned, on exactly the day she had planned, in exactly the place she had planned, it would all be over, and twelve years of running and eight years of hiding in New York would be for nothing and he'd come and he'd find her in the city, or she'd have to run again, this time with a baby.

She already knew what he'd do to Craig.

As for her and her baby, she couldn't imagine.

Or, rather, she could.

So she had to be perfect; she had to make Frank feel like it was all legitimate, this reunion, this reconciliation, after twelve years, even as she plotted the rest of the plan. Even as she lured Craig out to the woods for the week, even as she organized her actor friends, even as she engineered the various scenes and confrontations, the waitress in the parking lot, the hunter in the woods, the bar fight, the break-in, Shep's warnings, the final confrontation at the cabin—she orchestrated it all because she needed to reassure herself, beyond the shadow of a shadow of a doubt, that when the moment finally came to do what needed to be done, Craig would be there, he'd stand by her, he'd do his part, no matter what.

Because she couldn't do this alone.

Not alone.

She knew that, too.

So her performance had to be airtight, right from the beginning.
She had to be flawless.
Her performance perfect.
And it was.
Her masterpiece.

She typed.
  it's the perfect place
  ...
  where?
  ...
  plain ny
  ...
  i hate ny
  ...
  lol not the city its a town upstate
  quiet
  in the woods
  you'd like it
  ...
  ...
  ...
She waited.
Then typed.
still there?
  ...
i'm here
just 2 of us?
  ...
yes
well maybe my husband too
guess what. i'm married now
lol

...
...
...
hows that
being married
...
ok i guess
...
things happen. like i said, i forgive you
...
She stared at his words.
At his offer of forgiveness.
Then she wrote back.
so you'll come?

The invitation, the acceptance, the instructions.
The plan.
The lure.
The trap.

She gave him the location of the cabin and sent him prearranged times to text her over the week to check in as he made his way east. It was a two-day drive, at least, and she had everything planned so that he'd arrive on the morning of the sixth day, after the whole scene with Christian and Mike and Dan was over and done and they'd already left.

She made sure that Frank told no one.

our little secret then

In the end, she always knew he would come.

He still believed she loved him. Even after everything he'd done.

Even after all the ways he'd found to hurt her.

He still believed she loved him.

Those kind of men always do.

Now she sits next to Craig on the sofa in the cabin, staring at the red phone on the side table.

When she'd planned the week, she'd thought that, when they ended it, they would bury Frank deep in the woods.

Who would miss him? Who would mourn him? He'd told no one he was coming. The most anyone might know was that he'd gone on a hunting trip in New York State for a week and never came back.

Maybe one day, when he'd been missing long enough, maybe someone would come to comb the woods for him, maybe weeks later, maybe months, or maybe years. But the woods are large, and they swallow people up, and between the animals and the elements and the passage of time, if you bury a body deep enough, eventually all that's left is the secret.

And the woods never tell.

So that was her plan. She'd hoped that they'd come here, and they'd finish it together, and they'd bury him, and then they'd return to the city and start again.

Just the two of them.

The three of them.

Her, Craig, and the baby on the way.

D + C

+1.

That's what she'd hoped.

But she hadn't known that Christian would turn on her. She hadn't known about Alwyn's gun. Or that Craig would discover it, retrieve it, then hide it from her. She had told Craig *no guns,* in no uncertain terms, when he'd brought it up earlier in the week—there could be no wrinkles, no surprises, no X factors, she knew that—but she couldn't have known. She couldn't have known that Christian would come back and use the gun to threaten her. Or that Frank would kill Christian before they could kill Frank.

She hadn't planned on any of that.

Which means that now they have two bodies to explain.

She turns to Craig and takes his hands in hers.

Her eyes wet.

"I'm so sorry for all this," she says.

"You saved us."

"I lied to you."

"You did it for us."

"I put us both in real danger," she says. "By bringing him here. I know that."

"You were already in danger, every day. We had to do this. I'm glad we did."

"But Christian—"

"You tried to warn him. We both did," says Craig. "He didn't have to come back. He didn't have to threaten us. But he did."

"I know, but—"

"We did what we had to do," he says.

"I only kept it all from you because I wanted a different life for us," she says. "I wanted something new, with you. To start again. The three of us. That's all I wanted."

"I know. I want that, too," he says. "And we can still have it if we stick together. But we have to tell them the truth."

"We did the right thing," she says. "Do you believe that?"

"I do. Do you?"

"I do," she says.

He reaches a hand up to rest on her cheek. He considers a million more things he could say to her right now. But he says the only thing that seems to matter to him at all. It's very clear to him now, more than at any other moment in his life, so he says it.

"I love you," he says.

"I love you," she says.

This language feels new to them. These words feel newly minted in their mouths. Like this is a new language they're in the process of inventing together for them alone to speak. Like they're the first two people in the world to ever say these words aloud.

She lets go of his hands and gets up from the sofa.

She picks up the red phone.

She explains it all into the hotline. Her voice quavering.

"Something's happened. We need help. Come quick."

In tears as she tells the whole story.

Almost.

Almost the whole story.

The tears, though, are real.

When you're this good, they always are.

53

Kit and Bridget Arden sit in two chairs at the dining table, with Daisy and Craig sitting opposite. The room is silent. The sky outside is darkening into night. A clock ticks loudly from elsewhere in the cabin.

Near the door, Alwyn, the arborist, stands in his coveralls and trucker cap like a silent sentry, sliding a toothpick from side to side in his mouth.

The two EMTs in the private ambulance, the one with EDENIC FOUNDATION stenciled on the sides, have long since loaded up the two bodies on the pair of gurneys and departed.

All that's left now is to explain.

Kit kneads his gnarled hands on the tabletop, concern simmering in his clouded eyes.

"It should go without saying," he says finally, "that I am horrified by what happened here." Kit sighs heavily and stares a moment at the tabletop like there might be some further answers scratched into its polished surface. Then he looks up at them both, a scornful father. "Tell me, how did you two manage to get yourselves into such a mess?"

Daisy's heard that expression before. From her mother. In another lifetime.

"We did what we had to do," says Daisy.

Bridget sits at Kit's elbow, clad in a floor-length caftan, a kindly earth mother. She reaches out a bejeweled hand and places it on Kit's arm to temper him, as though calming an anxious horse. It's the gesture of a couple who know each other completely, who've been in each other's orbit for an eternity.

"I think there's a more important question here," says Bridget finally. "Are you two all right?"

"We are," says Daisy.

Kit gestures to Craig's leg, held straight at an awkward angle. "You sure you don't want one of my people to look at that?"

"It's not broken," says Craig. "It hurts like hell, but the EMT said it can wait until I get back to the city. Though Daisy will have to do all the driving." He laughs at his little joke. No one else laughs.

"I'm sure your people have their hands full right now," says Daisy.

Kit shakes his head, bewildered. "In all the years of the Edenic Foundation, we've never, ever had anything like this happen before."

Bridget clutches his arm, then leans forward, addressing Daisy directly. "I understand you two had a history. You and the assailant."

"That's right," says Daisy. "He's been following me for years. Stalking me. Since college."

"And how do you think he found you all the way up here, of all places?" says Bridget.

"He'd left a message for me a few weeks ago on the Internet. I'd done a TV show. That's how I paid for this retreat. After the show aired, I saw this message online and I just knew that it was from him. That he'd found me. And I knew he'd try to track me down. I'd hoped to come up here with Craig and tell him everything so we could decide what to do next. Frank must have followed us up from the city."

"And this other young man—Christian?" says Bridget. "What brought him here?"

"He's an old friend from school," says Daisy. "He knew about my history with Frank. He'd come to help us out. I wish he'd never come."

"Frank shot him from the woods," says Craig.

Bridget nods. "Then you killed Frank."

"That's right." Daisy clutches Craig's hand. "The two of us together, thank God."

Kit rubs his brow. "There are going to be questions. All sorts of attention."

"You can absolutely count on our discretion," says Daisy, glancing at Craig. "We're happy to do whatever you think is best."

"Absolutely," says Craig.

Bridget smiles, the diplomat, while her husband stews, troubled. "I think we can all agree that this went wrong in a way that none of us could have foreseen," says Bridget. "And I believe, once all the facts come out, it will be very clear to everyone what happened here." She delivers a summary of the events, like a binding agreement they will all sign off on. "This couple, our guests, were victims of terrible violence. This unhinged man, with an unspeakable history, came out here to do our guests harm. He brought a gun—his gun—and he shot a man. And, thankfully, our guests managed to overcome him. It's a miracle, really—it all could have ended so much more tragically, if you hadn't managed to stop him." She twists a ring on her finger and looks at Daisy. "I think that's exactly what happened here. I don't think it needs to be any more complicated than that."

"Honestly, we just want to go home," says Daisy.

Kit's still restless, unsettled. He tugs at his beard. Then he slaps the tabletop with an open palm. "We built a Paradise here, do you understand that? This is our life's work. And now? Blood's been spilled here. It's tainted." He glares at Daisy. "Do you understand what you've done?"

"Yes, we do." Daisy takes Craig's hand in hers and fixes her eyes on the old man. "We survived."

Bridget also takes her husband's hand and pats it, a mirror of Daisy and Craig. "Yes, you did. And we're so happy for that. As for the rest of it, we'll convey to the proper authorities exactly what happened here. It seems very cut-and-dried to me." She gives Daisy a look of deep understanding. "Assuming no other facts come to light."

Daisy thinks of her disposable phone and Frank's phone, both smashed to pieces with a painted rock. She thinks of how the phones are both bundled up in Shep's red windbreaker, the whole package now stashed in the trunk of their car inside of a packed suitcase, to be carted back to the city and buried, discarded, forgotten, lost in the city's infinite slipstream of trash.

"I don't imagine anything else will surface," she says.

Bridget smiles. "Then we're done." She stands. "I'm sure the local police will want to follow up with you. When they do, we'll definitely support your account."

Daisy rises and says to Bridget, "Thank you for your understanding."

"It's an old story, tragically," says Bridget. "In some ways, it's the oldest story. And, honestly, as a counselor, I've seen it too many times before. And it rarely ends well. I'm just happy for you that it's over."

Daisy thinks back to that day, the second day, when the four of them sat out on the porch—to Bridget's account of her years as a couples therapist, long before she moved out here with Kit. Of all the stories she'd heard, all the patterns played out. The frustration of watching something unfold and wishing she could somehow act, somehow intervene.

"Thank you," says Daisy.

Kit stands like a judge rising from the bench. Daisy offers to walk them both out to their car.

Alwyn gestures to Craig. "A word?"

Craig and Alwyn retreat to the kitchen. Once they're out of sight of the others, Craig hands him the gun, bundled back in the oilcloth.

"You have to believe me, we didn't expect this," says Craig.

"Just so long as no one got killed with my gun."

"It was never even loaded."

Alwyn opens the oilcloth, inspects the gun, then stows it in his coveralls. He looks up at Craig. "Don't worry, they'll make this go away. For all his grousing, the one thing Kit really cares about is protecting the reputation of this place—his slice of Paradise. And despite what he said, trust me, it's not the first time something like this has happened up here."

"Really?"

"When you stick couples in trouble alone in a cabin for a week, things have a way of going awry."

"But the police will have questions," says Craig.

"The Ardens have too much clout up here. It's basically a company town. And that's the beauty of living in the middle of nowhere." Alwyn smiles and shifts his toothpick. "Everyone knows everyone."

"Honestly, I don't know what you all expect to happen up here," says Craig. "Given those questions you made us answer."

Alwyn looks at him, curious. "What do you mean?"

"The seven questions."

"What about them?"

"Would you change for me?" says Craig, reciting them. "Would you sacrifice for me? Fight for me, lie for me, die for me? *Kill* for me? I mean, come on—" Craig leaves the rest unspoken, as though the implications hardly need to be explained.

Alwyn looks at him for a moment.

Craig can't be sure, but Alwyn seems amused.

"Those aren't the questions," Alwyn says.

They rejoin the others on the porch.

Kit says to Alwyn, "Are we good?"

Alwyn nods.

Bridget's retrieved a large wicker basket from their car, which she presents now to Daisy and Craig. "Usually this comes on the seventh day, as a parting gift," she says, "but I expect you might be eager to get home."

"We'll stay one last night," says Daisy, clutching Craig's arm. "We were promised seven days."

"Of course," says Bridget. She hands Daisy the basket, which is full of apples wrapped in cellophane, with a bright red ribbon tied around them. "From our orchard. Before the blight." There's an envelope perched on top of the apples.

On the envelope, in gold embossed letters: $Q7$.

"We also promised you seven questions," says Bridget.

Daisy takes the basket and thanks her. "I hope you'll believe me when I say that this week really helped us. It saved us. It changed our lives."

"I believe you," says Bridget.

Kit shakes his head, still troubled. "All we ever tried to do is build a Paradise. It's beyond me why anyone would want to spoil that."

"As far as I know," says Daisy, "only two people in history ever got the chance to truly live in Paradise. And they chose not to stay."

"Is that so?" says Kit. "What did they choose instead?"

"Each other," says Daisy, and takes Craig's hand.

Alone in the cabin again, just the two of them, Daisy unwraps the cellophane from the basket. She places it on the dining table like a centerpiece.

Craig stands by the hearth, stoking a fire, prodding it patiently with the iron poker. The fire blossoms as he watches intently. He gives the fire another nudge, then sets the poker aside.

He walks to the dining table and picks an apple from the basket. Takes a bite.

Chews.

"Tastes good," he says.

Daisy holds up an envelope. *Q7* written on the front. "Should we wait until tomorrow to open this?"

"Let's do it now."

They sit side by side on the sofa. She hands him the envelope. He tears it open and retrieves the question inside.

They huddle closer. Clutching the paper in their hands.

Question Seven.

54

Question Seven.

Would you forgive me?

That's it. That's all.
  You know what it means.
  Turn to your partner and ask it.
  Once you answer, you're done.
  You made it.
  Congratulations.
  Seven days. Seven questions.
  Forever changed.

55

He turns to her.

"Of course," he says.

"Me, too," she says.

They kiss.

Craig folds the paper up, slips it back into the envelope, and hands it to Daisy.

She stands and walks to the hearth and drops the envelope into the flames.

"You coming to bed?" says Craig at the foot of the stairs.

"In a minute. I want to watch the fire," she says. "I'll put it out and then I'll join you."

"Don't take too long," he says, with a playfully lascivious lilt. She listens as he mounts the stairs and hears his footfalls as he heads to the bedroom.

Once he's gone, she goes to the closet and stands on tiptoes to retrieve the Scrabble box from the high shelf.

She pulls the ancient cardboard lid off and, inside the box, under the game board, she finds six envelopes, identical on the outside to the envelopes they've opened and read together all week.

She pulls the seventh envelope, $Q7$, from her back pocket, where she'd folded it and stuffed it, unopened.

Seven questions.

The real questions.

Still sealed and stashed out of sight.

Swapped out each day for her custom substitutes.

She never intended for them to read the seven questions from the foundation. She doesn't even know what those questions are.

Instead, she had questions of her own.

Would you change for me? Would you sacrifice for me? Would you fight for me? Would you lie for me? Would you die for me? Would you kill for me? Would you forgive me?

Those are the questions she needed answers to.

She gathers the thick stack of envelopes from the box, the real questions, still unopened and hidden away in the one place she knew Craig would never look.

Craig hates Scrabble.

She adds the seventh envelope to the pile and also pulls out the weathered piece of paper, the one with her long list of words, the antagonyms, typed up at home and brought here and stashed in the Scrabble box as a conversation starter, to kick the week off right.

Cleave: to split apart, or to cling to.

Left: having departed, or having remained.

Bound: to be tied down, or to embark on a journey.

Weather: to be worn away over time, or to survive.

Her favorite words. Her Janus words. The two-faced god of looking to the past and to the future. Of gates and doorways. Of endings and beginnings.

She replaces the lid of the game box and puts it back on the high shelf. She closes the closet door.

She takes the bundle of unopened envelopes and her list of words and she tosses them all into the fire and watches them curl and burn.

The Seventh Day

||||

BLESSINGS AND REST

56

It takes hours of driving through the woods before they emerge and see the city.

It starts slowly at first: The buildings multiply, rising taller and taller as though in a jostling competition, until finally the city's skyline comes into view, jagged against the gray sky like an unstitched scar.

Woods at their backs.

City ahead.

The two of them, soon to be three of them, return.

Their home is exactly as they left it a week ago.

The life they left behind, undisturbed.

Craig opens the door with a hand on the knob, then steps in and puts down their luggage. Daisy places the basket of apples on the center of their dusty kitchen table. Arranges the basket just so.

The next day they start clearing out the so-called spare room, no bigger than a closet, really, which Craig had been planning to use as an office, as they prepare to give the walls a fresh coat of paint.

Not bad, they think, regarding the room, having moved out all the furniture and boxes and cleaned out the collected dust from the corners.

They stand in the doorway and look over the room together.

It's just big enough for a crib, they decide.

They've been back a week, maybe more, when they finally have some friends over for dinner.

It's a bit too early to reveal their big news, but they just can't wait.

Gasps and laughter. Smiles all around. Questions about baby names.

Daisy jokes that if they have a boy, they're going to name him Oscar. "I'll finally have my Oscar," she says.

"And if it's a girl?" someone asks.

Daisy looks at Craig, then looks at their friends, then says a name.

A normal name. A name no one there has heard from her before. A name with no particular meaning to any of them.

Only to her.

And to Craig now, too.

Because it was her name once.

A bottle of champagne pops to a great cheer and a fizz of foam. Champagne flutes are passed around for everyone, save Daisy.

Later, outside the kitchen, a friend pulls her aside. Slightly tipsy.

"So how was that week away?" the friend says, conspiratorial, her fingers grazing Daisy's arm.

"Good. Really good," says Daisy.

Her friend leans in. Gossip-hungry.

"So did it work?" She raises an eyebrow.

"Yes. I think it did."

The friend tips her glass toward Daisy's belly. Champagne sloshes. "Aren't you scared?"

"Of course. But we resolved a lot of things. I think we're ready for what's next."

"So you think you're going to make it? As a couple?" the friend asks.

Daisy smiles. "I do."

A timer goes off in the kitchen, ringing.

"Excuse me. That's the apple pie," Daisy says.

At the table, they all eat.

The apple basket holds flowers now.

"Apparently, you learned to bake in the woods," Craig's friend Kyle says to Daisy, with a loud laugh. He turns to Craig. "What about you? What did you learn in the woods?"

"I learned how to fuck up my knee." Craig taps his temporary brace.

"Bear attack?"

"Tripped over a stone."

"Go with bear attack. It's sexier." Kyle slaps him on the back. "You two bring back any souvenirs? I thought you'd have a buck's head mounted on the wall. Or maybe a bearskin rug for—you know." He bites his lip, thrusts his hips, makes a humping motion. The table chuckles.

"No, nothing like that," Craig says.

In fact, to the visitors, their apartment looks exactly as it did before.

Their life looks exactly as it did before.

Back from their week away.

Back from the woods.

And if anyone assembled at the dinner party, smiling and spilling stories, talking TV plots and workplace intrigue, happens to notice the one souvenir that returned with them, no one comments on it.

Sitting on the mantel next to a framed photo of their wedding.

In the photo, on their wedding day, Craig and Daisy feed cake to each other.

Laughing.

Looking as happy as they've ever been.

But not as happy as they'll be.

Next to the photo sits the souvenir.

A pink-painted rock, dusted red.

The red dots on the rock grow more rust-colored as the days pass.

The weeks pass.

The months.

The years.
A life.
On the rock, handwritten, among the rusted spatter.
D + C.
Forever.

IIII

ACKNOWLEDGMENTS

With gratitude to my agent, Elisabeth Weed, without whose expert guidance in every aspect of this process this book would literally not exist. To my editor and coconspirator, Zachary Wagman, without whose vision and acumen this would not be the book you are holding right now. To Howard Sanders, for being that rare and precious combination of exceptional creative collaborator and exceptional mensch.

To the crackerjack squad at Flatiron, including (but not limited to) Mary Beth Constant, Morgan Mitchell, Maxine Charles, Donna Noetzel, Keith Hayes, Megan Lynch, and Bob Miller. To Ali Lefkowitz, for patience and guidance, at Anonymous Content. To Michael Hingston at Hingston & Olsen, which published the first two chapters of this work in progress, in slightly different form, under the title "Happy Anniversary," as part of its 2020 Short Story Advent Calendar, where I was thrilled to be included alongside authors I consider heroes and inspirations.

This book was started in early 2019, before anyone (or certainly I) could foresee the cataclysmic global events on the horizon. In the years that followed, however, this story's themes of isolation, adversity, dread, resilience, loyalty, and love came to resonate for me in new and unexpected ways. So to my family and, especially, my wife, the fierce and fearless Julia May Jonas: You are the best copassengers, and copilot, I could ever dream of for this life raft, as we cling, survive, persevere, and thrive.

ABOUT THE AUTHOR

Adam Sternbergh is an editor at *The New York Times*. He is the author of *Shovel Ready*, nominated for an Edgar Award; *Near Enemy*; and *The Blinds*. He lives in Brooklyn with his family.